Settling The Score

Best wishes

[signature]

To Carol

WARWICKSHIRE v DERBYSHIRE
EDGBASTON AUGUST 20, 21, 22 1969

TEAMS

WARWICKSHIRE

P.W. Pywell
D. Weetman
B.R. Chatterway
C.J. Short
G.F.R. Ledbrook
R.T. Gledhill (Captain & Wkt)
P.M. Hastie
C. Stinton
J.K.L. Talbot
S. Hills
L.P. Upton

DERBYSHIRE

R.T. Hastie
N. Ibbotson
B.J. Picken
R. Brennan
R.C.S. Jephcott (Captain)
A.L. Crick
M. Shanks
D.K. Holliday (Wkt)
A.S. Badel
R.M. Turner
K. Colclough

Chapter One

1

Richard Hastie watched his captain press a thumb into the closely cut turf and sniff the air speculatively like a 'B' list television detective. 'The forecast said occasional showers then clearer. Did you hear it?' Hastie shook his head. Obviously Jephcott was angling to put the opposition in to bat if he won the toss. For the moment, the clouds were high and an unassuming breeze was barely ruffling the flags above the pavilion. Showers or no showers, the pitch looked full of runs and Hastie was not keen to share the blame with his captain if their batsmen made hay.

Both men turned to look at a figure applying the final touches to the crease markings. He was hunched inside a battered mouse-coloured jacket, trousers tucked into army surplus socks. 'The track's a bit greener than usual, Wilf.' Bristow half turned and scowled in the passive-aggressive manner handed down from one generation of groundsman to another. 'A belter for all that,' added Jephcott, fearing his words had been taken for criticism.

'You'd know about that would you, Mr Jephcott?' came the terse reply. According to Wilf Bristow, his field was one on which players appeared under sufferance and he believed in putting them in their place, especially visiting captains like Jephcott. 'If it's my opinion you want, the pitch'll be a bag of snakes the first day, a dust bowl by the second. You'll be doing the shopping with your missus by Friday.' Hastie exchanged a wry smile with Jephcott who drew deeply on his cigarette and resigned himself to judging the issue of the toss unaided.

As it happened, Richard Hastie was equally uncertain what his captain should do. Invariably he would opt to make first use of a pitch, especially at this venue where days of meticulous rolling would have gone into its preparation. But Jephcott was right, the track was more mottled than usual with patches of fine grass giving the appearance of lily pads separated by veins of buff-coloured earth. The unseasonably high rainfall had infused the soil with moisture and where there was moisture, bowlers worth their salt would always find movement off the seam.

Nevertheless, it was a risk to bat second. Even if the bowling side got early wickets, the weather might intervene to enliven the pitch when it was their turn to bat. Jephcott knew this, of course, but he was conscious of his team's position just outside the top four in the table, and was tempted to gamble. In what remained of the season, he believed a couple of wins would put his team in the prize money and a place that more accurately reflected its quality.

Since it was no secret that Richard Hastie was favourite to take over the captaincy in due course, Jephcott's habit of consulting him before start of play was taken to be a form of tutelage. The two men had emerged from very different backgrounds. The skipper was a Cambridge man and as near to a blue blood as could be found in that lugubrious swathe of the East Midlands between the toe-end of the Pennines and the Wash. His playing career had straddled the Sixties, a decade in which the notion of an amateur first-class cricketer had come to an awkward and faintly embarrassing end. Fewer of the former so-called 'gentlemen' could afford to play for 'fun'. Now all cricketers were 'players' and their initials, instead of appearing after the surname, were printed before it, as had always been the case for amateurs like R.C.S. Jephcott.

But even if the amateur and professional distinction had vanished from the scorecard, committee rooms were still bulging with brigadiers, local bigwigs and whiskery solicitors. The skipper was their sort of man. Marrying into a wealthy family with quarry interests, he had no need of a club stipend. Richard Hastie was in no such position. Married with two nippers under five and a house ninety percent owned by the building society, his current needs were palpable and his future prospects uncertain. If he was to assume the captaincy, he knew he would have his work cut out to loosen the famously tight strings of the treasurer's purse. Besides, he seriously doubted if he wanted the public glad-handing, the committee politicking, and the nose and arse wiping that went with the job.

'Take your feet off those markings,' growled Bristow to the ground staff lad who had joined him on the 'square'. Needing water to soften the stump holes, he had summoned the lad to make haste and fetch a bottle. On his return he had forgotten that treading on Wilf Bristow's pristine white lines before the start of play was forbidden. Bristow scrutinised the defiled 'popping' crease for signs of a smudge. His ground staff lads did not last long and this one was unlikely to prove an exception.

Drummed with a knuckle, the surface of the pitch sounded as hard as an oak table. Stumps fixed into such a surface stayed upright and sometimes split when struck by a fast-travelling cricket ball. The solution was to soften the soil so that the stumps could easily be uprooted and sent cart-wheeling back to the wicketkeeper. Loath though he was to indulge a bowler's ego, Wilf Bristow was not averse to a bit of theatre.

'Stand there,' Bristow directed as he took the bottle from the lad and poured water into each of three holes, taking care not to cause unsightly spillage. He slid the stumps into place and stood back to admire his work. A curt shake of his fingers dismissed the lad from the field and with Jephcott and Hastie heading to the pavilion, he was alone with his thoughts. In an hour or so, players would come to scrape and slide across his masterpiece. Every game, he felt, was death by a thousand cuts.

Set in a pleasant patch of suburban Birmingham, the Edgbaston ground had scale without grandeur and reflected an industrial rather than a sylvan aesthetic. Perched on top of the flat-roofed, two-storey pavilion were shed-like structures, one for the scorers, one for local radio broadcasters. Breaking the skyline beyond was a curtain of undistinguished poplars. A sprinkling of spectators had begun to dot the vast open stands, prematurely dipping into their picnic boxes. For a mid-week three-day Championship game, the crowd would be as meagre as Richard Hastie had come to expect. A steward detailed to herd them, stood dreaming of Test match days when the place would be packed and his crested white coat would confer on him more meaningful dominion over seats 'A' to 'G'.

'I'm thinking of playing young Badel,' Jephcott said as they walked. 'I've already talked to Mal about standing down.' Richard Hastie frowned. The skipper would be leaving out his specialist spinner in favour of a four-man seam attack. 'I think it will seam,' he added. 'We always end up carrying a spinner here but if I'm wrong, you can turn your arm over. Bad idea d'you think?' Richard shrugged. He thought his opinion was unlikely to make much difference. 'Perhaps you're right,' said Jephcott, implying he had expressed one all the same.

The changing room, which had been swept clean of any detritus left by the previous visitors, was once again a chaos of kit bags and coffin-sized cases. The spike-resistant melamine floor had been mopped and the citrus smell of cleaning fluid briefly masked the tang of dust, sweat, and grass. An opaque glass window prevented a view of the ground and restricted the daylight. There were concrete floors in the corridor, shower room, and lavatory. Together with the steel-framed windows, glass-brick divides and suspended ceiling, the interior of the pavilion resembled the staff rest-room of an engineering workshop.

Richard Hastie hurdled over the miscellany of bats, pads, and boots towards his changing place. Having hung up his blazer, he noticed that someone had squeezed into an adjacent corner. From the modest size of the kitbag, he deduced that Badel had chosen to change there. That was not the only clue. An odour strong enough to stun a mule exuded from a hanging Bri-Nylon shirt. This was not just the common or garden whiff of late adolescent armpit. Alvar Badel had travelled as Twelfth Man ostensibly to get a taste of the 'first-class' experience. Richard guessed that from the moment Jephcott told him he would actually be playing, Badel's sweat glands had switched to full-on terror mode.

Badel had come by his name through his mother's passion for the voice of Alvar Lidell, the wartime broadcaster. In a tough district, his mother's teenage fancy for the sonorous Swede had guaranteed her son plenty of playground ridicule. Cricket however had been his salvation. A senior club cricketer spotted the speed with which the lad could propel a ball and soon he was ripping out stumps for the county Second Eleven.

Barely willing to breathe, Hastie opened the dressing room door to excite a draught of fresher air and became aware of a

5

commotion in the corridor. Stepping out of the changing room, he saw Graham Murfin being ushered into the physio's room, a bloodied towel held to his head. 'Murf's taken one on the crust,' said Jephcott matter-of-factly. 'He's badly cut behind the ear. The doc's on the way but I'd say it's a morning in Casualty for him.'

The physio was dabbing a ball of cotton wool on a gash behind Murf's ear. 'What happened?' said Richard, knowing Wilf Bristow's practice net pitches were as blameless as those on his 'square'.

'I got pinged by Badel. Silly bugger was bowling flat out. I never picked it up. Must have ducked into it.' Holding his hand up, the physio asked Murf to count fingers then looked searchingly into his pupils. Richard surmised that full of fear and adrenalin, Badel's control must have gone awry.

The physio nudged Murf towards the treatment table and left him to staunch the wound while he went to search for a glass of water. With his free hand Murf made a token attempt to take off his pads then gave up. He was losing colour. 'I think the bugger chucked it,' he muttered before closing his eyes to watch the stars still twinkling on his retina.

Richard thought Murf's accusation was not without merit. Badel's loose-jointed bowling action had attracted whispers of suspicion after he had returned impressive figures in Club and Ground fixtures. As yet he was unknown to the wider world, but judging by his demolition job on Murf, that was about to change.

Anxious to earn his complimentary seat in the committee box, the home club's doctor breezed in. Pink and cheerful in a thorn-proof three-piece suit, he sent Murf post haste to hospital for stitches and a scan. 'Just a precaution,' he warbled. Experience told Richard that Murf would sit for hours outside

'X Ray', a figure of curiosity in his whites, signing the plaster casts of other accident victims. Nurses would park their bottoms on the nearest radiator intent on gossiping to a minor sports celebrity whose name they had never heard of before fate and a hard ball took a hand.

Luckily for Jephcott, Murfin's injury had occurred before he had officially announced his eleven but it still left him with the task of calling for reinforcements or using Mal Shanks. Ideally he would choose to draft in a replacement specialist batsman but since the Second Team was in the middle of a two-day match this was not without its problems.

It was accepted that at a moment's notice a second eleven player could be yanked out of a match to serve the colours. Journey time was crucial, but Jephcott knew that if a replacement could reach the ground by lunchtime it was the right decision. On the other hand he would have to be polite to the Second Team coach, an old sweat who ran things as if he were the warden of a Borstal. There would be the inevitable argy-bargy with him about Jephcott's preferred choice of stand-in. And then there was the question of transport. It was all too much trouble. Shanks, on the other hand, was already on the ground.

'I'll tell Mal he's playing,' Jephcott said to Richard. As is the way with captaincy, as soon as he made the decision, Jephcott sensed it would prove the wrong one.

2

'Wotcha, our kid,' said Philip Hastie, as he passed Richard en route to join his colleagues in the home team's practice nets. Awkwardly balanced on one knee as he buckled the bottom strap

7

of his pad, Richard Hastie was in no position to resist the nudge from his brother that sent him sprawling onto his backside.

'Pillock,' said Richard, finding tiny grass cuttings peppering his sweater as he gathered himself up. Philip Hastie had never been slow to demonstrate his physical superiority over Richard, two years his junior. As far back as he could remember, he had been Richard's hero, rival, and tormentor-in-chief. To Philip, nicknamed Speedy, his sibling had always been the 'clever-dick' who required a regular slap to keep him down. Now aged thirty, Speedy felt the same imperative.

'Where's he come from?' said Speedy nodding in the direction of Badel. Under instructions from nervous team-mates, Badel had halved his pace and was bowling a series of schoolgirl lobs.

'Alvar Badel?'

'Alvar?'

'It's Swedish.'

'Huh.'

'He's come out of the local league.'

'I hear he was too sharp for Murf?' said Speedy, grinning the grin of a bowler contemplating a batsman in pain.

'He's out of the game – gone to hospital.'

'Pity, Murf's usually one of my rabbits.'

People were fond of asking who was the fastest bowler Richard Hastie had ever faced. Around the country there were a handful of contenders. The bounding Springbok with the bandana; the giant West Indian propelling a blur out of a very black hand; old tombstone-face emerging white as a ghost out of a sea fret at Hove. These were bowlers who might dull an opener's appetite for a full English breakfast. And yet Richard Hastie would be hard-pressed to name a bowler who had terrified him more than his brother when a boy. On balmy summer evenings, Speedy would beat a fearsome tattoo on the garage doors with his express deliveries. His run-up, starting by the rhododendrons, accelerated past the begonias and ended in a delivery stride that took him beyond the bay window. Sometimes he would give up a second helping of tea in favour of starting his run-up from the cat's eyes in the road outside.

Put side by side the Hastie brothers were not obviously of the same kidney. At six feet two in his socks, Speedy still enjoyed the disparity in height he had exploited as a boy. His dark head of hair with a hint of curl was short and thick enough not to budge in a gale. Below it was a conventionally handsome face complete with ironic eyebrows and an engaging smile. His slightly too-long sideburns pointed to a decisive chin where a small pale worm of a scar supported no bristle. Irritatingly for Richard, whose uppercut had caused it, the scar embellished the cleft in Speedy's chin so admired by a string of pretty girls before Sheila, his wife, appeared on the scene.

Richard had learned to live with the comparisons. At five ten and twelve stone he could not match the breadth of Speedy's shoulders and chest, the size of his hands or thighs. But he was brighter, more nimble and better balanced – useful attributes in fending off Speedy and other maniacs propelling a hard ball from twenty or so yards away. The epic battles in front of the garage may have taught Speedy to bowl fast and straight but Richard had learned much more. To duck and weave of course, but also to pace a session, to wait for the bad ball, to take a blow to the body and not flinch. And when fatigue crept in with the dusk, he would seize the initiative and punish the wilting Speedy like a predator picking off his prey. On that patch of yard the brothers learned all they ever needed to know about the gladiatorial aspects of the game.

9

Having failed the Eleven Plus, Speedy left secondary school at the earliest opportunity to be apprenticed to his father, an electrical contractor. He was not short of intelligence but for a young man hell-bent on a cricket career, his path had been easy to choose. As long as he 'learned a trade', Hastie Senior could not summon the will or heart to promote an alternative strategy. In the summer of his nineteenth birthday, Speedy accepted invitations to play in Club and Ground fixtures for Warwickshire and was signed up on the strength of his performances.

In retrospect his decision had less to do with cricket considerations than with a desire to escape his hometown's parochial atmosphere and strut his stuff on a city stage. Progressive development of the Edgbaston ground had made it a Test match venue and Speedy always felt a stab of pride whenever he stepped into the arena. The downside was Wilf Bristow's benign pitches. A gently sloping square accommodated upwards of two dozen pitches, all of them shirt-fronts. It was a Mecca for batsmen and by choosing it as his home ground, Speedy had enlisted for years of hard labour. Pleas to make pitches more 'sporting' were met with the groundsman's intransigence. 'Put a bomb under it,' Speedy would sometimes shout as wicketless he trudged back to the pavilion.

'Try bending your bloody back,' would come Bristow's pitiless reply.

Unlike Philip, Richard jumped easily over the hurdle of the Eleven Plus but once at grammar school, he was notably unassiduous. Teachers attributed his low-octane academic performance to the distractions of sport. This was only partly true. What really put paid to Richard's motivation was the life his

10

brother was leading. Once Philip had left school the difference in their ages widened into a yawning gap. The 'brain-box' of the family could only watch with envy as his brother entered the grown-up world of pay packets, manly camaraderie, girls and sex. His own world seemed suddenly shrunken. He was beached and abandoned to his dull routine, his school satchel scored with the inky graffiti of a soul incarcerated.

Richard's sporting ability might have sustained him through the dog days but for the ramshackle provision of state school cricket where corrugated pitches made a mockery of the game. Beyond the school gates, League cricket offered much-needed respite, and when his performances were highlighted in the local paper, even his Headmaster was forced to take note. 'You must be quite good, Hastie,' he said, gathering his thoughts and assessing the unearned kudos for his school. 'What next, playing for a living?'

'Hope so, yes sir.'

'Waste of a good brain, isn't it? Your form master assures me you have one, albeit untouched by effort. I assume you'll be applying to university?' Such was his desire to emulate Speedy that Richard had not even contemplated further education. Yet what the Headmaster said seemed to make sense even to a recalcitrant adolescent. Within months he had salvaged his schoolwork and scraped together enough 'A' Levels to gain a place in the Economics Faculty of Nottingham University. During the university summers his text-books collected dust as the campus sports field played host to other red-brick universities and county Second Elevens. As a lynchpin of the side, he consolidated his reputation as a technically sound batsman with a useful line in bloody-minded obduracy. This was never truer than when Speedy, undergoing a fitness test, turned up to play for a Warwickshire Club & Ground XI. Despite his brother bagging a handful of wickets, Richard remained undefeated to deny the opposition victory.

Always subsequently described by the hacks as 'a match within a match', the Hasties' sibling rivalry was destined to run and run when Richard signed a contract with Derbyshire after graduating. In Hastie Senior's view, Derbyshire, a county renowned for its misty moorlands, was fit only for sheep and seam bowlers. But the offer of a job from a Derby-based printing company giving him summer sabbaticals to play cricket, was one too good for Richard to refuse. And so, just as unresponsive Edgbaston tracks blunted the bite of Speedy's bowling, the moist pitches of the Peak District gave Richard no easy tenure of the crease. Proud though he was, Hastie Senior believed both lads had inherited a rogue gene that predisposed them to making life hard for themselves.

To Richard Hastie's irritation, Speedy was in no hurry to join his own team-mates in the nets.

'Tessa alright?' he asked.

'Yup.'

'The folks were asking.'

'Asking what?'

'If she's alright. They'd had a call.'

'Tessa's fine,' said Richard, feeling the clammy hand of family speculation. He had always felt disinclined to discuss his marriage. His parents treated intrusion into their own privacy as bad manners and he had inherited the trait. Not that his folks had ever had much to hide. Marital perturbations in the Hastie Senior's household were as rare as rain clouds over the Gobi, and Richard looked for no other template in his approach to married life. When he and Tessa had stepped down the aisle, happiness was their uncertain goal, procreation the norm, and making one's bed and lying on it the imperative. But things had changed. The clamour for equal women's rights had been as much a soundtrack to the 60s as the Stones and the Fab Four.

Richard felt he had successfully assimilated many of the new mores. As long as Tessa's contrariness was proportionate, he usually admired her inclination to speak her mind and take no bullshit from him or anyone else. Yet that very morning she had perversely chosen to debate the relative merits of quotes to tile the bathroom – just as Ken Colclough had pulled up outside the house. The Senior Pro was a stickler for time-keeping, and there would have been hell to pay if Richard was not ready for their journey to Birmingham.

'Not now, Tess. Another time.'

'You've had time,' she had snapped. 'Time and again you've had time.' Youngest daughter, Jessica, was engrossed in catching cornflakes from a spoon and pushing them into her mouth with her fingers. Sarah, five, was more attentive, sensing the temperature rising to a point where swearing might be added interestingly to the mix.

'Look, I've agreed we should do it.'

'I need an answer now. If we don't get on, it won't be done before Christmas.' Bloody Christmas, he had thought. How often must he be coshed by the Yuletide log?

'Tess, that's four months away.'

'You can't get tilers just like that. They're booked up months ahead.'

'We'll talk when I get back.' Tessa chewed the inside of her bottom lip and her dark blue-grey eyes flashed in irritation. It was fortunate that whenever he conjured up her face in his mind's eye, it was not the one confronting him. Her smile would be perfectly formed around even teeth, chin elegantly defined, eyes clear and welcoming, skin creamy smooth bar a small clear mole close to a dimple on her cheek. Now her chestnut hair was scraped back behind her ears and her neck was slightly mottled, a sign of anger bubbling below the surface. 'Sorry, got to go.' He drew her into a placatory hug and planted a kiss. 'Be good for mummy, you two.'

'Trouble?' enquired Ken Colclough, watching Richard load his gear into the rear seat.

'How d'you mean?'

'Your missus, she's got a face like a smacked arse.'

'The girls are playing her up.' The arch of KC's eyebrows made it clear he was not fooled.

The Austin Cambridge glided out of the suburbs onto the dual carriageway, the needle glued to a sedate 60 mph on the dial. The car, bought second-hand with testimonial money, had a two-tone paint finish and enough chrome accessories to give purpose to KC's polishing compulsion. With its leather bench seating and column gear change, a third front-seat passenger could be accommodated with ease. Since the fixture list required teams to criss-cross the country for days at a time, KC was fond of promoting the car's armchair comforts as an aid to arriving at games fully fit to play. A sequence earlier that season had seen Jephcott's team travel from Gravesend one Friday to play a three-day match at Taunton, packing their bags again on the Saturday evening to drive to Manchester for a Sunday League game before returning to Taunton to complete the last two days of the Championship fixture. Given that they were transporting themselves in their own cars, the risks to life, limb, and sanity were obvious. The chance to ride shotgun in KC's Austin was therefore not one to be passed up lightly.

For a moment Richard was tempted to confide in KC but the impulse passed and they travelled in silence. He accepted that on the first morning of a match he might be tenser than usual and less patient with the girls. Then again, his was no ordinary job. He was not a shopkeeper, a bank cashier, or a bathroom tiler. Doubtless they too had their moments of crisis, but not in front of a clutch of hardened sports writers and spectators. Rightly or wrongly, he felt entitled to some special pleading. However, as his annoyance subsided, he was forced to accept his own culpability. He had teased out the decision on the bathroom décor, convinced that another more essential item of expenditure was bound to arise. What the hell, he would phone her as soon as possible and give her a free hand.

At the side of the practice nets Speedy was continuing to exercise his jaw rather than his limbs. 'Tessa's got all on. Kids are bloody hard work at that age.'

'How's Sheila?' said Richard, hoping to deflect the conversation.

'She's well. Tessa, you and the kids must come over for Sunday lunch as soon as the season's over. Who knows we might have something to celebrate?' Speedy cocked an ironic eyebrow and smiled. 'I just ran into Gil Atkins heading for the Committee Suite.'

The sighting of an England selector was not an unusual event in itself. With only seventeen counties to choose from, players bumped into them on a regular basis. But it was the middle of August and the stakes were higher than usual. Not only was the team for the last Test match about to be announced, but also the party for the winter tour to the West Indies.

'Well he's not here to check on Paul Pywell, is he? He's a cert. So is Topsy Turner – if he's fit.'

'So who?'

'Me,' said Speedy. 'Well think about it.' Richard did not want to. It made him feel queasy. He was always surprised how quickly the worm of sibling rivalry wriggled up inside him. His brother already had experience of Test cricket. Sadly for Speedy, he had worn his England cap only once a long way from home, an event remembered only by a handful of sports trivia nerds. He had been coaching in New Zealand and coincided with an England touring party struck down by a virulent sheep-borne infection. Speedy had rushed to the colours and performed with quiet efficiency, taking two wickets, a fact he reprised at every family gathering.

Richard thought Speedy was a long shot for England selection. His pace, so fearsome in his youth, was latterly reduced to military medium and unlikely to trouble batsmen on the unforgiving tracks of Sabina Park and Bridgetown. And yet, once he allowed himself to be more objective, he had to accept that Speedy was among the top dozen bowlers in the averages. No fluke either. He had bowled a lot of overs and achieved an impressive strike rate. As the tabloids might say, if the England XI were ever again ravaged by bug or blight, he would 'let nobody down.'

'Put a show on today and you might be in with a chance yourself,' said Speedy, surprising Richard with his generosity.

'Nah, too many good openers about.'

'Too many easy runs, you mean?' said Speedy, alluding to the way in which England's batsmen had been filling their boots against docile Indian and New Zealand attacks. It would be different in the West Indies where the throat-ball, delivered at pace, was the standard offering. For that the nation required men who were prepared to take it uncomplainingly on the chin, the chest, and in the groin.

'You can play the quicks as well as anyone and you've got guts. You might not open but you could dig in at Number Six if they needed the cavalry.' Richard allowed Speedy's words to excite his unspoken aspirations. Atkins was, after all, on the ground, eyes peeled, asking to be convinced. But timing was all. As everyone on the circuit knew, once Gil Atkins had taken lunch and liquid hospitality, his head would roll back leaving any afternoon heroics unwitnessed. 'Yes, I think it's more open than you think,' continued Speedy. 'Course, I doubt if Tessa would let you go.' He gave his brother a scurrilous wink and ambled off to join his team-mates.

3

'What's the Skipper playing at? He's put the buggers in,' Ken Colclough thundered. 'Why didn't you stop him?'

'It was *his* idea, that's why,' said Mal Shanks who had become head stirrer after his temporary demotion to Twelfth Man. It was clear that Jephcott's invitation to join him for a tête-à-tête at the wicket had made Richard complicit in any madcap scheme he had in mind.

'Nothing to do with me,' said Richard, deferring to 'KC' whose voice was the only one likely to carry much weight with the skipper. Not that KC would ever admit to pressing his opinions. 'I don't get paid for making the captain's decisions,' he would say while reserving the right to chunter about them long after the event. 'Think about putting the opposition in, then bat,' was an adage KC might have coined had it not been handed down by generations of seam bowlers before him. Pace bowlers preferred not to be disturbed on the first day of a three-day match. A thirty-minute burst at six o'clock was permissible, but the rest of the day should be just that, a day of rest. KC had already examined the lunch menu. With a bellyful of steak and kidney pie and the best bread and butter pudding on the county circuit, he was planning the sort of slumberous afternoon Gil Atkins famously enjoyed. Now KC had a face like a small boy whose ice cream has been snatched by a seagull. The day was ruined. It would involve work, sweat, and sore feet.

'Nothing to do with you?' KC said accusingly to Richard. 'So what were you doing out there with him?' It was a fair enough question.

'A second opinion,' sneered Mal.

'The Skip thought we might get rain.'

'Rain, my arse.'

'He's heard a forecast,' said Richard, labouring.

'I'll give you a forecast,' said KC. 'Runs, hundreds of bloody runs.'

'Where's 'Topsy'? Does he know?' said Mal, hopeful of enlisting a new source of dissent.

'You'll find him on the bloody treatment table as usual,' said KC exiting, possibly to amend his lunch order to something lighter on the stomach.

Chapter Two

1

'Is that rain?' asked Jephcott hopefully after Topsy Turner had bowled his first over. It had included three lacklustre deliveries well wide of the off stump. 'I'm sure I felt a spot,' he continued to an arc of sceptical slip fielders.

Handed the first use of an Edgbaston pitch, Paul Pywell, Warwickshire and England's Number One, could hardly believe his luck. He had nudged Topsy's fourth ball for a single and was leaning on his bat in an ominously assured manner. It was the 'nudge' that gave it away. A gentle push to cover's right hand off a half-volley. For a batsman of Pywell's class it was a ball asking to be hit for four, instead he had eschewed the risk of a full-blooded drive so early in his innings in favour of absolute certainty. For an hour he would check his shots and ignore any balls bowled wide of the stumps. He was like a purse-lipped surgeon laying out instruments on a tray before an operation. And when the 'op' got underway, the scoring would be so deft, the incisions so fine, that a bowler would discover the loss of his vitals only when he saw his analysis at the end of the day.

Taking their lead from Pywell's self-assurance, others in his team had adopted, in Richard Hastie's view, a superior attitude

19

when it came to opponents from less prosperous counties. Their expansive well-equipped venue, sited on the edge of a thrusting metropolis had, he felt, encouraged feelings of self-importance. He suspected his own team was considered a poor country cousin even when games between them were evenly contested.

Though he had ceased to fulminate about Jephcott's decision to bowl first, Ken Colclough's features remained as chiselled as a German woodcut. Normally keen to make a mate of the umpire, he made do with a curt nod as he handed over his sweater and measured out his run-up. In his pomp, KC ran twenty strides to the bowling crease, now he made do with ten. There had never been any vanity in his action. There was too much heaviness in the thighs for that, too much clumsy articulation of the arms. The efficiency of the end result, however, was never in doubt. Batsmen the length and breadth of the country said KC bowled a 'heavy ball'. They felt its jarring force on the splice of their bats or in the bolt of pain that shot through them when struck on the tender inside of the thigh. Day in day out he had been one of the best half dozen bowlers in the country. Contemplating the runs against tally on a hot afternoon, Jephcott always knew he could lob a ragged ball to KC and immediately put a brake on the scoring.

'What's this, Skipper, a bag of snot?' KC would snarl, examining the ball. As senior pro he saw it as his job to enforce among the team an ethos of respect for the ball. Each and every man was expected to spit, polish, and pick debris from its seam. A well-kept ball not only encouraged the bowlers, it was also a sign of communal endeavour. In bygone days KC never needed to articulate this to fellow team members. As former military conscripts they had accepted their stint of 'bull' unquestioningly. But things were different now. 'What're you doing, Topsy? Don't just tickle it, polish the bloody thing!' Topsy Turner's languid stroll back to his mark reduced KC to tears of frustration. 'He's just a lazy streak of piss,' he would say as the ball came back to him at the end of an over unloved and neglected. But even KC recognised that Topsy's natural talent more than compensated for his shiftless disposition. His height and suppleness gave his bowling the bounce and pace that won matches.

Jephcott did not need to consult KC about his field setting. It was routine. Nothing fancy. Two slips, a gully, cover, mid-off, mid-on, a third man and a fine leg to sweep up the nicks. The only sign of out-and-out aggression was a short square leg. Somehow Neil Ibbotson had got lumbered with that position until someone else could be fooled into replacing him. Standing at 'social' within arms reach of the batsman's back pocket was a place for reluctant heroes. 'Ibbo's' good hands and quick reflexes made him a leading catcher, principally off Topsy whose steep bounce induced edges onto a batsman's body or ricochets off his gloves. Ibbo swallowed these morsels like a sea anemone hoovering up passing small fry.

From the end of his run-up KC saw Pywell taking recon-naissance of the field placings before twirling his bat and stooping into his stance. One of the best batsmen of his generation, KC knew it took a good ball to dismiss Pywell, especially on his home turf. He glanced at the ball in his hand, its shiny lacquered surface already crazed. He swung his arms for the first time that morning. The previous day he had been sitting playing cards at Chesterfield as rain washed out play. Now, despite his inactivity or perhaps because of it, he felt stiff. August, he reflected, was a cruel month for a bowler. Rationing what energy he had for the final fixtures, KC would avoid pre-match net practice and warm-up routines. He claimed a mug of tea and a fag hit the spot just as effectively. But when he began his run up he felt a stranger to his limbs. All the connections and cartilages were knocking and his feet seemed attached to his legs by puppeteer's string. Even his teeth did not feel his own. In time past he had a truculent bristling approach to the wicket, now he felt like an old woman shuffling to catch a bus. As his right foot landed, his left arm reached for the sky, the body rotated and down into the delivery stride came his large left boot. The groan as he released the ball left no doubt about the effort expended. The resulting delivery, of no great pace, dropped on a length and was patted back down the pitch by Pywell in an overly deferential manner.

KC stared at the ball as it rolled towards him. How he longed to take the smug look of competence off Pywell's face. Another couple of looseners he thought, and perhaps he could find enough nip to dig one into his ribs. 'Making the buggers jump,' had been an essential part of his trade, but in the corner of his eye he saw Jephcott urging Richard Hastie to step up a yard at second slip, a sign of his fading capacity to make the ball zip. Two brain boxes together, thought KC, seething at their stupidity in choosing to put the opposition in.

Though his body continued to protest, KC wheeled around and bowled four more deliveries of perfect line and length. Such control against the odds was little short of a miracle. On the other hand the ball had done nothing either in the air or off the pitch. Each time Pywell had dotted the 'I's and crossed the 'T's on the batmaker's insignia. More out of irritation than intent, KC called Jephcott to take mid off away and put him close in at leg slip.

'Don't think so, KC,' came the captain's defensive response. KC's expression closed like a fist. Muttering darkly he walked back to his mark. The lacquer on the ball was still too new to reward a polish but some thumbed-in spit would keep it clean. Though his shin soreness would take a couple more overs to disperse, his feet felt more connected and his thigh muscles had begun to flex. With less choke needed, he turned and ran in, a sense of grievance sharpening his stride. Outwardly there was nothing to distinguish this from the previous five deliveries. It was the same off stump line just short of a length. But as Pywell moved confidently forward to smother it, the ball pitched on the seam and lifted, deviating enough to take the edge of his bat and fly towards Richard Hastie at second slip.

Richard saw the ball coming all the way. It was at that awkward height between waist and chest where a catcher's hands could point either up or down. Richard's did neither. Instead of nestling into a cupped web of fingers, the ball smashed into the base of his thumbs and fell to the ground. KC stood and stared in disbelief, one hand on his hip, the other hooked behind his neck as though about to tear his own head off. 'Well fuck my old boots,' he groaned.

'That is 'over', gentlemen,' said the umpire, drily re-imposing decorum. Feigning sympathy, Pywell nodded to KC in acknowledgement of the injustice. Richard, however, knew to keep his apologies for later. In the past KC would have merely glared and told him to 'catch the next one' in the sure knowledge that another chance would come soon enough. But on that strip of turf and with Pywell in prime form, the drop was likely to be costly. Richard had been done for pace and he silently cursed Jephcott for moving him closer to the bat earlier in the over.

KC snatched his pullover from the umpire and headed for the boundary. The brooding set of his shoulders admonished every-one on the field. If he caught wind of Jephcott's commiserating 'bad luck, KC', he did not acknowledge it. Still furious, he took up his position at fine leg and heard a boy's voice behind him.

'Can I have your autograph?' During Topsy's opening over KC had been dimly aware of a man sitting with a boy amid a bank of empty seats. KC put his head down and counted grass. The boy called out again. 'Oi, can I have your autograph?' There was no 'please' or 'Mr. Colclough.' KC gave the boy a sour look. He was about twelve years of age.

'What's he say, Steven?' KC heard the man call in sing-song Brummie.

'Nothing.' KC stepped forwards a few yards as Topsy bowled then backed onto the rope again without turning.

'Yow could at least answer the lad.' KC turned his head, his hands on his hips. An apology would have diffused the matter in an instant but the dropped catch had driven a stake through his heart.

'Can't he see I'm working?' KC said.

'Yeh, and it's may who's paying yow're wages.' KC bit his tongue.

'I'll sign at the end of the session.'

'Yow can stuff it. Who are yow anyway?'

Over the years KC had earned his share of crowd appreciation but he had never enjoyed an easy rapport with the public. He was too socially awkward to work a crowd. A rueful smile or a nod of the head just about exhausted his repertoire of responses. The celebrity of his situation never occurred to him and the new demands of the public to 'know' about players rather than just follow their performances left him bewildered. He blamed the introduction of short-form Sunday League cricket for bringing a new sort of crowd to the game. Sunday used to be a day for players to spend with their families or on the golf course. Now it was a workday. And not even proper work but hiss and boo entertainment for folk who, in his opinion, knew no better. Instead of being allowed to graze peacefully in the outfield, KC was expected to gallop and hurl himself about. A mis-field or a futile dive was greeted with abuse and ridicule rather than polite sympathy.

While at one end Topsy worked up enough pace to hurry both batsmen, KC kept it tight at the other. In the sixth over, Weetman, Pywell's opening partner, drove lavishly at a ball which nipped back to take the inside edge. This time KC was grateful to see the ball land safely in Holliday's gloves behind the stumps. It was an obvious 'nick' and the appeal to the umpire was perfunctory. Weetman angrily banged the toe of his bat into the ground and took his leave. 'Well bowled, KC,' said Jephcott, ambling to the stumps to confer. 'I thought the track would do a bit.'

'He played outside a straight one,' lied KC, determined to deny his captain any credit for opting to field first. 'Straight' or not it was a wicket and Richard Hastie saw his opportunity to eat humble pie.

'Sorry about the catch, KC.'

'Sorry? I could've caught that in the nick of me arse,' retorted KC. Neil Ibbotson smirked behind KC's back and leaned consolingly on Richard's shoulder. Firm mates, Ibbo and Richard came from a different era to that of the senior pro and the captain whose best years had been the late Fifties and early Sixties. Many called the period a Golden Age. Certainly the England selectors had a wealth of new ball bowlers to choose from and despite KC's consistently fine figures he was considered only when a freak sequence of injuries forced their hands. He had appeared in just three Tests and never made an overseas touring party. Fair-minded followers would tell him how shameful it was that lesser bowlers often got the nod. KC merely shrugged his shoulders like a man born to expect injustice as his due. Cricketers of the Gentlemen v Players era accepted unquestioningly the right of 'gentlemen' at HQ to pick the England team. Accordingly someone as unyielding, taciturn, and devoid of natural grace as KC would always be at a disadvantage.

The adage 'character is destiny' was never more valid than when applied to KC. Perhaps The Powers That Be feared his hands would be too coarse to meet Her Majesty, his manners too untutored for Government House.

It was different now. The wholesale decline and retirement of a generation of proven bowlers had opened the door to a wave of pacemen like Topsy. Products of the post-war baby boom who, despite their early infusion of NHS orange juice, had no endurance.

'I doubt if you can manage fifty off the wrist,' KC would taunt Topsy lewdly as yet another muscle spasm confined him to the treatment table. People said he had grown too fast for his body. He needed time to fill out and toughen up. It never happened. Topsy remained a six feet four inch beanpole with ligaments that went 'twang' in the night. In pre-season training KC relished being paired with Topsy for one-to-one lifting exercises that exposed the difference in their core strength.

'I were pushing coal wagons when I were your age, not supermarket trolleys.' In fact KC had every reason to be grateful for Topsy's contribution even if it meant accepting uphill-against-the-wind duties himself. Less resolute batsmen escaping from Topsy's pace would relax their concentration and succumb to KC's more insidious probings at the other end.

Weetman's dismissal had brought in Brian Chatterway, a nervous starter forever fidgeting with his gear and yakking to any fielder in earshot. Deciding that this compulsive talking was his way of settling in, Jephcott ordered his men not to respond. Richard Hastie, for one, found it hard to comply since he and Chatterway had always got on well. In his debut season when Hastie had asked his advice, Chatterway had not hesitated. 'Take care not to score too many runs, they'll come to expect it. If you've scored twelve hundred runs by mid August, think about next season's contract negotiation and go lame.' His was the authentic voice of the professional.

'What's it doin', Dicky?' Chatterway asked.

'Swinging,' lied Richard.

'Which way?'

'Both.'

'Any tips?'

'Keep your ground shots low and score if you can.'

'Thanks, you're a mate.' Jephcott tapped his foot irritably but the badinage continued as deliveries from both KC and Topsy went past Chatterway's bat without making contact.

'Just hold your bat still and we'll try an' hit it,' chuntered KC. Chatterway smiled and went about his business, steering and nudging the score along in Pywell's slipstream.

With only one wicket down and the early hardness leaving the ball, Jephcott was contemplating a failed gamble. Intent on keeping Topsy fresh, he took him off after five fruitless overs and brought Badel into the attack. As he talked to him about his field placings, he was alarmed to see the lad's flannels quivering with fright. All the usual expressions of encouragement deserted him. He simply gave Badel a pat on the shoulder and joined Richard in the slips.

Badel could barely grip the ball let alone run in and aim it at a set of stumps. The process of bowling suddenly appeared to involve an impossibly complex sequence of movements. That one of the finest batsmen in England was waiting at the other end never entered his head. The looming question was whether he could get the ball down there at all.

Pywell may have seen Badel's first ball but it was hard to know. England's Number One did not have to stir out of his stance as the ball whistled past Ibbo's nose at short square-leg and raced for four wides to the fine leg boundary. Down on the rope,

KC barely moved before the ball hit the sponsor's name. A petrified silence hung in the air. Badel's mouth was sandpaper dry but his hands oozed sweat. Behind the stumps, 'Doc' Holliday mentally put on his flying boots. 'Well it was quick,' offered Richard. Jephcott said nothing. Legs braced apart, a hand on each knee, he waited to see what horrors might follow.

Like any established county batsman, Pywell was quick to attune himself to the visual quirks of opposition bowlers. Their run up might be straight or curved; the ball held low in one hand or sometimes across the chest. The delivery action could vary from a model of metronomic efficiency to a slapstick agitation of arms and legs. The speed with which Pywell's eye 'picked up' the ball as it emerged finally from the bowler's hand was the key to his success or failure. He would take a cautious look at new boy Badel but he had already seen enough to expect rich pickings. However, Badel confounded everyone by landing his next three deliveries on the cut strip. Not only 'landing' but forcing Pywell into some uncharacteristically hurried blocks.

'Well bowled, Alvar,' Jephcott called up the pitch, the conjunction of cricket and Sweden making the captain feel faintly foolish. Pywell went prodding up the pitch and stared at the sightscreen in search of an explanation for his sudden discomfort. Next ball, he made sure he got enough bat on it to pinch a single and seek the sanctuary of the other end.

'Alvar – is that a Derbyshire name?' asked Chatterway. Obeying captain's orders, Ibbo made no reply but Chatterway went on regardless. 'Alvar, it's a funny one, is that. Is it Derbyshire for 'bloody quick' or something?'

Observing Badel's bowling from fine leg, KC chewed over the prospect of having a new seam bowler on the block. He had resigned himself only recently to playing second fiddle to Topsy and another demotion would see him lose the new ball. Jephcott was already using him as a stock bowler rather than a strike weapon. 'Keep it tight, KC,' he'd say. 'Just give me a couple more overs.' Sweat running down the nick of his arse just so Topsy could be kept fresh. It was not simply the loss of status that KC feared, he knew that first change bowlers rarely got a sniff of the second new ball when it was due. Without that he would be deprived the chance of cleaning out the rabbits at nine, ten, and jack, a perk which often redeemed a bowler's analysis.

For all Chatterway's nervous antics, Badel was not accurate enough to finish him off. The bowlers had not performed badly but the pitch had not misbehaved in any way since KC made the one delivery jump at Pywell and saw the catch spilled. Ominously, Jephcott had given up looking for rain. Having put Topsy on for a second spell at one end, he reasoned that a variation of pace was called for at the other and tossed the ball to Mal Shanks. It was tantamount to waving a white flag.

Shanks had first played for the county club at the age of twenty and now sixteen years later he was drawing on the dog-end of his First-class career. His short stocky frame had wheeled out thousands of overs of left-arm spin. Uphill or against the wind it was all the same to him. Three short hops to the wicket and over came his arm. He seemed to have perfected the frictionless delivery. Over sixteen seasons it was inevitable that he had enjoyed good days but lately his entry into the attack had been the batsmen's cue to dip their bread in some very sluggish gravy.

The captain listened to Shanks's fanciful ideas for an attacking field then ignored them. Addicted as he was to bowling at least one bad ball an over, Jephcott was anxious not to let things run away from him. While Topsy bowled a good second spell with no luck, Shanks served up his customary quota of good and bad. Pywell, who was the main beneficiary, took care not to be too punishing in case Jephcott took him off. But then as everyone's concentration was winding down in anticipation of the interval, Chatterway got himself out. Shuffling back and across to an innocuous-looking ball from Shanks, he got his bat caught behind his pad and the ball hit him 'plum' on his back leg. As shocked as anyone, Shanks let out a shrill and successful appeal.

A second wicket before lunch might have saved the captain's blushes but it fooled nobody. Both batsmen had got themselves out and a hundred and ten runs were on the board. Out on the field under a big sky the players' collective reaction had been diffused, but once they were closeted inside the dressing room it coalesced into one big cloud of negativity. Jephcott had boobed and KC for one was going to tell him so. But then KC found himself on the backfoot instead.

Denis Slingsby's bespectacled face appeared round the dressing room door. 'Could I have a word, Robin?' Jephcott looked up from untying his boots. Slingsby's smile, intended to allay anxiety, achieved the opposite. Nobody got between a player and his lunch unless something was seriously up.

2

Jephcott slipped on his Hush Puppies and followed Slingsby out of the dressing room to the adjacent club secretary's office. Though the room had a picture window onto the ground, Slingsby's desk faced the opposite wall. On it were hung a series of framed photographs of past county teams. The early sepia-tinted pictures of hirsute unsmiling faces gradually gave way to shy post-war smiles and on to the natty blazers, full-on beams and long hair of combines from the Sixties.

'There's been a complaint,' said Slingsby apologetically.

'Oh?'

'A spectator says Ken Colclough swore at his young son.'

'When was this?'

'When Ken was fielding on the boundary earlier today. The lad asked for his autograph and Ken told him to 'piss off'.'

'How old is the boy?'

'About twelve I'd guess. I appreciate he shouldn't have approached a player during play but you know how it is.'

'What would you like me to do?'

'Well, up to you Robin. It would be nice just to nip it in the bud. The thing is, he and dad came in on a British Leyland Group membership ticket. We don't need to bow and scrape exactly but they are biggish sponsors of ours.' Hoping to draw a politic gesture out of Jephcott, Slingsby's eyes twinkled behind his lenses.

'What will this chap settle for – forty lashes?' said Jephcott. Slingsby smiled indulgently.

'I'm sure he'd be happy with an apology and a scorecard signed by both sides. If you can persuade Ken to be available at close of play, I'll go ahead and fix it.' Jephcott nodded and left. Brusque and belligerent though he could be, KC had always been the consummate professional and he did not relish the prospect of taking him to task.

The dining room was designated a spike-free zone and Jephcott knew he would find KC having his lunch in the changing room in preference to taking his boots off. 'A man and a kid? Yeh, I remember them.' KC frowned and downed a forkful of steak and kidney pie. 'What about them?'

'The father said you swore at the boy.' KC's jaw dropped in surprise. For a moment Jephcott had a clear view of half-masticated pie. 'Did you swear?'

'I don't think so.'

'The father says you told the lad to 'piss off'.'

'If I didn't say it, I thought it,' said KC unhelpfully and shovelled in another forkful.

'They came in on a group membership card – one of the club's biggest sponsors.'

'Who's that then?'

'British Leyland.'

'British Bloody Leyland!' KC almost choked. The company had become a byword for chaotic labour relations and shoddy manufacture. It had something like twenty different unions and several thousand militant shop stewards, a large proportion of them labelled 'reds' by the Press. KC assumed the complainant must be one of them.

'I expect he's bored of running his own company into the ground so he comes here on a 'sickie' to muck us about.' Jephcott offered a shrug of his shoulders to convey sympathy without suggesting the matter was closed.

'Denis Slingsby wondered if there was something we could do?'

'Like what?' said KC.

'An apology perhaps?'

'What for?'

'You didn't sound sure – about the swearing.'

'Well I am now. British Bloody Leyland, I'm not kidding.'

'Slingsby's not a bad sort. It would help him out of a corner.'

'He's never done 'owt for me.'

'He's arranging for a scorecard to be signed by both teams. I'd like you to give it to the boy at the close of play.'

'No apology,' said KC firmly.

'See how you feel when the time comes', said Jephcott, hoping KC's mood would soften as the day wore on.

Chapter Three

1

When Richard Hastie went to use the phone in the pavilion corridor, he found Topsy relaying bets to his bookmaker. One or two of his team-mates also used his credit account, copying his habit of broadcasting their rare triumphs while burying a persistent stream of losses. It still surprised Richard that otherwise sane individuals could be duped into believing they had inside knowledge via 'a lad at the yard'. Just as professional sportsmen expected to enter night clubs free of charge on account of the celebrity testosterone they supposedly brought to a venue, an inside racing tip was somehow considered one of their perks. Sadly for Topsy and Co, the deficit balance on their account suggested the lad at the yard had a wicked sense of humour.

Aware that players would soon be finishing their lunch and exiting the dining room, Richard pointed to where his wrist watch would normally be in the hope of hurrying Topsy along. He needed a private word with Tessa and his window of opportunity was small. 'What colour are they today?' said Topsy, flirting lewdly with the bookmaker's assistant. 'My favourite. I look forward to getting a flash of them. Got to go, someone's waiting.'

Richard dialed home. Though his message was to be a magnanimous one he felt a tickle of apprehension in his gut. After his cool parting from Tessa that morning, three days of non-communication would probably lower the temperature to freezing. As absences went, a three-day stay in Birmingham involving two overnights was relatively short. In past seasons Richard had chosen to travel from home each day rather than stay in the team hotel. However, traffic snarl-ups had made the journey time unpredictable, and though Jephcott was no dressing room tyrant, anyone arriving at a ground less than an hour before the start of play could expect a stiff rebuke and a fine on top.

Tessa took an age to answer the phone and was breathless when she did. 'I was putting the girls into the car,' she said in a tone that implied he should have known. 'What do you want?' Already his gesture of conciliation seemed the minimum requirement.

'I'm sorry about the way we left things this morning.'

'Well you agreed weeks ago that I could get the quotes.'

'I know – my fault. Why don't you just get on and book the job?'

'Right,' said Tessa, trying not to sound surprised.

'Whatever tiles you're happy with,' he said over-egging it.

'Okay, fine.' She saw no point in telling him she had already decided to do just that. 'I'd better go or the girls will be creating.'

'Yes, right.'

'See you when I see you.' Her phone went down and Richard held the receiver for a moment. He might have been dismissed for nought before the lunch interval or scored a blistering century but she had not enquired.

He could not blame Tessa for her apparent indifference. From April to September a professional cricketer led a strange stop-start existence. Mazy car journeys up and down the country were interspersed with yawning days in the field or sessions holed up in a pavilion. Days of listless inaction suddenly spiked with bursts of tension, fear, and excitement. Soldiers describe their own deployment in similar terms and cricketers' wives would have no difficulty in finding common ground with their army sisters. Tessa Hastie, like other wives, put her married life to one side for half the year and became a single parent.

From the start she had more or less accepted this as her lot. The introduction of Sunday cricket, however, had given oxygen to her unacknowledged resentment. At first she had joined the other wives in trying to make a social event of Sunday one-day fixtures, but the children required constant supervision at venues bustling with spectators and ill-equipped for family amusement. Finally Tessa had preferred the peace and containment of her own back garden to the hassle of match day involvement.

Sunday play had brought other consequences. On the one hand it was seen as an innovative way to bring in the crowds and sell the game to a wider television audience, but to the die-hards it was the thin end of the wedge. 'Mickey Mouse' limited-over cricket not only corrupted the game, they said, its association with tobacco sponsorship also tainted the players who took part. Even the 'John Player' branding mocked cricket's eager acceptance of the money.

Richard was no smoker, neither were most of his team-mates, but leggy promotions girls made sure they were stocked up with packs of cigarettes which they in turn could give away as favours. In their smart-as-paint yellow and black uniforms, these pushers of the weed were a cross between cosmetic counter assistants and air-hostesses. Their glamour was as good a reason as any for players' wives to drag themselves and their kids along to keep an eye on their partner. They sensed that on the Sabbath of all days, the chugging nature of county cricket had suddenly become more febrile.

Of the single men only Rod Brennan, the club's overseas signing, could lay claim to success with John Player's playmates. The Tasmanian's big lopsided grin, broad frame and tanned skin, proved an irresistible combination to young women looking for action. Not that Rod was one to trumpet his triumphs. He thought too much of his fiancée back in Hobart to ever let her down by relating his off-duty encounters to team-mates. Such an attitude left ten men, the physio, the scorer, and the dressing room attendant with their tongues hanging out to dry. It was unsatisfactory not to say unsportsmanlike. Fellow players had no option but to imagine the moment when Rod unbuckled his belt and presented what was widely accepted to be the largest white member on the circuit. Even in its flaccid state, Rod's todger stuck out at forty five degrees from the vertical like a baby's arm. Weary of the ribaldry, Rod took pains not to exhibit himself, further diminishing his comedy value in the dressing room.

Richard shelved plans to go back into the dining room for dessert and opted to read his newspaper for the ten minutes remaining before play resumed. In the dressing room he found KC reading a newspaper. 'This yours?' he said, gripping Richard's *Daily Telegraph*.

'When you've finished with it,' said Richard, searching in vain for another broadsheet.

'I see Lycett's tipping your kid for the Windies?' Things have come to some'at.'

'Speedy's figures aren't bad,' replied Richard loyally.

'They need a batter who can bowl a bit, not t'other way round. Still it's a wonder he's got a mention. Normally you have to play for Middlesex to impress Lycett.' Richard obliged with a smile of agreement but knew he was unlikely to avoid a canter on one of KC's hobby-horses. Julian Lycett was the doyen of cricket correspondents. He was knowledgeable, elegant in his prose, and authoritative. Some players, particularly those north of Watford, believed he held undue sway over the national selectors. 'He never shifts his lard-arse out of London unless it's to cover a Test,' KC observed. 'Even then the snooty bastard has to put a peg on his nose. What does he know? He's never played the bloody game.'

It was fatal to put up a counter argument once KC had found his groove. Years before, Lycett had promoted the selection of a Kent bowler of modest achievement but impeccable manners to travel as fourth seamer on an M.C.C. tour. He was a player destined to carry the drinks and be the ambassadorial face of the M.C.C. abroad. To have been overlooked for a bowler so much his inferior had been an insult to KC and it still stung. 'That's why Atkins has come to see your kid. He's just jumping to Lycett's voice.'

Richard gave up looking for something sensible to read. He had already read the report in the *Telegraph* of the previous day's play at Chesterfield. Since rain had intervened to wash the game out after lunch, Richard's batting in the morning had won undue prominence. His unbeaten innings of eighty to set up the declaration was 'calm and measured with hardly a false stroke'. He had 'used his feet and eased the ball into gaps, punishing anything erring in length.' One to save for the scrapbook, thought Richard, aware that KC was in danger of trailing the report across the gravy residues on his lunch plate.

'They could do worse than take you to the Windies,' said KC without looking up to inspect Richard's look of surprise. 'Another nice write-up in the paper. Plenty of runs in the bank.

37

Why not?' he said, as if Richard had contradicted him. 'Just learn to catch the bloody ball before you go.'

2

As Jephcott led his team out after the interval there was a suspicion of rain in the air. The blue morning sky had given way to a sulky grey and spectators had migrated to the covered stands. After finishing his lunchtime husbandry in the middle, Wilf Bristow halted on the boundary edge and willed the clouds to open properly so he could wheel on the covers. At that moment he had the worst of all worlds – rain too light to stop play but heavy enough to send players skidding across his turf.

Such as it was, the rain had come later than Jephcott had hoped. The ball was thirty five overs old and its seam already discouragingly flat. He needed a sharp shower to tip the odds in favour of his bowlers. As it was, the modest spits and spots would merely make the ball greasy to hold and do nothing to alter the nature of the pitch.

Buoyed by his pre-lunch dismissal of Chatterway, Mal Shanks bounced onto the field like a man about to cut through the opposition like a scythe through buttercups. Jephcott, however, threw him the ball more in the hope of lightning striking twice than a vote of confidence.

Chatterway's replacement was Curtis Short, Warwickshire's West Indian middle-order batsman. Short was one of a number of gifted West Indians who had adapted quickly to English conditions. The Weekes, Worrell, and Walcott era had spawned a raft of players whose defensive skills were as sound as their attacking shots were flamboyant. Curtis Short was hungry for runs and prepared to graft like the most obdurate English stonewaller. A compact player in his stance – backside out, shoulders hunched – as Shanks bobbed in to bowl. After using three innocuous offerings as sighters, Short leaned back to the fourth and with a flick of the wrist, dispatched it square of the wicket to the leg-side boundary. Shanks held up his hands in disbelief as if the batsman had been bamboozled into a misjudgement even as the ball hit the rope.

A stand between Pywell and Short wasn't something Jephcott wanted to contemplate. Deciding to persist with a combination of spin and pace, he brought on Topsy. A good lunch, he thought, might be lying heavy on Pywell's stomach and softening his resolve. This strategy fatally assumed that Topsy himself had been careful with his portions. 'Give 'em three overs of hell,' said Jephcott. Topsy nodded without a trace of enthusiasm. 'Knock 'em over, fella,' urged the captain, pretending to find some shine on the ball.

When challenged, Topsy would claim with some justification that he needed to refuel at lunch. He was not a one-meal-a-day mutt. He needed stamina and if it took a few deliveries to shake a meal down, then so be it. It astonished 'civilians' to learn that county cricketers routinely tucked into a three-course lunch of meat and two veg followed by sponge pudding and a cheeseboard. Only during festival weeks on outlying grounds did a wan ham salad make an appearance, usually eaten under canvas in a field canteen.

So having assessed at nil his chances of extracting life from the pitch, Topsy had taken more 'stamina' on board than was perhaps wise. Pywell, on the other hand, had visualised an afternoon of run-plundering and prudently slipped cream crackers and cheese into his napkin for later. The contest, already uneven, thus swung further in favour of the bat.

Richard swore he could hear bread and butter pudding

sloshing about inside Topsy as he ran in to bowl. It was unlikely that KC could hear the same from his position on the boundary, but he could see the result in Topsy's output and began to stretch his legs in anticipation of an early return to the attack. His fears of a long afternoon of stiff-upper-lip bowling were allayed, however, by a sharp downpour which brought Wilf Bristow scurrying from his lair beneath the Priory Stand. By the time the umpires had made the decision to retreat to the pavilion, the covers for both ends were half way to the middle. And once on, the umpires knew they would have a devil of a job getting Wilf to take them off again.

3

Despite the hospitable bowling of Shanks and Topsy, the truncated session had yielded only forty one runs and Jephcott reasoned that rain could only make the pitch more difficult to bat on. For the moment, he was happy to sink into a corner with a newspaper and let the weather do its worst.

Two coffin-shaped cases placed one on top of the other made a card table and a 'school' quickly gathered. KC declined the chance to recover his losses of the previous day, preferring to snipe at Topsy from the sidelines. 'I hope Gil Atkins was asleep when you opened up after lunch. My Aunty Beryl could've bowled quicker.'

'Leave him alone, he's nursing a niggle in his groin,' said Ibbo, tongue-in-cheek.

'Then he should see the physio instead of playing cards.'

'Put a sock in it, Ken, I'm trying to concentrate,' said Topsy.

'First time today then,' muttered KC before moving off to autograph a stack of new bats brought into the changing room by Colin Stinton, the Warwickshire beneficiary. Destined to become raffle prizes, the bats already bore the home team's autographs, and those of two other county teams. It was a chore nobody begrudged since the award of a tax-free benefit seemed to be the goal of most county cricketers. Richard and Ibbo thought the system was essentially feudal. Because the registration rules restricted players from moving between counties for better wages, they had become in effect tied employees and the benefit system further shackled them to one club by holding out the possibility of a distant payday for loyal service.

If the beneficiary was fortunate, a committee of friends would help to arrange pro celebrity matches, dances, and sports dinners. But more often than not, the fund-raising burden was borne by the player himself. As a result, virtue was rarely rewarded. A player who had given outstanding service on the field of play might possess the organising acumen of a dyslexic librarian. Thus the great KC's tax-free bonanza had realised no more than half that of Mal Shanks, who had proved murderously adept at squeezing the last pip out of each and every benefactor. 'No coin too small' had been Shank's battle cry as he raided piggy banks and bludgeoned booksellers into selling his benefit brochure.

4

Signatories to Colin Stinton's benefit bats had left a space below Jephcott's name in recognition of KC's status as senior pro. It was rather wider than his reticent signature required. KC's confident capitals were followed by child-like lower case letters including a 'g', the tail of which underlined the previous letters of his name. It was a surprising, albeit ineffectual, display of pretension. Richard and Ibbo surmised that he was determined not to be out-curlicued by Topsy Turner, who set about embellishing his autograph the minute he won his first England cap.

Out on the square, the umpires parlayed with Wilf Bristow. The rain had stopped and spectators were promenading beyond the shelter of the stands. One or two shouted their displeasure at the delay in removing the covers, but Wilf was a master of obfuscation. After assessing the direction and strength of the wind and the type and altitude of the clouds, he forecast another bout of rain in ten minutes. As the umpires appeared to be ignoring his expertise, he added that the light was too gloomy in any case.

'Get 'em off,' shouted a khaki-coloured anorak sitting alone in the stands. His frustration found an echo on the other side of the ground.

'What're you waiting for?'

'Get 'em off,' repeated the anorak, spurred on by the show of Black Country solidarity.

'Get on and play the bloody game.'

The umpires turned their backs on Wilf in an attempt to convince the spectators of their independence of action, and after a moment or two squinting at the sky, decided to take an early tea.

'Bloody disgrace,' cried the anorak.

Denis Slingsby frowned from his office window. He had become inured to members' complaints concerning the players' aversion to rain. He had reasoned with people that cricket was not an easy game to play in the wet. The counter argument that it was the same for both sides cut no ice because rain invariably favoured the batting side. Bowlers charging in to bowl had to be sure of dry footholds or risk injury. Fielders were disadvantaged if the ball was wet and slippery. Only when poor light made visibility a problem did the balance swing against the batsman. Even so, Slingsby sometimes suspected a degree of collusion between umpires, groundsman, and players. He had been detailed by his committee on more than one occasion to remind Wilf Bristow of his obligations to the paying public.

'What, all five of 'em?' Wilf replied when approached on the matter. 'I don't make the decisions,' he had said disingenuously. 'Talk to the umpires, not me.' Not on your Nelly, thought Slingsby. A club secretary appearing to criticise or influence the umpires' judgement would be keelhauled at HQ. Umpires were sensitive souls when made to defend their integrity. They also tended to be ex-professionals with a well-seasoned distrust of committee 'suits' and salaried outsiders like Slingsby.

The news of an early tea was greeted with no great surprise in the dressing room. Ibbo was on a roll and eager for another hand of cards but others beat a retreat. Topsy's race tips had flopped as usual and they had lost enough money for one day. Richard thought about calling Tessa again, but when he went to the phone he found Rod Brennan leaning against the wall cradling the receiver to his chest. From the warm confidential tone in his voice, he guessed that one of Rod's compliant female playmates was on the other end. If he stuck around in the hope of persuading Rod to wind up his conversation, he would have to be party to the unctuous bullshit he was dripping down the line. Richard withdrew to the dining room and resolved to try Tessa later.

5

A lack of physical activity since lunch had dulled players' appetites and tea was a desultory affair. Gil Atkins had invited himself into the players' dining room and sat between the captains on the top table. Like other England selectors he viewed county captains as his accomplices in the quest for the best Test team. They were normally out of the running for selection themselves and therefore in an impartial position to judge the capabilities of contenders. This was particularly the case when it came to temperament. A player had to be a sound team man in the dressing room as well as on the field. The ability of a player to lift the spirits of others in times of crisis could bring preferment over a player with superior figures.

It may have been his imagination but Richard got the impression that he was the subject of discussion between Jephcott and Atkins. While Jephcott seemed engaged in an extended reply to a question, Atkins maintained a glassy stare over his shoulder, nodding intermittently. Speedy's comments in the nets and those of KC later had slyly taken root in the hopes and dreams corner of Richard's brain.

When Richard confided his thoughts to Ibbo, he had them quickly dispelled. Atkins's rheumy gaze, explained Ibbo, was like that of a blind man, scoping everything and seeing nothing. But minutes later Richard felt a warm hand on his shoulder and turned to find Atkins.

'My spies reckon your knock at Lord's last week was as good as any they'd seen all season,' said Atkins.

'Not good enough though,' said Richard straining for modesty.

'Well the win may have gone begging but you did more than your bit. You've not done much bowling lately?'

'No.'

'It's always useful to a skipper if you can turn your arm over. Just a thought.' Richard nodded solemnly as if Atkins had said something profound. Out of the corner of his eye he saw Speedy intently observing their exchange.

It was true, Richard had neglected his bowling, but with runs coming thick and fast he thought it best to conserve his energy for batting. Jephcott seemed to think so too. He had been asked to bowl his off spin only to effect a change of ends for the regular bowlers or as a brief variation to break a stubborn stand. 'A batter who can bowl a bit,' he recalled KC saying. Was he really in the frame? The phone in the dressing room corridor was available but concerned by Atkins's observations, Richard sailed past regardless to the dressing room.

Irrespective of whether or not he was in the selectors' thoughts, Richard had good reason to be satisfied with the season now drawing to a close. May had been uncharacteristically dry if not especially warm and he had surfed a wave of good fortune to post sizeable scores. He had no doubt that he owed a great part of his success to the arrival of Rod Brennan. Pre-season nets had shown the Tasmanian to be a strong clean striker of the ball and Jephcott decided to make him Richard's opening partner.

It was generally accepted that the openers' task was to see off the opening attack and establish a firm foundation. A conservative approach to batting was therefore the order of the day. Rod Brennan showed no such inclination. If the ball was there to be hit, he was going to hit it. It was a simple enough idea that in English conditions was less easy in the execution. Even modest bowlers could make the ball wobble enough in the air and off the pitch to make full-blown attacking shots something of a lottery. But from the first delivery, Rod was willing to charge the seamers and thump the ball into the yonder. 'Plenty of room in the sky,' he explained as yet another massive mis-hit fell shy of a shell-shocked out-fielder.

The benefit to Richard of having Rod and his thunderclaps at the other end was that bowling sides were completely discombobulated. Respectable deliveries being smashed to the boundary was no surprise in the closing stages of a run chase, but in the first overs of a three-day match? There was something unseemly about it. Bowlers were affronted, all dignity lost. Meanwhile Richard could travel inconspicuously in Rod's slipstream, taking advantage of the opposition's disarray. As gaps opened up all over the field, he nurdled and nudged to set himself up for a long stay at the crease.

Of course, it could not last. As word got round the bowlers' union about Brennan, the more width they gave him to hang himself. After chasing one too many wide deliveries and perishing, Jephcott pushed him down the batting order to save his explosive talents for when the ball was older and moved less off the seam. By that time, however, Richard was on such a roll that he found himself in the first half dozen batsmen in the national averages.

With the reinstatement of Ibbo as his opening partner, Richard felt responsibility settle again onto his own shoulders. But something fundamental had changed in his approach. Without forsaking his tried and trusted technique, he experienced a new freedom. Something of Rod Brennan's attitude had rubbed off. Hitherto when he had gone out to bat there had been a self-effacing air about him. Perhaps it was a survival strategy, an anticipation of failure to ward off disappointment. Whatever the reason, he now found himself stepping onto the field in the expectation of success and more often than not it proved to be the case.

The ups and downs of a sports pro's career naturally enough create corresponding tensions in their personal lives. So it seemed perverse that Richard's success on the field had brought friction rather than harmony between Tessa and himself. Was it arrogance and self-absorption on his part or was it simply the kids going through a difficult stage? He had begun to wonder if personal conflict actually fuelled his desire for success, even sharpened his reflexes. On occasions, all night rows or separate beds had been the precursor to his most accomplished performances on the field. The glowing press reports next day merely added salt to Tessa's wounds. It confirmed her belief that she and the family came a poor second to his ambition.

Back from hospital, Graham Murfin was shrugging off expressions of sympathy like an old trooper. Yes, he'd had his head X-rayed. No, they hadn't found anything, ha ha. Alvar Badel hovered uneasily and apologised for the umpteenth time. 'Save it for the opposition in future,' said Murf, aiming for locker-room wit and missing. He was not feeling as chipper as he was making out. The injury behind his ear was an awkward one to dress. He had been spared the full wrap-round bandage in favour of a thick pad of gauze battened down with sticky tape. It looked as if it might fly off as soon as he blew his nose. Faced with the prospect of spending the thick end of three days on twelfth man duties, Murf toned down his stoicism when Jephcott came into the dressing room.

'How're you feeling, Murf?'

'Bit shaky.'

'D'you want to go home?'

'Up to you, Skip.'

'What did the hospital say?'

'They suggested taking a couple of days off,' said Murf,

thereby giving Jephcott no choice but to let him go. Of the players only Rod Brennan would be heading back to Derby after the close of play but he did not immediately warm to the idea of giving Murf a lift, involving as it would a sizeable detour round the city ring road to drop him off.

'Sure,' agreed Rod bending to fasten his boots and hiding the irritation on his face. Ibbo winked at Richard. Clearly Rod had urgent business back home and did not want to deprive the female in question for a moment longer than necessary.

6

Tessa Hastie lay on the living room carpet staring at the ceiling. She had taken Sarah to play with her neighbour's daughter. Not needing to compete for her mother's attention, Jessica was content now to ignore Tessa and concentrate on arranging the interior of her Fisher Price doll's house, chatting non-stop to the miniature occupants. Mum, dad and child in their little plastic chairs, baby in a rocker, the family placed neatly round a tiny gingham-covered table.

Five years of child rearing since Sarah was born had eroded a sizeable chunk of Tessa's sense of identity not to mention her brain cells and stamina. It seemed a whole lifetime since she had worked as a conveyancer for a firm of solicitors, a senior partner of which, James Egan, happened to be the county cricket club's lawyer. When Richard Hastie asked his advice about purchasing a flat, Egan introduced him to Tessa as the person who would handle the paperwork.

She had been made aware of Richard previously from a newspaper photograph of local sporting celebrities attending the opening of a car showroom. Tessa's closest work colleague,

Maggie, had enthusiastically put names to the faces and though she had no interest in sport, Tessa could readily appreciate why her friend was so smitten. The half dozen twenty-somethings were at the peak of their physical condition. Photo-savvy and crisply dressed in suits and ties they projected a relaxed virility. Maggie fancifully compared them to the L.A. Rat Pack. Her mock swooning from the wings during Richard's subsequent visits to Tessa's office never failed to amuse, and as her attraction to him deepened, Tessa got a buzz from others openly coveting the same prize.

After a whirlwind of dates, Tessa moved into Richard's flat – a conveyancing service not normally afforded to clients, she assured him. They married within months of living together in deference to her parents' sense of propriety, and a year later she was pregnant. She now realised that the time selfishly to savour their life as a besotted, fun-loving couple, had been all too brief.

Neither had she grasped then the nature of a professional sportsman's existence. She had no inkling of the rivalries, self-absorption and nervous tension that went hand in hand with the job. Despite this lack of understanding she had been happy to offer Richard a sympathetic ear when he had sacrificed his wicket in a doomed run-chase, or when capricious umpiring had cut short a promising innings. But as she became bored and exhausted with the day-to-day grind of motherhood, she felt less disposed to share his woes and the separation of their roles became ever more pronounced.

At first Tessa believed this drifting apart could be arrested in the winter months when Richard became a nine-to-fiver. Instead he seemed intent on giving his out-of-season job more attention than was absolutely necessary in order to check criticism from colleagues about his part-time status. His continued absences in those niggling scratchy hours between the girls' tea and their bath time had eaten into her reserves of goodwill. Their partnership, she thought, had declined into an allotment of duties, their dialogue into a series of corkboard messages.

7

'Okay fellas, let's shake 'em up.' Jephcott's post-tea exhortation as he led his men onto the field might well have come courtesy of the public school handbook marked 'officers for the use of'. Similar utterances had been used as readily in armed conflict as on the games field. Transparent though Jephcott was in affecting the vernacular, nobody seemed to take exception. Accordingly nobody had openly questioned his decision to put the opposition in to bat. A tacit understanding existed that players would go wherever he led and however barmy the strategy. This mute acceptance of a natural officer class, Richard thought, had cost the lower ranks dearly down the years. Yet there was no mistaking the respect in which Jephcott was held, and over the past six seasons he had melded a disparate bunch of characters into an effective team.

It helped that Jephcott was a handy player. A captain not worth his place on playing ability might survive for a time, assuming his judgement was sound, but the rigours of a long season exposed the lack of a more measurable contribution. There were still some in the cricket establishment who believed the 'gentleman' and 'player' model worked best. A man of independent means, they believed, was free to be his own man in a team of hired hands. But cricket had not been immune to a decade in which old patterns of behaviour had been swept aside. Players had always been motivated by win bonuses and now they expected to be led by a captain who could get runs and wickets rather than one who had the right connections.

Jephcott lobbed the ball to KC. 'Give me a quick blast.'

Whether or not KC inwardly bridled at the request, Richard could only guess. KC's blasting days were long gone. KC knew it and so did Jephcott. With the score at 151 for 2 there was a brief window of opportunity to take advantage of any effect the rain might have had on the pitch. Two or three quick wickets would change the complexion of the day, but Jephcott needed accuracy from his bowlers to exert some pressure. Normally after an interval he would call on Topsy in the hope of him slipping a fast delivery through the defence of a batsman restarting his innings. However, the light had deteriorated under a lowering sky and he was afraid Topsy's extra pace might force the umpires to intervene on the grounds of safety.

Accordingly, Jephcott nominated all-rounder Tony Crick to bowl his medium-paced inswing. Crick had murmured his dissatisfaction at being overlooked in the morning session. He was what the trade called a 'bits and pieces' player. As such he had the best and the worst of it. If he failed with the ball he could make a contribution with the bat and vice versa. On the other hand, his position at six or seven in the order often left him shoring up the innings while running out of batting partners. As for bowling, he rarely got hold of the ball before it had been battered into a soft dog-eared lump.

Though he would never admit it even to himself, the 'bits and pieces' life suited Crick. As long as he chipped in with a half-century now and then and a couple of wickets here and there, his place in the side was assured. Though limited-over cricket was a curse to traditionalists like KC, it was tailor-made for Tony Crick and his all round skills. Recently a quick-fire forty and a three-wicket haul had brought him a Man of the Match medal in a sixty-over contest. It was a welcome moment in the spotlight for someone who believed he was more leading-man material than Jephcott seemed to recognise. However to move up a notch in the skipper's estimation he would need to show more dedication. As he was nudging thirty years of age the odds were long on him changing his spots.

For a start Crick did not do early nights. He and middle-order batsman, Barry Picken, were the nighthawks of the team. Married as they both were, the County Championship enabled them to lead a varied double-life whenever and wherever they played away from home. KC had observed disapprovingly that the duo were so addicted to chasing 'skirt' that cricket had become a sideshow. He would recount how, during a match at Lord's, he had spotted Crick fondling a woman in the Rose Garden behind the pavilion. 'On top of her, he were – during the bloody match – at Lord's!'

Naive observers had even broached the possibility of Crick succeeding Jephcott as captain. It was an opinion primed mainly by Crick himself who suspected that despite his educated background, Richard Hastie was not a shoo-in for the job. Appropriately for a conman and serial philanderer, Crick possessed a useful measure of plausibility. He made a habit of treating hacks to drinks at the end of a day's play and fed them tit-bits in return for favourable write-ups. That he combined a public image of decency with unsavoury private tastes was no drawback. After all, it was common enough among politicians, captains of industry and royalty.

After a fruitless over from KC, Crick wiped the ball dry with a cloth and with some vigorous polishing up and down his thigh, tried to work up some shine. Jephcott needed wickets but he could not afford to give away easy runs so his field setting was a compromise. Crick routinely swung the ball into the right-handed batsman. If the ball failed to swing in the air he would revert to off-cutters. Whichever it was to be, Jephcott felt comfortable in weighting his fielders to the leg side.

Crick's first ball was an in-swinging half-volley. Pywell fastened onto it and drove it crisply to mid-on where Richard was fielding. The elegance of the stroke belied its power and he had to drop down quickly on one knee to form a barrier with his lower leg. The ball smacked into his calf just below the knee-cap. 'Wakey, wakey,' shouted Ibbo, amused by his discomfort. The second delivery was a replica of the first. Pywell shaped to play the same stroke, but like the class batsman he was, he turned his wrists at the last moment to find the gap, ten yards to Richard's right. Pywell did not bother to get out of the blocks. From the moment it left the blade it had 'four' written on it. Richard jogged towards the boundary hoping a spectator might pop out of the stands and lob the ball back, but nobody appeared.

Crick measured out his run-up again. It was a familiar ploy meant to convince those not acquainted with the ruse that the two bad deliveries were the result of an error in calculation rather than schoolboy incompetence. He picked up his marker disc and moved it back an inch. Off the field Crick's self-belief was impressively resilient. Drawing on a reservoir of charm, he could win over the most sceptical of doubters. On the field, things were different. There his performance was exposed to scrutiny and summarised in statistics that precluded any fakery. Courtesy of the good book *Wisden*, his career would be summed up in a single stark line of figures that would dog him for life like a prison record.

In his determination not to serve up another full-length ball, Crick over-compensated and pulled his next delivery down short. Anticipating this, Pywell leaned onto the back foot and with a dismissive flourish, stroked it through the covers. Ibbo dived full-length but succeeded only in stinging the tips of his fingers as the ball scorched past en route to the rope. Crick hung his head and air-kicked the ground in disgust. He glanced sheepishly at Jephcott standing arms folded at slip, tapping his foot in fury. Another half hour of this, thought the captain, and they would be deep in the mire.

Pywell issued a little throat-clearing cough, a subconscious sign to himself not to be too greedy. The swagger in Crick's shoulders had vanished. He badly needed a dot ball to stop Jephcott's irate foot coming loose from his leg. Almost to a man the fielders knew where the next ball was going. Behind the stumps, 'Doc' Holliday braced himself to take the face-saving delivery down the leg-side. When it came it was almost a wide that had Holliday scrambling on all fours to collect it. Crick held a hand up in apology. 'Sorry, 'Doc',' he shouted. Jephcott swopped grimaces with his keeper. If he did not know that Crick had slept in his own bed the previous night, he could have been forgiven for thinking that sexual incontinence had taken its toll.

After Pywell had eased Crick's last ball through mid-wicket to steal the bowling from his partner, Jephcott approached Crick as he put his sweater back on.

'Problems?'

'Wet ball,' said Crick.

'Do you want another man on the rope next over?'

'Hope not.'

'So do I,' came the frosty reply.

A sepulchral gloom had begun to envelope the ground as KC prepared to bowl again. Crick's hapless over had fuelled KC's contempt for those who let their standards drop. He would have no truck with it. And just to prove the point, his next over alone was worth the admission money. The first two balls struck Pywell's bat high up near the splice jarring the knuckles of his thumb and first finger. The third cut in off the seam and smacked him on the hip above his thigh guard. Pywell hopped about as if he had been shot, half-grimacing, half-laughing it off. KC returned a grisly smile and came back with more of the same. Pywell fended off the fourth ball and called for an implausible run.

'Stay!' screamed Short, unwilling to sacrifice his wicket. Pywell nodded an apology. Within the space of four balls, the balance had shifted. In his heyday KC had regularly turned games on their head with a sudden incisive spell. Jephcott clapped his hands, a signal to every fielder not to make an error that might release the pressure he hoped was about to build on the batsmen.

Pywell rubbed his bruised hip, prodded the pitch and watched Jephcott change the field to bring two men closer to the bat. KC noted the changes with quiet satisfaction. For a moment the years rolled back. His body was no longer an obstacle to be surmounted but an imposing propulsive force, the ball his accomplice rather than a tool.

KC's fifth and sixth deliveries lacked only their due reward. The first was a shade short of a length forcing Pywell onto the backfoot but giving him no time to adjust to a break-back. He jack-knifed at the waist as if the ball had cut him in half before zipping through to the keeper. The second seemed to hit exactly the same spot, but as Pywell pushed forward to minimise lateral movement, he found himself playing at air as the ball broke the other way to beat the outside edge of his bat. A collective groan went up from the in-fielders at Pywell's good fortune. KC simply stood hands on hips. He was much too proud to claim mere moral victories, but there was some satisfaction in showing who was boss.

For the benefit of the umpires, Pywell blinked exaggeratedly at the clouds. There was no doubt that the rain and dank atmosphere had 'greened up' the surface of the pitch. While it was a pity to forego another helping of Crick's erratic bowling, KC was a different proposition and it was clear Pywell wanted to go off before he was undone. However the umpires made no move to confer. KC took the ball to Crick. Disdainful though he often was about Crick's personal conduct, KC was a team-man first and last and he knew a few words of encouragement went a long way.

'Line and length, Tony. Let the ball do the work.' It was nothing that Crick did not know already, but he accepted the advice with a sombre nod. He realised another bad over would loosen the grip KC had begun to apply. Jephcott fiddled with the field but rejected the more defensive options and much to his relief, Crick got his radar working and began to pose Curtis Short problems of his own. As a result, Short joined Pywell in grimacing at the umpires in a non-too-subtle attempt to get off the field for bad light. Usefully for their cause, lights had been switched on at points around the ground and the pavilion was glowing like a cruise ship at twilight.

Having contrived a single from a leg-bye, Short found himself facing up to KC's next over. The expectation that something was about to happen was almost palpable. KC stood pawing the ground at the end of his run up before anyone else had taken their fielding positions. Close to the end of a long and successful career, it surprised Richard that KC could still summon up such bloodlust for his prey. Richard wiped the palms of his hands on the grass. Just as the prevailing gloom made batting more difficult, so it was for slip-catchers. While many players had the good-sized hands and sharp reflexes required to field at slip, very few had the temperament to remain static yet alert hour upon hour. Days might pass before a chance presented itself but the good slip-catcher reacted as if it had come by appointment. No surprise, no grabbing in haste, just the welcoming cradle of soft hands. Despite KC's caustic comments, Richard had become a reliable member of the slip cordon, but his earlier drop had punctured his confidence. One mistake had created doubt, and once tension crept in, further chances were likely to go begging.

Curtis Short stopped KC's first ball with a statuesque back-foot defensive shot, holding his body shape, elbow high, bat straight, until a fielder came to pick up the ball. The next ball caught him neither forward nor back and rapped him on the pad. The in-field went up in a concerted appeal, but Short had got a sliver of bat on the ball. As it squirted out to the leg-side, Short called for a comfortable single.

'No!' Pywell bellowed. Short slammed on the brakes but lost his footing as he spun round to recover his ground. He scrambled to his feet and dived for the safety of the crease. He got up and spanked dirt from the front of his pullover and pads. The whites of his accusing eyes glared from under the peak of his cap but the rebuke sailed over his partner's head. Pywell smiled and twitched his nose as if the call had been unduly speculative. 'Too tight for me, Tiny,' he said.

'Pillock,' replied Short, not quite under his breath.

Jephcott put in a third slip as Short composed himself to face KC again. Every ball in his last two overs had pitched more or less on the same spot and done something testingly different. The next delivery would have been too good for most batsmen even in daylight. Pitching on off-stump and holding its own, it was effectively a fast leg-break. How Short managed to get a touch on it was a miracle. KC saw the ball arrowing fast to Jephcott at first slip. The trajectory of the ball was higher than that of the catch dropped earlier but still awkward and in the gloom Jephcott failed to judge its speed. The ball broke through his hands and cannoned into his chest. Knocked back on his heels, Jephcott's hands wafted desperately to snatch the ball as it rebounded in front of him. In anticipation of another catch going down, KC threw up his arms in despair only for Richard to launch himself full-length in front of Jephcott to catch the ball an inch above the turf.

Short shoved his bat angrily under his armpit and marched off. He had been stuffed by KC, by the umpires, and by Pywell. He was so furious that at first he seemed to be walking not to the dressing room but directly to the secretary's office to tear up his contract.

Next man in, Geoff Ledbrook, emerged reluctantly from the lights of the pavilion but stopped when he saw the umpires removing the bails to signal a stoppage of play. How long they would have continued had Short not perished, Richard could only guess. Certainly another few overs in the prevailing conditions would have enabled the visitors to claim some parity in the contest. As it was, Pywell's unbeaten eighty eight out of a total of 171 for 3 had put the home side in the driving seat and on course for a three hundred plus score. It was not the outcome Jephcott had hoped for at the start of play and despite his athleticism in catching Short, Richard felt the burden of his own culpability in giving Pywell a 'life'.

Wilf Bristow wasted no time wheeling on the covers and directing his ground staff to roll tarpaulins over the square leaving just the pitch exposed to the elements. It was twenty past five and with close of play scheduled for six-thirty he saw little chance of further play. He was particularly keen to protect those pitch ends that bore evidence of the season's wear and tear. Wilf knew he had to squeeze three new pitches out of the 'square' before he could rid himself of his summer lodgers and get on with the autumn repair work. Though he had explained many times the importance of back-end restoration work, his long-suffering wife could never understand the embargo he put on a September or October holiday. 'Are you the only one who knows anything about grass?' she would ask. 'Why do you have to do everything? I'm sure they'd cope for a week.' But Wilf was deaf to her reasoning and allergic to foreign food, which meant she was condemned to an annual off-peak anorak adventure in Blighty.

The players had come to the same conclusion as Wilf about an early abandonment and began to untie boots and make plans for the evening. Word went round that Colin Stinton wanted some of the visiting players to join those of the home side at a benefit 'social' in Bordesley Green. Stinton had asked Holliday to supply two 'volunteers', knowing 'Doc's' own benefit was due the following year and that he would expect a quid pro quo. 'Don't all rush,' said 'Doc', faced with a wall of silence. 'Stint's an okay fella. A couple of hours won't hurt you.' Everyone looked down at their feet except Alvar Badel. 'You up for it, Alvar?' Badel blinked in surprise. 'Didn't have any plans, did you?'

'No.'

'Good lad. That's you and me then and bugger the rest of 'em.' Badel knew he had been lumbered but as a new boy he felt like a spare part anyway. The problem of how he was going to spend the evening had been solved for him.

Chapter Four

1

While KC went to mollify 'Mr British Bloody Leyland' and son as requested, Richard killed time by phoning Tessa. The pavilion was deserted but for himself and the dressing room attendant flitting back and forth with glasses to wash and boots to whiten.

'Hi, it's me. Thought I'd call again since we had to cut it short earlier.'

'Oh.' Her tone was still a little cool.

'How have the girls been?'

'Bit stroppy. Jess especially.'

'The season will soon be over.'

'Yes well…' she said in a weary drawl. 'I'm not sure that will make much difference. Their squabbling is driving me to drink.' Jessica was in her terrible-twos phase and Sarah, three years older, was trying to top her for tantrums. 'Sheila phoned. She said you'd been tipped by one or two papers for a place on the winter tour.'

'Stupid paper talk,' he said, keen to douse her fears. 'There must be a dozen more players who are on the fringe. Reporters don't decide anything.'

'So you are on the 'fringe'?'

'It's idle speculation, Tess.'

'Don't you want to go?'

'Yes, of course, but it isn't going to happen, so forget it.'
Richard knew that Tessa was unlikely to have got wind of the
paper talk had it not been for Sheila's call. As a grass widow
herself, his sister-in-law must have known the impact such news
would have on Tessa. The prospect of him extending his absence
from domestic duties during the summer for four more months
in the winter was bound to meet resistance. And since he was at
best a long shot for selection, any aggravation on that score was
gratuitous.

'How much would you get?' asked Tessa.

'How much?'

'For touring the West Indies?'

'No idea.'

'It would have to be a decent amount, wouldn't it?'

'Probably, but don't go breaking the bank on a rumour,' he
said, surprised by her pragmatic reaction. He doubted if she had
yet worked out that a player selected for a winter tour had only
two or three weeks break after his return home before he
reported back to his club for a new domestic season. If Richard
went to the West Indies, Tessa would have to spend many more
months as a single mum on top of the summer she was now
enduring. Her folks lived in Lincolnshire and were in no
position to offer anything but occasional help with the kids. His
own parents, though well enough disposed, were no better
placed geographically.

'Where are you?' she asked.

'I'm still at the ground, waiting for KC. How's the grass?'

'Similar to how it was this morning. Do you want me to get
someone to cut it?'

'No. It can wait 'til I get back. Here's KC now. Shall I call you from the hotel?'

'No point. I'll be out.'

'Oh?'

'I got the offer of a babysitter, so I took it.'

'Right. Well, have fun.'

'I'll try. Bye.'

'Bye, love.' KC's arrival had foreshortened the conversation but Richard had the feeling that Tessa was the one who had done the dashing.

'Stood like a lemon, I've been,' growled KC.

'Is everyone happy?'

'Aye, everyone but me. The Skipper dropped me right in it. He told Slingsby I'd give the lad a signed scorecard after close of play. But him and his dad, from British Bloody Leyland, were nowhere to be seen. Slingsby says they'd been in the club hospitality suite all afternoon getting smoke blown up their arses. So he asks me to wait and he'll go and get them. Comes back ten minutes later to tell me Paul Pywell's had a word with them instead, so everything's 'tickety-boo'.'

'Well at least you didn't have to apologise. Leave the creeping to others, eh?' said Richard.

'Right enough. Pywell's so bloody smooth he shits marzipan.'

2

The Aloha Hotel stood back from the Hagley Road behind a low brick wall. A handful of trees, stunted by traffic fumes, relieved its aspect and partially obscured the car park running the length of the frontage. The club secretary never knowingly spoiled the team with luxury accommodation and the Aloha was par for the course. Once a substantial Edwardian residence, it had spread sideways via annexes into adjoining properties so that the original entrance, though porticoed, lacked the proper scale for the large mongrel building it had become.

KC swung his Austin into the car park. The heavy clouds that had brought play to a premature close continued to provide a sombre backdrop. 'The Bates Motel?' suggested Richard. But KC had always seen worse. At the drop of a hat he would regale younger players with grisly tales of the 'digs from hell' in the late-Fifties.

'Just to have a roof that kept out the rain was cause for celebration. Portsmouth, Liverpool, Cardiff – the club put us up in places where you wouldn't kennel a dog. No breakfast, just a gas ring in the corner to mash your own brew. Naked bulbs, bed bugs, mildewed blankets, the bloody bog miles away.'

The Aloha Hotel therefore held no terrors for KC. Quite the opposite. The swirling red carpet in the entrance hall gave him the comforting sensation of stepping into the lounge of his local pub in Bolsover, a feeling quickly dispelled by Mal Shanks, standing at the reception desk.

'You'll never guess,' said Shanks, salivating with bad news. 'It's a temperance hotel.'

'What?' scowled KC.

'No bar.'

'For pity's sake!' KC was not given to journeying far from his lodgings once he had booked in. The flesh-pots of the city were a mile or so away and had long since ceased to be an attraction, so the lack of a bar was a major aggravation. Judging from the smell of boiled vegetables rolling like mustard gas from the kitchens, Richard guessed he might not relish the table d'hôte either.

'Plus all the singles have gone,' said Shanks, trading exclusively in misery.

'What d'you mean?'

'No single rooms just doubles.'

'So who's had mine?' said KC.

'Can I help you, gentlemen?' said a rickety-thin man who had emerged from a small back-office. His head was balding in wayward tufts like a decommissioned lavatory brush.

'I want to book in. The name's Colclough. There'll be a single room down for me.'

'I'm sorry, sir, not according to the correspondence.'

'If one of the team is in a single you've got my say-so to chuck him out,' said KC, pulling rank.

'None of your team is in a single, sir. Only the elderly gentleman – your scorer, I believe?'

'Are you sure?'

'Absolutely, sir. The room rate quoted was for doubles.'

'I'll swing for those buggers in the office,' said KC.

'I told you,' said Shanks drifting away.

'So who am I rooming with? Mr Hastie here normally rooms with Mr Ibbotson,' said KC, getting tetchily formal.

'He's already booked in with a Mr Shanks,' said the lavatory brush consulting the register. Richard wondered what on earth Ibbo was playing at. He felt the mustard gas settling on his chest. KC turned to him.

'It's you and me then. Weren't thinking of going on the 'razz' were you?'

'One slight complication,' said the man. 'The room has a double bed.'

'Come again?' said KC.

'It's a double room, with a double bed.'

'One bed?'

'Correct.'

'Between two?'

'Yes.'

'What d'you take us for?'

'Late arrivals?'

'You have no other rooms at all?' asked Richard with a rising sense of dread.

'I'm afraid not, sir. We're fully booked. You might find availability elsewhere in town, though it is a busy time for business conventions.' KC's broad shoulders slumped. He seemed drained even of bile.

'If the Skipper were here I'd give him an earful. But he's not stupid, is he? He books in with old school chums or friends in the 'county set'. If he stayed in the same bloody digs as the rest of us, standards would soon improve.'

'There is something I can do,' offered the lavatory brush. 'I could put a camp bed in the room?' Both men stared at Richard. Clearly the younger man was expected to know his place and in this case it was on a camp bed.

'What d'you think?' said KC.

'Well I don't fancy trailing round without a car looking for a room,' Richard replied, making a mental note to confront Ibbo about his jackmanship.

'I'll see to that immediately, sir. There will be just enough space.'

But when they eventually acquired the room key, they found the camp bed jammed between a wall of floral wallpaper and the double bed with barely an inch to spare. It had a wooden zed frame guaranteed to creak if the occupant so much as breathed deeply. For a large part of the day Richard's thoughts had been waylaid by the prospect of his selection for an England tour and the fame and glamour that came with it. Now he found himself in a dismal hotel on the Hagley Road contemplating a night on a makeshift bed. Nothing new there, he reflected. From his earliest days as a budding cricketer, his feet had never been allowed to leave the ground.

Downstairs the swirling red carpet in reception clashed violently with a heavily patterned green and gold design in the hotel lounge. There Richard tracked down Ibbo, sitting cross-legged behind a newspaper. He kicked the sole of Ibbo's dangling right shoe. 'Thanks for that, mate.'

'First come, first served. What kept you anyway?'

'I had to wait for KC. Now I'm stuck with him and his snoring.'

'You know the drill with a snorer. Kiss him full on the lips and he won't sleep a wink.'

'Where is everyone?'

'At the Berni.'

'KC and Mal are eating here.'

'Christ, they must have no sense of smell.'

3

The pub, circa 1930, stood four square on a generous slab of tarmac. Its morose brickwork was strapped and bounded by mock-Tudor beams and the latticed windows obscured rather than revealed the interior. Not that Richard or Ibbo needed a preview. Wherever they were in the country they knew a Berni Inn would be a home from home. The signature decor of dark wood tables, red upholstered chairs and vellum-shaded lamps was sure to be enveloped in a swirling fug of smoke from the chef's griddle. The brothers Berni had ventured out from their Bristol beginnings to colonise every sizeable town in the country and itinerant cricketers looked no further for a meal that fell just inside the limits of their expense allowance. A few were tempted to spend their per diem on alcohol alone, but an outdoor life generally demanded something more sustaining. Even Tony Crick and Barry Picken believed a Berni steak was the essential precursor to a night on the prowl.

As Richard and Ibbo sat down at an adjoining table, Crick and Picken together with Topsy were leaning back in their seats to scrutinise the waitress who had come to collect their finished plates. She was a plain but pleasant girl of about twenty.

'Nice bit of rump, love,' said Crick, winking at Picken and Topsy across the table. Both hands full, the girl made no response other than to blow away a stray lick of hair that had fallen across her eyes.

'What time d'you finish?' he continued.

'After your bedtime,' said the girl with practised brevity.

'What would you know about my bedtime? My bedtime's flexible. Are you flexible? You look nice and flexible.'

'Apple pie, ice cream, or cheese and biscuits?' recited the girl in a bored monotone.

'No, thanks,' said Picken, saving his witty remarks for later.

'Nor me,' said Topsy. The girl put her tongue in her cheek and waited for Crick.

'What was it again?' he said.

'Apple pie, ice cream, or cheese,' Richard interjected, irritated by Crick's infantile joshing and wanting it over.

'I wasn't asking you, I was asking our lovely serving wench,' said Crick, fixing the girl in a beam of false attraction.

'That's a 'no' then, is it?' she said.

'Yes a 'no'. But I'd like to leave you a tip – you should smile more.' The girl turned abruptly on her flat heels and scooted. 'Didn't you two want to order?'

'Bugger off, Tony, and pull someone your own age,' said Ibbo.

'Why?' said Crick feigning bemusement.

'We'll leave you to it,' said Picken rising from his seat. 'If you're interested we're going to the Calypso Bar for a quick one then on to Billy Bigtime. Topsy says he can get us in free.' Topsy smiled smugly. Derbyshire's own Billy Bigtime. Ever since he had pulled on his England sweater he had milked the freebies that went with it. Crick and Picken thought their credibility with impressionable females could only be enhanced by their association with an international 'star' and they were more than happy to hook up when the offer was made.

'We'll see,' said Richard cautiously. 'We might have a long wait here now you've upset the staff.' The three men sauntered to the bar to pay their bills. Richard observed Crick resume his pestering of the waitress. Why couldn't he see she wasn't interested?

'Don't mind our friend,' he said when finally the girl came to take their order.

'Is he always like that?'

'Pretty much, yes.' As she scribbled on her pad, Richard found himself noting her neat cupid's bow lips and her breasts straining at the too-tight white blouse. A waitresses pouch pocket emphasized the lubricious declivity of her belly and he felt an unbidden tingle in his groin, one that set him calculating the days since he and Tessa had last made love. A Sunday morning, he remembered, when for once the girls had overslept. Even then he had forced the issue and ignored her insistence that they would be caught in the act. He had done everything that normally gave her pleasure, yet her muted responses conveyed perfectly the current state of their relationship.

It was eight-thirty when Richard glanced at his watch. They would finish the meal and be out of the Berni by nine. Away from home the problem of how to spend the hours before a sensible turning-in time was one he and his fellow teammates routinely had to negotiate. The more senior players tended to opt for a quiet drink in the hotel bar while the junior contingent preferred to venture away from constraining influences. Richard and Ibbo felt they had a foot in both camps. Not yet old enough to settle for the slippered somnolence of the lounge but someway past the cattle-market shenanigans of the local Locarno. In any case there were financial as well as physical implications and a sequence of nights on the town was not sustainable for either reason. However, since the Aloha Hotel was a teetotal establishment, Topsy's offer to gain them free admission to a club was not to be sniffed at.

'The drinks will cost an arm and a leg,' said Richard when he caught Ibbo's drift. 'We could find a pub near to the digs.' But clearly Ibbo fancied something less predictable.

On recent visits to Birmingham, Richard had accepted his brother and sister-in-law's invitation to stay at their Edwardian semi in a leafy avenue not far from the ground. This time the guest bedroom was in the throes of redecoration and the offer of the bed-settee had not appealed. Though a night at the Aloha Hotel on a creaking camp bed now seemed no more enticing, Richard consoled himself with the knowledge that he had evaded Sheila's chilli con carne signature dish that previously had proved an unexpected laxative. In addition, her conversation was stuck in a groove of such domestic aspiration that only like-minded females could stay the course for the duration of an evening. His freedom to roam, however, was restricted by Ken Colclough's routine of tucking himself up by eleven o'clock. A bungling entrance in the small hours would not go down well.

Dropping a clanger as well as a sitter in one day would be more than the senior pro could probably stand.

Ibbo drove into the centre of town and parked in Queensway. The gloom of the day had lifted and there was warmth in the evening air. The smell of oil and dust rose from the tarmac as they climbed out of the Cortina. Up and down the street Richard could hear laughter mingling with the click-clack of sling-back shoes on pavements and the clinking of glasses from a nearby bar. The night seemed suffused with undefined promise.

'The doorman's always a Mick round here,' warned Ibbo. There were two Micks to be precise. Pat and Pat stood across the threshold to Billy Bigtime's.

'Topsy Turner – who would that be now?'

'Mate of the owner,' said Ibbo, hopefully.

'I doubt that,' said Pat with a smirk.

'Punters, yes,' said the other Pat. 'Family, yes. Mates, no. Not Billy.'

'He's an England cricketer,' said Ibbo surrendering all dignity.

'Tall fella, thin as a fiddler's bow?' said Pat.

'That's him,' said Ibbo.

'He said nothing about yous.'

'Let's go,' said Richard, embarrassment overcoming his venality.

'But seeing as it's Wednesday night, I'm tinking Billy wouldn't fuss.' The other Pat nodded in sly agreement. 'If you're down in the casino, you'll have to be signing the book. If it's just pussy you're after, that's upstairs. There's a couple of old tails up there might suit you.'

Ibbo and Richard climbed the staircase to the 'cabaret room', newly refitted to reflect Billy's notion of what a bigtime in Brum should look like. Exposed brickwork, glove fabric seating and jet black tables projected a stripped-down glamour. There were enough reflective surfaces to please the most compulsive narcissist and the floor twinkled beneath a myriad of pin spots.

The place was sufficiently quiet for the barman to instantly spot the new arrivals and wait, hands on the bar, for their order. Richard scanned the room. He deduced that the business convention that had condemned him to sharing a room with KC had spewed out enough delegates to populate half a dozen of Billy's black tables. Blowing out smoke and belly laughs, they kept watchful eyes on three gogo dancers simulating upright sex to the beat of a Motown standard. Having catered so dutifully in dark and dingy venues to the needs of Mods, Rockers and Punks during the Sixties, Brum had finally succumbed to Middle-Of-The-Road music in a place that evoked the 'nighterie' of a holiday cruise liner. It was, Richard concluded, the upscale version of the Locarno for white-collar clubbers who had a bit of money and a few miles on the clock.

'No draught beer,' said the barman.

'Two bottles then,' said Ibbo digging deeper into his pocket. There was no sign of Topsy, Crick or Picken. Billy's was one of the few places where gamblers could play American crap, so Richard guessed they were in the casino. Crick, he imagined, would be rolling the dice with a lot more conviction than he displayed with a cricket ball but with much the same result.

'Do you want to find the others?' Richard shook his head.

'They'll come up here soon enough, nursing their losses and looking for spare.'

'Best get in quick then. What about those two?' Ibbo nodded in the direction of the dance floor where the gogo girls were surrounded by a miscellany of the clientele whose dancing was markedly less frisky. 'The one in the white-topped dress. Her mate's in a flowered jumpsuit.' Richard focused on two women stepping in and out of the spots. Uncertain though he was at assessing women's ages, he thought the pair were about par for a Wednesday night. Younger clubbers would be skint until Friday while this older shift of divorcees and footloose husbands exuded a stale aura of hope over experience.

'D'you want to break them up?' said Ibbo.

'What for?'

'A dance.'

'Then what?'

'A drink perhaps and a cuddle in the corner?' Ibbo was pragmatic when it came to sexual indiscretions. After living with Val for two years, much against her parents' wishes, he had finally agreed to get married. Selected as Best Man for the nuptials, Richard felt a nagging obligation to put the brake on Ibbo's off-campus activities. Val was the love of Ibbo's life, no question. Nor would he break sweat to go astray. But sex offered on a plate was something he did not feel arrogant enough to refuse. And once the deed was done he was blessed with the capacity to move on without looking back. In Ibbo's book, copulation was nothing more than a more interesting way of kissing. Richard, in comparison, was a tortured soul whenever he had been tempted to break faith with Tessa. Sex was not just kissing, it was an awkward fumbling business with buttons, fastenings and elastic. It was muscle-seizing contortions in tight corners and stickiness and smells and guttural responses − an unsavoury smorgasbord of the senses not easily erased from his memory. Yet the urge did not diminish but simply bided its time for a surfeit of alcohol, a row with Tessa, or just plain vanity to cut it loose.

Two salarymen lumbered onto the dance floor and tried to split up the two women. The one in the dress smiled falsely and shook her head. The suits sitting at the black tables guffawed.

'Losers,' Richard heard one shout. One of the men smiled, shrugged his shoulders and headed back to his seat to be greeted with a chorus of taunts. The other man stayed on the dance floor intent on returning the snub by mimicking the women's movements. When, as a result, they stopped dancing and stepped off the floor, the man continued to gyrate oblivious to the embarrassment of his colleagues.

The room was filling up and the two women had to slalom their way towards the bar. 'Nice one,' said Ibbo ironically as the one in the dress came alongside.

'Yeh, a real dickhead,' she replied in a Brummie drawl. 'There's always one.'

'You and your friend like a drink?'

'Why not? Bacardi and Coke for me and the same for her.' Richard's heart sank. What was the fool doing starting something there was no earthly chance of finishing?

'I'm Neil, this is Richard.'

'Sandra and Lesley.' Lesley, in the jumpsuit, fixed her eyes on the dance floor in a practised show of detachment that gave Richard the opportunity to scrutinise her. She had dark hair falling just above the shoulders. Despite her attempts to shape it with hot tongs, unruly curls had broken out at the ends. Flicking the hair back, she revealed a smooth neck and neatly shaped chin. The flowered jumpsuit was halter-necked with a broad waistband. The pants fitted closely over her backside and flared from the knee. Compared to Sandra's two-tone mini dress, the outfit was bang up to the minute though seemingly proof against any action a fondler of body parts might pursue. Not that Richard was venturing mentally down that road. His major concern was how to extricate himself from a situation barely begun but capable of running quickly out of control. A quiet moment to knuckle-rap his mate was required but Ibbo seemed stuck to the bar and more worry-ingly stuck on Sandra.

Richard visualised the possible scenarios. If he was lucky, Sandra and Lesley were just a couple of locals who knew they could accept a free drink before vanishing into the crowd, no harm done other than to Ibbo's wallet. Equally common, though a shade more perilous, would be the sudden appearance of regular male partners. Depending on the hostility of said parties, this scenario could end in a ruckus or an invidious escape via the fire door. The requirement for a pro cricketer to turn up fit and able to play, heavily favoured the latter solution. No more palatable was the possibility of Sandra and Lesley latching on to them for a whole evening of free-loading before disappearing to the loo never to be seen again. Less likely was the notion of Richard working Lesley into a lather of sexual desire, spiriting her unseen back to his hotel room, and without disturbing the senior pro's slumbers, shagging her brains out on a camp bed that creaked like a door at the Hammer House of Horror.

How much more sensible it would have been to have gone with 'Doc' Holliday and Alvar Badel to Bordesley Green to raffle off an autographed bat. A couple of beers, a chat with the local cricket obsessives, and the undying gratitude of the Warwickshire beneficiary. What could be better? Instead he was being finagled into a no-win situation with two women who undoubtedly knew their way round the forest better than their would-be predators.

'No-win? What're you on about?' said Ibbo when Richard finally cornered him in the Gents. 'I'm well in. What's up, don't you like her?' Richard despaired of Ibbo's artlessness. 'She likes you.'

'Who says?'

'She told Sandra. She must fancy miseries.'

'Come on, let's cut and run.'

'Don't be such a pillock. They're gorgeous.' Richard suspected the fizzy beer had corroded Ibbo's brain.

'Gorgeous or not we don't have a hotel room to take them to. So what's the point?'

'What's wrong with the car? Besides they might take us back to their place. Think positive. Just a couple more dances then I'll pop the question.'

'You've already popped the question. Val said 'yes', remember?'

'You're bloody boring,' said Ibbo.

'Boring and married.'

'Double boring.' Richard dug his hands into his pockets and pondered the accusation. In truth the drink, the music and the naff ambience had done its work and softened his resolve. These women were not 'gorgeous' as Ibbo claimed but they had an unrefined sensuality that was hard to ignore. He realised that he fancied Lesley and if she fancied him then he could at the very least be sociable.

The struggle Richard had waged with his conscience was immediately rendered pointless however when he and Ibbo emerged from the Gents to find the two women on the dance floor with Crick and Picken.

'Thanks mate,' moaned Ibbo.

'I needed a slash.'

'You dragged me in there with you instead of leaving me to mind the coop. It'll take a pressure jet to prise those two off them.' Despite a feeling of relief, the sight of Crick's fraudulent smile washing over Lesley made Richard's stomach heave. Now out of the running, he was safe to indulge in self-pity. Resting his chin on his fist at the bar he could smell Lesley's perfume on his hand and speculated on a good time snatched from under his nose.

4

Tessa Hastie returned home to find every room in the house lit up. 'They said they wanted the light left on,' said the whey-faced teenager, rousing herself from sleep. She had straggly jet-black hair and looked like Snow White on acid. She rolled her legs off the sofa and sat up amongst a litter of women's magazines.

'Did they play you up?'

'Not really.'

'What time did they get to sleep?'

'I heard nothing after nine.' Call it 'ten' thought Tessa but let it go. Babysitters were not easy to come by and she did not want to sound critical. Besides, the vacuousness of this particular girl, real or affected, suited her fine. There was no cheery probing into her evening out as there might have been from an adult neighbour. It was eleven-thirty and past the time Tessa could dissemble with confidence.

She paid the girl and let her out, then checked upstairs. As usual Sarah was as neat as an entombed mummy, while Jessica, sprawled head down, appeared to have been the victim of a violent crime. She folded Jessica under the sheets and stroked her hair. It had been a fractious day and her evening out had not lifted Tessa's mood. There had been time only for two drinks in a dowdy and suitably remote pub before a wearisome return journey. But now, listening to Jessica's breathing, she found comfort in its steady rhythm.

5

Richard reacted to the urgent knocking at the door with a nimbleness that belied his lack of familiarity with the bedroom.

His synapses had mapped the layout well enough for him to find his way, semi-conscious, in the dark without colliding with a single fixture or fitting. He opened the door one eye's width to find Tony Crick fully dressed and unusually agitated. Behind him, leaning with the sole of his shoe against the corridor wall, was Barry Picken.

'Those birds you were with?' said Crick without preamble. Though Richard had made the journey to the door with preternatural precision, his mind refused to catch up.

'Birds?'

'The barman said you and Ibbo were with them.' Afraid he might disturb KC, Crick lowered his voice without losing intensity. 'Called themselves Sandra and Lesley.'

'What about them?'

'Have you lost any money?'

'Why?'

'One of 'em lifted my wallet. I had almost a ton in it.'

'A ton!'

'Yes,' said Crick, irritated by his own foolishness rather than Richard's bleary incredulity. 'We've been with the cops for the past two hours.'

'What the hell's going on?' KC reached past Richard's shoulder with a sausage-fingered hand and levered the door wide open. Richard moved aside. Even in pyjamas, KC's physical presence was undiminished. If anything the multi-striped fabric seemed to add bulk to his shoulders and chest.

'I've lost my wallet,' said Crick, hoping to avoid embarrassing details.

'Well it's not in here, is it?' said KC grumpily.

'No but Dick might know something about it.'

'Do you?' asked KC.

'No.'

'Right, then bugger off to bed,' said KC.

'A policeman downstairs wants to speak to him.'

'Why?'

'My wallet was stolen by a bird I met in a bar.' KC's eyes, only now fully open, narrowed again. He thought 'A Bird In A Bar' could be the title of Crick's autobiography if one ever came to be written.

'She nicked it while we were dancing.'

'She must have seen you coming. But what's that got to do with Dick?'

'He was with her earlier.' Richard felt a tightening in his throat and a burning sensation in his cheek-bones. It wasn't just the effect of KC's accusing glare but the realisation that he was being drawn into a situation requiring explanations and third party scrutiny.

Dressed in his pyjamas, Richard gave a short statement to a policeman in the hotel lounge along with Ibbo. It added nothing to what had already been established but it placed him at the scene. Innocent though he may claim to have been, he would be found guilty by association of drinking, gambling, and womanising.

Ibbo was inclined to be more relaxed. As long as Tessa and Val did not learn that they had bought drinks for the women, their involvement in anything unworthy could be refuted. Accepting that a united front was the safest option, Richard resisted the urge to remind Ibbo that it was he who had bought the drinks.

Given Crick and Picken's appetite for sordid adventuring, it was ironic that exposure and punishment should come at the hands of pickpockets rather than irate fathers, boyfriends, or husbands. Since the start of the season they had already spiced up their usual catch of blousy divorcees and willing shop girls by debauching two sixth-formers in Bath and going halves on a randy grandma in Gravesend. Picken affected a demeanour of quiet discretion about his doings, leaving Crick to satisfy the prurient interest of the dressing room with lurid reports of their encounters.

'She just bent double over the settee and said, 'take your choice big boy.'' Even KC was sometimes forced to shake his head and laugh. At such moments, Robin Jephcott, ever the gentleman, would find ways to distance himself, burying his head in a newspaper or some correspondence. He was not averse to blue jokes, nor was there any reluctance to tell them if he was in earshot, but it was generally accepted that he was not 'one of the boys'. This detachment extended to his family life of which Jephcott spoke little. His wife, Pamela, was an alert clear-eyed woman, her pretty face blighted by a severely styled bob. No slave to fashion or cosmetics, she would turn up once a year in the same satin ensemble for the annual players' party and know everyone's name, wives and girlfriends included. Richard imagined the cramming session necessary for such a feat – the Jephcotts huddled over photographs and memory cards the night before. They had two children, a boy and a girl both at prep school, the primer for a private education that would perfectly replicate their own.

Richard and Tessa had once been invited to a dinner party at the Jephcotts' where they learned that Pamela's greatest, perhaps only, interest was her horse. Richard recalled two cocker spaniels in front of an inglenook fireplace, brooding oak furniture, large lumpy sofas, well-worn carpets, and stiff gins in cut glass beakers. Why an invitation had been extended to them he could not fathom. He thought maybe it was the social part of his induction to the captaincy? Having journeyed from their four-bed new-build on a small housing development, the rambling Jephcott residence set in tree-fringed grounds represented another world. The Jephcotts' social ease and their casual disregard for anything up-to-the-minute, identified them as certifiably Old Money. Tessa Hastie, a state school product to her fingertips like Richard, had been a particular success, wearing a mini dress that revealed plenty of thigh while sitting on the sink-in sofas.

'Gosh Tessa, what smashing legs,' enthused Pamela, herself wearing a dull ankle-length number.

'Absolutely,' agreed James Egan who with his wife made up the sixsome. Besides being the cricket club's solicitor and a chum of Jephcott's, Egan had been Tessa's boss at the law firm where she worked before getting married. With a boyish good-natured face and a body erring to podgy, he had a disarming way with the opposite sex that he deployed whenever the opportunity arose. Perhaps as a reaction to his unreserved admiration for Tessa's legs, Egan's wife flirted with Richard for the rest of the evening. Not until Richard and Tessa were travelling home did he learn that Egan had been squeezing Tessa's thigh throughout the meal.

'I bet he got the Skipper to invite us so he could get his paws on you.'

'It's just his way.'

'Why didn't you stick a fork in his hand?'

'And risk a huge fuss?' she said, not unreasonably.

'The randy goat always said he shouldn't have introduced us.' Tessa had smiled and patted Richard's leg. In hindsight a more demure outfit for dinner might have been more appropriate, though he suspected she had not found Egan's attention unflattering. Nonetheless he thought a faux pas had been made and that they had come across as lightweights.

The memory of that evening lodged uneasily in Richard's mind as he padded barefoot back to his hotel bedroom. Although he had done nothing heinous, he did not relish Jephcott learning about his part in the night's events. The spotlights, the mirror-glass, the sultry Motown sounds and swanky black tables might have suggested night-time glamour, but in the shaming transparency of day, he knew Billy Bigtime's would be seen as nothing more than a pick-up joint.

He tiptoed back into the blackness of the bedroom. Afraid of waking KC, he stood still until his eyes became accustomed to the dark. Once by the zed bed, the major obstacle was lowering himself onto it without it groaning like a Man O'War in heavy seas. Holding himself taut half in half out of the bed, he almost suffered a muscle seizure. Only when he was down did he discover that KC was fully awake.

'Tony Crick,' KC grumbled, 'more like a crick in the bloody neck.'

6

There was a studied silence about KC at breakfast. While Mal Shanks kept up a steady stream of conjecture, KC buttered his toast with the deliberation of a judge determined to learn the full facts before pronouncing sentence. In Jephcott's absence the senior professional was, as he put it, in 'loco capitano' and he took the job seriously. He was no mother hen but neither was he inclined to treat team members like responsible adults. Each season produced too many episodes of delinquency to adopt such a policy.

Crick and Picken attempted to demonstrate their professionalism by making an early appearance in the breakfast room, chins smooth-shaved and hair sharply parted. They routinely contended that late nights did not adversely affect their performances. Crick claimed to have tried the early-to-bed method on one occasion and emerged runless from the game in question. A 'king' pair in fact. Case proven. There was no way he would risk a repetition. Picken was more plausible, blessed as he was with a constitution that seemed to shrug off the need for sleep. But now both men would have questions to answer in public. The Deep Throat who resides in every police station would waste no time retailing the circumstances of the previous night's incident. There would be news columns of feigned outrage denouncing 'supposed professionals' for boozing the night before a match, betraying the supporters and employers alike. The captain and the club would be expected to comment. As for wives, there was plenty of grovelling in prospect there. It was all so silly, said Crick, when for once they were more sinned against than sinning.

Crick had already constructed a rickety story in mitigation. The eponymous Big Billy, he suggested, had invited Topsy to round up a few team-mates to help publicise the refurbished venue. He would deny dancing with the women, despite a host of witnesses to the contrary, and claim that his wallet had been lifted as he made his way through a crowded bar. Whatever merit the story had as a smokescreen, it roped Richard, Ibbo, Topsy and Picken into the deception. Richard doubted if those closest to them would be fooled. Certainly not Jephcott or Tessa. Yet clearly it would be a breach of team spirit to refuse Crick support, however reluctantly.

At the Edgbaston ground, KC doled out Crick's sanitized version of events to Jephcott in the glass-fronted enclosure outside the dressing room. Even as he spoke, KC had a nagging feeling there was something nastier in the woodshed. Jephcott though seemed surprisingly content to take the story at face value. Like a superior officer informed of a bar-room brawl by his squaddies, he saw no harm as long as each man was fit to perform his duties. KC imagined that if the day went badly, Jephcott might choose to review the matter.

'Too bad about your cash, Tony,' said Jephcott.

'Yes, Skip, I was bloody livid,' said Crick.

'Two tarts working in tandem – I thought that would be right up your street?' quipped Shanks, unhelpfully.

'KC said you lost a hundred?'

'I got paid a backlog of expenses the day before.'

'Good job you lost a wedge on the crap table or they could've nicked that as well,' said Topsy, finding amusement in Crick's loss now the skipper's humour had been established. Slingsby's head popped round the door.

'Tony. Someone from the Constabulary to see you.' Trouserless, Crick exited the dressing room, his flannel cricket shirt long enough to hide his bits and pieces both fore and aft.

'They seem to know who they are,' said Picken.

'I hope not,' chuntered KC to Richard, 'we might find out what really happened if they catch 'em.' He seemed eager for someone to know he was no mug. Even if Jephcott had swallowed Crick's account of the previous night, KC for one had not.

Chapter Five

1

'Hi, how are you this morning?' Tessa frowned quizzically at the other end of the phone. Richard sounded extraordinarily bright.

'I'm fine. Is something wrong?'

'No,' he lied. 'Just touching base.'

'Right,' said Tessa still perplexed. A call from Richard in the hour before play was due to start was unusual unless there was an emergency.

'How was your night out?'

'Fine, thanks.'

'What did you do?'

'Oh we just went for a drink,' she said vaguely.

'Who's 'we'?'

'Maggie.'

'Maggie?'

'The one I used to work with.'

'Don't remember her,' said Richard. 'Long time no see?'

'Yes, it was good to catch up.'

'Not thinking of going back to work are you?'

'It's an idea,' she said, ambivalently. Now that a phone conversation presented a rival for Tessa's attention, Jessica had

84

begun tugging at the legs of her mother's flared jeans.

'I've had an eventful time,' said Richard, getting to the purpose of his call. He knew any delay would give his sister-in-law the opportunity for mischief once Speedy had relayed the gossip to her. 'Tony Crick had his wallet stolen in a club. The owner invited Topsy to take a few of the lads as a publicity stunt. I went there for a drink with Ibbo, just to be friendly, but Tony stayed on and had his wallet lifted.'

'How much was in it?'

'Getting on for a hundred pounds.'

'A hundred?' she gasped.

'The police are on the job but I reckon he can say goodbye to the money.'

'Why was he carrying that much money? Was he gambling?'

'I don't know. We didn't stay long. Anyway you're okay?'

'Yes.'

'And the girls?'

'Yes.'

'Good. Well I'd better go then. Take care.'

'And you.' She put the receiver down, looked at herself in the hall mirror. She would have to get in touch with Maggie as soon as possible.

Tessa had surprised Richard with her lack of curiosity. Perhaps the inquisition would come later? Certainly the chances of keeping things quiet were nil. The 'fuzz' had turned up mob-handed just to convey the news that Crick's wallet had been found in an alley close to Billy's. It was empty but for a photograph of the owner's wife and kids and had gone to Forensics for examination. Topsy said they were unlikely to find Crick's fingerprints on it on account of his renowned reluctance to buy a round.

2

Still mortified by his role in the friendly fire incident of the first day, Alvar Badel was again bowling dolly drops in the nets. According to 'Doc' Holliday, he had been a more or less silent companion on their visit to Bordesley Green the previous evening. For all he knew the lad was a livewire among his peers but he rather doubted it. There was something about him that was unformed, amoeba-like, as if his body and features were still deciding which direction to take. Incipient acne was present and his lips were indistinctly outlined and pale, a cold sore in one corner adding to the confusion. His hair was a dirty flax colour with wispy sideburns curling unassertively towards a chin of soft stubble that rarely saw a razor. This and a slender frame of no more than five ten in height gave no hint of menace.

As Richard made his way to the nets he heard Speedy call from behind. 'Heh, our kid.' Richard paid no heed until Speedy came alongside. 'What've you been up to? You and Tony Crick?'

'I'd left by the time it happened,' said Richard, correctly assuming Speedy knew why a squad car happened to be parked at the rear of the pavilion.

'Sheila wondered why you didn't want to stay with us,' said Speedy suggestively. Richard did not rise to the bait. 'Billy's of all places.'

'We had one drink and left.' After his phone conversation with Tessa, Richard had almost convinced himself that he could side-step any unpleasantness but already he could sense the futility of his story. Even if Speedy did not apprise Sheila of the details, she was bound to find out. The wives' bush telegraph would see to that. Besides, the boys in the Press Box would be on the ground soon and sniffing for angles.

'The cops say Tony had his trousers round his ankles when his wallet was nicked?'

'Rubbish. He was dancing,' said Richard, suddenly skewered by doubt.

'Yeah, the knee-tremble tango.'

'That's bollocks.'

'How would you know? You said you weren't there.' Enjoying Richard's discomfort, Speedy winked and put a spurt on to join his team-mates. Richard may have cursed his foolishness in being anywhere in the vicinity of Crick, yet it could have been a whole lot worse. If it had not been for Crick's intervention, his own wallet might now be under the microscope in Forensics. He began to pad up. He could see Crick talking animatedly to anyone who cared to listen. The police's sleazier version of events now seemed the most likely. Trust Crick to fan a barely smoldering fag-end into a significant conflagration? Was his hunger for the limelight so great that he was willing to invite disgrace? Yet Crick was no Pywell or Topsy. The escutcheon emblazoned with three lions was not about to be besmirched by scandal. If it appeared at all, Crick's journeyman status would surely consign his story to a footnote at most in the match report. But even as Richard comforted himself with this assessment, the flaw in his logic became clear. Though Crick's international status was non-existent, his own had become a matter of newspaper speculation. Who was to know how the selectors might view a sordid tale of late-night roistering featuring an England hopeful?

'Are you netting or not?' demanded Topsy, ambushing Richard's nascent paranoia. He went into the net and took guard. Unless he cleared his mind and focused on his game, consideration for England's winter tour was guaranteed to remain a pipe dream.

Though below full pace, Topsy came onto the bat with just enough zip to awaken Richard's reflexes. Bowling twirly stuff, Shanks and Jephcott completed the quartet together with Badel. A favourable forecast had brought some fair-weather fans out to watch. They stood behind the nets clutching tuck-bags, their lugubrious scrutiny further sharpening Richard's concentration. After late-cutting Shanks with the deftest of caresses, he went to retrieve the ball from the back corner of the net and heard a familiar voice.

'Morning, Richard,' said Ron Grimley, not bothering to take the cigarette from his mouth.

'Hello, Ron.' Richard did not care to dwell on the reason for Grimley's appearance among the gathering of jobless gawpers behind the net, but there was no denying he fitted in perfectly.

'Fun and games, I hear?' Normally at the start of the day Ron Grimley would be having a cough and a spit in the Press Box, browsing the previous day's match reports for grammatical howlers or statistical slip-ups committed by his fellow hacks. As his 'Sports Supremo' byline in the local rag implied, he was not only expected to report on county cricket matches both home and away but also on soccer, basketball, table tennis, speedway, and because he passed the Drill Hall on his way home, badminton. It was claimed he refused to write the angling column because he knew nothing about it. The players reckoned this was rich seeing how Grimley's knowledge of cricket could be written on the back of a bus ticket. Technically they were right. Judging by the shape of him, it could safely be assumed that Grimley's schooldays were spent as an over-sized bystander while others played. But Richard for one was aware that his knowledge of sporting facts, figures, and personalities was compendious and his prose effectively trimmed to the demands of the afternoon edition.

'Ron wants a word with you,' said Jephcott as Richard left the confines of the net. 'He's got wind of what happened last night. I don't think he'll drop anyone in it so be co-operative. Hopefully you can use him to halt any mischief-making in the Press Box.' Richard nodded though he doubted if Grimley enjoyed much credibility among the hacks. They were a cynical bunch and treated most snippets from fellow scribes as booby-traps.

As he took off his pads, Richard glanced at Grimley shambling towards him. He had worn the same threadbare hacking jacket all season complementing it with a pair of sagging elephant-arse trousers, spattered brown suede shoes, and a pair of spectacles 'invisibly' mended with Sellotape. Grimley, he observed, had gone beyond journo cliché into the realms of homelessness.

'You looked in good nick,' said Grimley, a newly lit fag wagging like an admonishing finger in the corner of his mouth. One of his eyes was almost shut against the upward licks of smoke. 'I hear Gil Atkins had a word with you yesterday?'

'Yes.'

'Did he have anything interesting to say?'

'Not really. Just a passing nod.'

'You got the nod, eh?' said Grimley teasingly. His interest was entirely legitimate. If a local player was to be selected for an England tour party his job was to ensure home town readers got to know about it first. More often than not this was a forlorn hope given that the player himself might first learn of his selection from the BBC radio news.

'What was going off last night then?' Grimley tried to make the question sound chummy.

'Talk to Tony Crick.'

'I have. He said you were there.'

'Not for long.'

'Yeh?'

'I'm rooming with KC. It's more than my life's worth to wake him up after bedtime.' More convinced, Grimley smiled and nodded.

'I'd just like to give chapter and verse to the lads in the Box. Tony says you were all there to publicise the club's refit but apparently that was done eighteen months ago. The local 'nick' is leaking gossip like a broken piss pot. They're saying Billy's is a knocking shop and Tony and Barry got turned over by a couple of toms. I'm just telling you what's on the wire.' Richard felt his scrotum tighten. If the story continued to develop, it was guaranteed to send sports editors into paroxysms of tub-thumping sanctimoniousness. Grimley took a notepad from his bulging side pocket. 'You were there, Ibbo, Tony, Barry, and Topsy? What about Rod Brennan?'

'No.'

'Unusual for a swordsman like Rod to miss the fun?'

'He's not staying.'

'He's travelling each day?' Richard nodded. 'What about the Skipper? Where was he?'

'No idea. He's staying privately.'

'Keeping his nose clean, eh?'

'Like me,' said Richard with more hope than expectation.

3

When Jephcott led his team out at the start of the second day's play, Topsy was unusually buoyant. Unattached as he was, none of the scandal-mongering circulating the ground was likely to embarrass him unduly. True he was an England player, but a playboy image was not something he was averse to cultivating.

An even more plausible explanation for his good humour was Jephcott's plan to keep him back to attack the opposition's tail, leaving the immediate heavy lifting to KC and Alvar Badel.

Geoff Ledbrook had to face the remaining three balls of the over abandoned by KC the day before. Though now a little past his best, Ledbrook was a solid middle order batsman who had always been disinclined to sell his wicket cheaply. He and Pywell took advantage of KC's loosening deliveries to get the scoreboard moving again and when Badel opened from the other end he seemed tentative and a yard slower in pace than on the previous day. Pywell sailed to three figures helped by two streaky boundaries off KC that aroused such disgust in the bowler's breast he could barely join in the applause for Pywell's ton. At the end of KC's over, Jephcott took the opportunity to have a quiet word with Badel. 'A bit stiff?' he asked, trying to mask his irritation at the lad's guttering start.

'A bit.'

'Better now?' Badel nodded. 'Then give it full throttle. Okay?' Badel nodded again, realising belatedly that the captain was not best pleased with him. Both batsmen had comfortably negotiated the first overs of the day and were rolling up their sleeves like diners about to tuck into the main course. Unless a break-through was made soon, Jephcott feared his team would struggle to stay in the match.

Badel ran in, light soundless steps culminating in a swivel of his hips and a whiplash jerk of his arm. The ball spat off the pitch and reared at Pywell's throat. Done for pace and with no time to duck or sway, Pywell instinctively raised his hands as if to parry a punch to the head. The ball crunched into the shoulder of his bat and flew over gully for two runs. 'Well bowled,' shouted Jephcott. Pywell batted his eyelids in a parody of surprise. Smiling mirthlessly, he went down the track to tap down the spot where he thought the ball had pitched and peered quizzically at the sightscreen.

Badel ran in again, lifted by Jephcott's praise. This time he pitched the ball shorter. Not quite bouncer length but on the evidence of the previous delivery, one demanding immediate evasive action. However, the ball was onto Pywell before he could shape any sort of response. He had time only to turn his back and the ball hit him in the soft tissue below the shoulder blade. Pywell made a sound like the dry retch of someone about to vomit. Heartened though he was to see Pywell's discomfort, Jephcott refrained from broadcasting his congratulations to the bowler. Instead he stepped solicitously towards Pywell who was squatting down using his bat as a prop.

'You alright, Paul?' Pywell offered no response. As Jephcott moved in to offer closer attention, Ledbrook sauntered down the pitch to confer with his teammate.

'Never saw it,' said Pywell.

'D'you want the screen moved?' said Ledbrook.

'There's nothing wrong with the screen.' The insinuating tone of Pywell's reply and his dirty look in Badel's direction left no doubt about his meaning. A conspiracy of glances passed between fielders. Only Jephcott and Badel seemed unaware of the unspoken question hanging ominously over the proceedings. Taking time to put his gloves back on, Pywell turned to eyeball the square leg umpire. Time-served, Jim Rook was having none of it. He could spot an attempt to exert pressure a mile off and declined to look at Pywell's eyebrow-raising antics. Whether or not Badel was a chucker he was not about to judge with the naked eye. In such cases, Rook had learned that even evidence provided by a film camera could make an umpire look a right Charlie.

The outcome of Badel's next delivery was as predictable as it was lethal. Despite his commanding three-figure total on the scoreboard, Pywell had become ruffled. He played suicidally back to a fullish length ball and was rapped on his pads bang in front of the stumps. Badel let out a surprised LBW appeal so shrill he might have had an untrained ferret trapped in his trousers. Pywell was on his way to the pavilion almost before the umpire could raise his finger.

As later order batsmen struggled to handle Badel, those escaping to KC's end adopted a desperate muck or nettles approach and perished. Hoping to catch Gil Atkins' eye, Speedy lasted only three balls before a Badel delivery shot through his balsawood defence and sent the middle stump cart-wheeling to the keeper. As he turned grim-faced to the pavilion, Richard knew his brother would look in his direction. The split second exchange of glances embraced an aeon of rivalry – a primitive instinct refusing to be cowed. 'Don't dare to take pleasure from my downfall,' signalled Speedy. But framed within a blandly fixed expression, Richard's eyes betrayed his delight. Brotherly love had always involved lashings of harsh retribution. Chinese burns and dead-legs at the very least. Somehow Speedy would find a way to make Richard suffer.

KC wound up the innings to finish with six wickets for eighty six. Expensive by his standards but a 'six-fer' felt satisfyingly like old times. The opposition had subsided from one hundred and ninety for three to the comparative poverty of two hundred and thirty six all out. Seeing the tail disappearing so rapidly, Topsy had ostentatiously loosened his limbs to attract Jephcott's attention. He was usually more than willing to see others expending energy rather than himself, but he drew the line at Badel having first dibs at the rabbits. The kid would have to be watched.

Jephcott paused at the picket gate and invited KC to lead the team off the field. It was a gesture to which both men had become accustomed over the seasons – KC modestly accepting the pats and plaudits in the manner of someone 'just doing his job', the captain barely nodding his appreciation. The fact that he held KC in high regard was so embedded in their relationship nothing more was needed. To make a fuss would imply KC's performance was in some way unusual. Though KC did not return Jephcott's admiration with unconditional subservience, he had respect for a gaffer who led his men from the front. Prodded forward, Badel shyly followed KC through the gate. His debut figures of three for twenty eight had got Jephcott out of jail after his decision to field first. The captain had seen young fast bowlers come, fizzle out, and disappear. Very few managed to sustain and justify the coach's hyperbolic claims. Badel, however, certainly had something different.

4

From the fall of the eighth Warwickshire wicket, Richard had felt a tightening in his throat and a spike of agitation in his guts, signs of his body marshalling its resources for the fray. He had once seen a *Punch* cartoon depicting a fast bowler running in to bowl. A thought-bubble above his head showed the stumps shattered by an express delivery. In ironic contrast, the thought-bubble above the batsman's head showed the batsman being carried off on a stretcher. Though visualisation as a means to self-improvement had become a new addition to the coaching manuals, it was something Richard had always done in an unselfconscious way. Contemplating the bowlers he would have to face, he recalled his past duels with them to familiarise himself once again with their strengths and weaknesses.

Seymour Hills he knew would take the new ball. Six feet four inches of West Indian brawn, his bandy legs cantering to a frenziedly climactic delivery stride. He was ranked in the leading half dozen West Indian quicks. Four of the six were plying their trade in English county cricket, discolouring batsmen's bodies wherever they went. John Talbot shared the new ball but none of Hill's supple athleticism and trampoline-bounce. He had a heavy-limbed gait and large feet with a pronating tendency that inclined him to knock-knees. Whereas Hills' torso was an inverted triangle, Talbot's fell squarely from shoulders to hips. He was an English heavy-horse, durable but in his case not overly biddable. Richard knew that unless he was roused, Talbot became easily bored, content just to get through his quota of overs as a preliminary to sinking some pints later in the day. Given due respect he could be milked for runs without taking an undue risk. Speedy was a different proposition. Coming on as first change, he would bust a gut to atone for his failure with the bat, and claiming Richard's scalp would be high on his wish list.

After the team's morning of success, the mood in the dressing room was buoyant. The citrus tang of cleaning fluid, so pervasive on the first day, had been obliterated by the aroma of men at play – a sweet sour cocktail of sweat, damp wool, embrocation, grass, rubber and buckskin. Ignoring the exasperated tutting of the brown-coated dressing room attendant, the team had quickly made the room their very own midden.

With only ten minutes allowed between innings, there was no time for a wardrobe malfunction. Without removing his boots, Richard climbed out of his fielding flannels taking care not to snag the turn-ups in his boot spikes. He slid a shell-shaped polypropylene guard into the pocket of his jock-strap, its padded leather surround ensuring a snugger fit into the groin. For thigh protection Richard used a thin slab of high-density rubber sewn into a cotton cover. Straps attached to it top and bottom tied at the waist and round the leg above the knee. The thigh guard was shaped at the bottom to accommodate the top flap of the left pad. But first Richard had to get into his batting flannels. These were flannels he thought too shabby for public exposure in the field but sound enough to take the pinch and creasing from tightened pad buckles. Superstitiously he always put his left pad on first. Bending forward to secure the bottom buckle, the rush of blood to his head created a hammering pulse at his temples. With practised dexterity he pleated and tucked his flannels behind the three straps and buckles leaving the top one slacker to enable a flexing of the knee. He repeated the exercise with the right leg as now team-mates, easing their boots off, lolled about and chatted, uninvolved and seemingly indifferent to his efforts to get ready.

Richard had perhaps three minutes remaining to gather himself. He laid out his gloves, bat, and cap on the bench, wrapped a towel round his shoulders and headed for the shower-room. In a lavatory cubicle Ibbo was engaged in his customary nervous evacuation. Lost in their hurried preparations, both men went about their business without speaking. Richard ran a bowl of water. For a minute or so he cupped cold water into his hands and, dousing his face, tried to cool his eyes and clear his mind.

Chapter Six

1

For a delivery to be fair the ball must be bowled, not thrown or jerked; if either Umpire be not entirely satisfied of the absolute fairness of a delivery in this respect, he shall call and signal 'No Ball' instantly upon delivery.

Denis Slingsby half sat, half perched, on the corner of his office desk. One hand held the phone, the other worried change in his pocket. From the picture window he could observe, if inclined to do so, the umpires ambling towards the middle followed by the home team's captain, Gledhill. Increasingly, however, Slingsby had found himself in favour of turning his back on the field of play. Ten years before, he had stepped down as managing director of a minor metal-bashing company to become County Club Secretary. It had seemed like a dream job for such a cricket enthusiast as himself. A natural administrator, he was a round peg in a round hole. Too much so perhaps? His very competence appeared to hoover into his office every conceivable problem from playing staff to catering, from toilet provision to ground maintenance. It was hard now to reconcile the idyllic sinecure he had envisioned with the complaints and pay demands that daily winged across his desk.

'Have you talked to the umpires?' came a cultured voice at the other end of the phone.

'No, there wasn't time. Ray Gledhill came to see me between innings. They're back on the field now.'

'Gledhill's a sound sort,' said the voice from HQ. Sound enough thought Slingsby, though he was sure Paul Pywell had made the bullets for his skipper to fire. 'The young man's first game, you say?'

'First First-class game. It's probably a bit premature to blow the whistle just yet?'

'Well yes and no. We're taking such reports very seriously. If this bowler's action is suspect we'd better take a look at him sooner rather than later – if only for the young man's sake.' Slingsby had not enjoyed making the call to Lord's, now he felt positively grubby. HQ's hidden agenda in its campaign to rid the English First-class game of throwers was its fanciful belief that other countries would follow suit. The 'Powers That Be' were particularly anxious in view of the forthcoming tour of the West Indies to have paceman Chester Deeds excluded from selection.

Judging whether a bowler's action was legal or otherwise was fraught with difficulty. Certain players were double-jointed which made judgement unreliable even when filmed evidence was available. On the question of Deeds however there was unanimity of opinion. He was a chucker, no question, but there was dissent about whether he threw every ball or just the occasional killer delivery? Batsmen like Pywell or Graham Murfin, now nursing a sore head on the sidelines, fully accepted the physical danger of facing up to the quicks as long as they were playing within the laws. Where they drew the line was in being crusted and laid out by a rogue delivery. A layman might reasonably point out that a hard ball bruises the same whatever the mode of delivery, but as Pywell had implied, it was not only speed that a thrower gained, the ball was also less easily sighted out of his hand. At speeds of 85/90 mph this posed a serious problem. The sensation of being dismissed by a delivery which seemed to come from nowhere was a common one even to a batsman as well set as Pywell had been.

'If the umpires think his action is doubtful we'll need to have him filmed,' said the voice. 'Do you have anyone handy?'

'I'll see what I can do.' Slingsby regretted the words as soon as he had uttered them. If the lad had simply fed Pywell easy runs nothing would have been said. His mistake was in taking wickets and there was nothing like success for bringing the knives out. Slingsby knew that secretly filming a bowler's action was a grisly business. The thinly populated stands around Edgbaston provided no concealment for a cine cameraman and once discovered, the attempted subterfuge would cause bad blood between the two counties for seasons to come. He toyed briefly with the idea of phoning his opposite number at Derbyshire in a spirit of comradely openness, but since his own club captain had instigated the complaint his concern would sound decidedly hollow. Perhaps if the umpires were equivocal about Badel's action he could legitimately leave the issue in abeyance thereby lobbing the hot potato onto someone else's plate?

2

Milky rays of sunlight slid intermittently through the cloud cover but failed to burn off the haze that had hugged the distant city tower blocks since early morning. Faced with an awkward fifteen minutes batting before the lunch break, Richard and Ibbo had hoped the pitch might have dried from the previous day's rain, but the way in which KC and Badel had cut through the Warwickshire batting indicated otherwise.

It helped that none of the tail-enders had stayed long at the crease. There was nothing an opener hated more than to see seam bowlers nicking a few runs. A little larking about in the middle not only limbered them up, it allowed them to get above themselves. Cold, miserable, and stiff in the joints was how Richard preferred his opponents.

As Richard and Ibbo approached the middle, Seymour Hills paced out his run-up in the opposite direction, his final stride a cartoon leap reminiscent of the Pink Panther. Richard and Hills had confronted one another on a number of occasions and the honours had been even with Richard gaining the upper hand of late. As he was to face the first ball, he walked to the batting crease at the City end poking the toe of his bat at imaginary bumps on the track. Jephcott had opted for the light roller between innings to avoid squeezing more moisture to the surface, but at the ends at least, the pitch was firm and dry. Sometimes pitches were so hard Richard wondered if he would be able to move his feet once his spikes had penetrated the surface.

'Two legs, please, Jim,' Richard called, hiding leg and middle stumps behind the width of his bat. Jim Rook pointed to the off-side as a signal for Richard to inch the bat to the off before declaring himself satisfied.

'That's two,' said Rook. Richard scratched the position of his guard with his spikes. Though he knew from habit what field would be set for Hills, he swivelled three hundred and sixty degrees to make sure. Gully, three slips, and a wicketkeeper, a short-leg stationed within two yards of his backside, a fine leg on the rope, a mid-wicket, a mid-on, and a cover point patrolling the square. Holding his arm as a barrier across the bowling crease, Jim Rook watched the pavilion clock and waited for the ten minutes to elapse before play could be resumed. The enforced hiatus gave Richard another opportunity to register his racing heartbeat. Unwisely he let his attention shift to the committee box where he could see Gil Atkins among the club-tie worthies enjoying a pre-lunch drink. He took a deep breath, tugged at his gloves, fiddled with the top flap of his pads, nudged the peak of his cap – a repertoire of twitches that he would repeat before every ball as an aide-memoire to his muscles. Rook lowered his arm and called.

'Play.'

Richard bent his back into his stance, checked the position of his feet against the mark he had scored on the crease, and focused on Hills beginning his run-up. A crucifix on a neck chain had escaped from the bowler's shirt and was swinging from side to side in opposition to the bustling roll of his shoulders. Bowed legs notwithstanding, Hills' urgent acceleration was impressive. Richard however saw that the bowler's eyes were not on him but trained anxiously on the fast approaching bowling crease. Like most bowlers off a long run, until he had delivered a few balls in match conditions, Hills could not be certain of the precise measure of his run-up. Running uphill or downhill could alter his stride length. Similarly if he was bowling with or against the wind. The window for Richard to take advantage of this uncertainty was usually short. Once the calibration was complete, the bowler's focus shifted quickly from his own feet to the batsman's stumps.

Hills' run up culminated in a convulsion of arms and legs. The ball, propelled from a high arm action, bounced short of a length, half a yard wide of the off stump. Richard moved to cover his stumps with his pads and watched the ball carry through into the gloves of Gledhill. Hills scrutinised his footmarks to confirm that his feet had landed well within legal bounds. These first deliveries were looseners for him and sighters for Richard – two men groping for compass and range. Richard had never had much problem seeing the ball early out of Hills' hand. Besides he was in prime form. After carefully sizing up Hills' first five balls, he clipped the final delivery off the back foot. The crisp report of cracked lacquer echoed round the ground as the ball came off the bat and sped between cover and gully to the boundary. It was a favourite shot of his, achieved with little back lift and using the bowler's pace to power it.

'Shot,' said Ibbo walking up the pitch to meet Richard at the end of the over. 'Is it swinging?'

'Don't know. He bowled too short to give it chance.' Ibbo nodded. Chewing a wad of gum, he affected the insouciance of a movie gunslinger before the shoot-out. Richard hoped the deception worked more successfully on the opposition than it did on him. Every player had his own way of coping with nerves. Richard preferred to find a moment of quiet in the dressing room and to keep his movements to a minimum once he was out in the middle. In contrast others might pace, whirl their arms, squat, bounce or kick their feet to ease the tension.

Ibbo strolled back to his crease and took guard. The right and left-hand partnership of Richard and himself posed the usual problem for bowlers trying to find a consistent line. The batsmen were aware that the more they rotated the strike with singles the less likely the bowlers were to settle. Not that they were particularly good judges of a run. A number of recent calamities had made Richard determined to call the shots in this aspect of their partnership. Safety first was his watchword even if it did mean turning down a run to get Ibbo off the dreaded mark.

John Talbot was having one of his gobby days calling down the pitch to have his captain move fielders here and there, sparing Ibbo none of the detail. 'Third Man wider for this cock, Skipper. He pokes it there a lot. Why's mid-off so straight? He's never played one there in his life, have you, Ibbo?' Refusing to be drawn into the debate, Ibbo chewed the cud and waited for the verbals to cease. 'Round a touch, Speedy,' said Talbot directing Richard's brother to move squarer at cover.

Talbot was a waster but no mug. He was a master at bowling within himself, a useful discipline on Bristow's benign surface. Aiming for accuracy rather than pace, he bowled nothing in his first over that Ibbo could either leave or nudge for runs. Richard chose not to engage in conversation with Ibbo at the end of the over. They both knew their job was to stick it out until the interval or suffer the wrath of Barry Picken batting at first wicket down. Richard had calculated they would need to survive at least two overs of Hills and two from Talbot before lunch. However, the pavilion clock told him Talbot's maiden had taken only a little over three minutes. Unless he could slow the game down a tick tock or two, there would be time for a third over from Hills before the interval.

'Can I check the screen again, umpire?' asked Richard. Since Hills was already at the start of his run-up, Jim Rook stepped from behind the stumps at the bowler's end and raised his right arm to mimic Hills' delivery position. Rook knew the screen was perfectly well sighted but was quite prepared to condone a bit of time wasting at this juncture. As an enthusiastic trencherman, the lunch break was the high spot of Rook's day and he liked to enjoy every second of it. Within the time remaining, if Hills were to bowl the first ball of what would be his third over, it would condemn everyone on the field to overtime while he completed it. Two club members jumped up and pushed the sliding screen in the direction indicated by Richard's semaphore.

'Thank you,' said Richard re-arranging his pads, gloves, and cap before settling into his stance. His gamesmanship may have used up some time but it risked disturbing his concentration. 'Head still. Balance,' he repeated to himself. Irked by the contrived delay in starting the over, Hills put something extra into the first ball. As Richard moved back and across, the ball kissed the pitch and lifted, bouncing above the meat of Richard's bat and striking the splice before dropping and rolling slowly to meet Hills as he followed through.

'How's the screen, man?' Hills asked pointedly, knowing the pavilion sightscreen was redundant wherever it was sited since his vertiginous arm would always be above it. Richard ignored the gibe and busied himself, tapping the pitch like a bird pecking for worms. The delivery had been testing enough to put him on alert, which was just as well because Hills then produced a swift bouncer that narrowly shaved his nose. Having thus pushed Richard twice on to the back foot, Hills next ball was an attempted yorker landing almost in the batting crease. Anticipating the variation, Richard's bat came down with the clunking certainty of a meat safe door, smacking the ball into the ground. The resulting ricochet off the track, shot past Hills' flailing right boot en route to the fence for four.

Richard had always found these opening salvos of an innings scarily exciting. Whenever he had batted down the order, he found that the hardening effect of the roller had worn off, the ball was softer, and the bowling less mettlesome. Compared to the bounce and zip of the opening exchanges, there was a sluggish feel to the proceedings, as if he was playing underwater.

Teasing up the tension for the last over, Talbot fiddled with the field, asking Gledhill to bring another two fielders close to the bat. Though Ibbo did a passable impersonation of someone who could not care less that he was not yet off the mark, Richard imagined his guts were coils of windy agitation. Talbot slanted the first three deliveries across Ibbo. He jabbed each one square on the off-side where Speedy strolled in and collected the ball without fuss. On each occasion Richard shouted an over-emphatic 'no'. Nerves jangling, Ibbo fidgeted and prodded the pitch. Changing up a gear, Talbot fired his fourth and fifth offerings down the leg-side where they sailed past for Gledhill to take. Ibbo spotted the groundstaff waiting on the boundary edge with brushes, buckets and paint. The prospect of going into lunch without a run against his name did not please him.

Talbot turned with a little skip that seemed at odds with his burly physique and bowled a ball of fullish length across Ibbo's body. The ball hit a thick outside edge and squirted square on the off-side. Ibbo saw enough daylight between the ball's path and Speedy's right hand to spring out of the blocks. 'Yes,' he shouted. Having resolved to do all the calling in that segment of the field, Richard's responding 'no' stayed stillborn on his lips. With Ibbo steaming towards him, he had a split second to make his choice – to go back to the safety of his own end and allow Ibbo to perish, or commit belatedly to a dash up the pitch in the hope of a schoolboy fielding error. 'Run!' screamed Ibbo, bearing down on him.

Richard picked his knees up and raced for the far crease. He could see Speedy swooping on the ball. He needed more revs but he was running through porridge. In one smooth movement, Speedy plucked the ball off the turf and with a flick of the wrist, threw at the one stump he could see from that angle. As Richard launched himself full-length to make his ground, Gledhill was tearing in from the opposite direction to collect Speedy's throw should it miss the stumps. If it hit, Richard was dead, but the throw was a whisker off target. A younger, nimbler keeper might have made it faster to the stumps and Richard would have been done for. Now as he lay flat out measuring his length along the pitch from his tiptoes to the furthest reach of his bat, Richard was 'home' by an inch.

'Over and lunch,' said the umpire impassively. Everyone sauntered towards the pavilion leaving Richard face down in the dust. He did not budge until he heard Ibbo's voice.

'You okay?'

'Marvellous, yeah. Smashing.'

'If you hadn't stopped for a crap, you'd have got home easy.' Richard clamped his jaws shut and got to his feet in stages. How much of his dive for the crease had been pure skid was now evident from the scorch marks down his whites. The upper flap of one of his pads had been forced back on itself and his shirt buttons had been yanked out of their eyelets. Worse, the impact had jolted the polypropylene box hard into his groin. Far from protecting his tender parts, the box itself had given him a fearsome thump. When he regained the vertical, a sickly pain invaded his pelvis and radiated to his back making him stoop again. All this, he thought, just to get Ibbo off the mark. He glanced at the committee room window where he saw Gil Atkins taking liquid refreshment. Ibbo was a good mate and somehow that bond had disarmed Richard's instinct for self-preservation. He could not wholly despise himself for it but on reflection he doubted if a true England contender would have done the same.

3

If Speedy had spent the morning in the middle creaming the ball to all parts of the ground, he might not have had time or inclination to phone his wife. But as it was, the big fat zero against his name on the scoresheet had given him all the rancour he needed to dish the dirt. And Sheila, in her turn, could hardly wait for him to put the phone down before calling Tessa.

'I think the club's called Billy Bigtime,' she said. 'I haven't been there myself, but I gather it has a reputation. We said Richard could stay on our sofabed but he turned it down. He might've saved himself a lot of trouble if he hadn't been so fussy.'

'What trouble's that?' asked Tessa.

'I'm not sure. Speedy thinks there's more to come out. Anyway I thought I'd warn you.'

'Well thanks but Richard's already told me about it.'

'Oh.' Sheila tried not to sound cheated. 'What did he say?'

'That Tony Crick had his wallet stolen. Richard was in the place earlier with Neil Ibbotson, just for one drink.'

'That's alright then,' said Sheila, less than convinced. 'We have to take a lot on trust, don't we, what with the stories you hear. Blokes are all the same, I suppose, 'specially when they get in a crowd. Not that I worry about Speedy.'

'That's alright then,' said Tessa, mimicking Sheila's less than reassuring tone.

'Seriously, I think we're lucky, you and me. But some women don't like to talk about it, do they? They'd rather not know what goes on. Out of sight out of mind for both parties. Well it wouldn't do for me.' Tessa shifted her weight to her other foot in anticipation of a lengthy peroration. 'If Speedy was fooling about I'd want to know about it. Quite apart from anything else there's the health issue.'

'Health?'

'Nasties. VD, and all that.' A mental picture of Speedy submitting to Sheila's forensic examination swam into Tessa's mind. 'It's not nice but it's there, isn't it?'

'I suppose so,' said Tessa evenly. She felt slightly chastened by the realisation that she had spent little time fretting about her husband's fidelity. Given her own behaviour it seemed unrealistic not to admit the possibility of him attracting and being attracted to other women. Certainly he had given her no cause for doubt, but absorbed in the hurly-burly of early stage motherhood, neither had she had the inclination to question that trust.

'I know for a fact that Geoff Ledbrook gave his wife VD,' Sheila went on. 'The club doctor tried to keep it quiet but it came out after they split up. They say he caught it on an M.C.C. tour, so that's another worry for us, isn't it?'

'Is it?'

'Well both Richard and Speedy have been tipped to go this winter. So fingers crossed, eh?' Tessa could not say if Sheila was wishing for Speedy's selection or immunity from the clap. 'And next time make sure Richard stays here with us.'

4

Everyone else having made an early break for the dining room, only next-man-in, Barry Picken, was in the dressing room when Richard and Ibbo returned. Richard took off his pads and went to the shower room where a mirror above the sink showed the full extent of his skid-scarred frontage. Inspecting the underside of his forearm and elbow he discovered a dust-encrusted graze. After only fifteen minutes at the crease he looked a wreck. On the other hand he had been lucky to escape dismissal and though not overly superstitious by cricketers' deranged standards, he did not want to slap fortune in the face by changing his shirt and flannels in mid-innings.

'Put your short-sleeve pully over it, it won't look so bad,' said

Ibbo, reading his thoughts. It was a typical Ibbo solution. In the winter months he was an estimator for his father's plastering firm. From the stories he told Richard, the firm spent most of its time covering over shoddy workmanship. 'It was a good run, you know,' repeated Ibbo.

'Was it balls,' said Richard. 'In any case it was my call.'

'It was wide of Speedy, mate.'

'Not wide enough. You know he's got a good arm. If Ray Gledhill wasn't such a camel, I'd have been a goner.'

'Well he is and you're not,' said Ibbo, plastering over the dispute with a smile and a wink.

'Cutting it fine, weren't you, lad?' Gil Atkins commented as he and Richard went into the dining room together. 'A good fielder, your kid, you should know that.' Atkins smelt of pre-prandial alcohol but evidently it had not dulled his powers of observation. In the blink of an eye he had noted Richard's lack of judgement and Speedy's skill in the field. If they really were rivals for an England tour place, the score read Speedy two, himself nil.

Richard watched Ibbo pile his lunch plate high with spuds. 'Soon run this off,' said Ibbo, seeing his look of incredulity. Richard envied Ibbo. His apparent lack of imagination freed him from the fear of potential pitfalls. While Richard became distracted by thoughts of the future unknown, Ibbo lived resolutely in the present. His ambition was simply to play well enough to stay in the team. He was brave and stubborn against the new ball and unselfish when asked to take risks. Added to a safe pair of hands in the field and a clubbable nature in the changing room, it could be argued he was a more important member of the team than those whose contribution in terms of pure figures was superior. And while some might be fooled by his self-deprecatory utterances, an indestructible self-belief glued the whole package together.

'Here, have another,' said Ibbo forking a spud onto Richard's plate. 'You're eating like a girl.' Richard thought he was probably right. If he stayed on the field for a stretch of the afternoon, he would soon be running on empty. Traces of blood on the tablecloth told him the graze under his arm was still weeping. He held a paper napkin to the wound and turned round to get another napkin from one of the women serving on table. Instead, he caught the eye of Speedy sitting on the table behind.

'Tessa's been on the blower to Sheila. Very worried about you.' Speedy's tone was joshing and treacherous at the same time. 'She's got wind of what you get up to when you're away from home.'

'Who phoned who?' asked Richard.

'Sheila didn't say. She wants to know what you're doing tonight.'

'Who does?'

'Sheila. She says you've got to come and have a meal with us.' Richard's heart sank.

'Thanks but Ibbo's got something planned. Haven't you?' Ibbo hid behind a forkful of potato and nodded.

'That's exactly why she wants you to be with us for the evening,' said Speedy, glancing sardonically at Ibbo.

'Can't be helped,' shrugged Richard.

'She won't take 'no' for an answer, mate.'

'Sorry, I promised Ibbo.'

'Is that right. So what's the plan, Ibbo?'

'We were thinking of going to the flicks,' said Richard, cutting in quickly to fill the empty thought bubble above Ibbo's head.

'Yeh,' agreed Ibbo.

'What's on?' asked Speedy. Richard looked at Ibbo who had cannily filled his mouth to overflowing and was in no position to answer.

'Not sure,' said Richard, 'but it's ages since we saw a flick.'

'Whatever's on, it starts well before you'll get away from here. Tell you what, why don't you bring Ibbo along? Sheila does a wicked chilli con carne.' Richard sensed that Ibbo was about to turn tail and head for the hills.

'Don't worry about me, I'm fine, thanks. You must have loads of family stuff to talk about,' said Ibbo in full flight.

5

Looking small behind a big desk, Slingsby peered at Rook and Chambers over his steel-rimmed specs. It seemed to him that even without their white coats they were readily recognisable as umpires. Former First-class players and now approaching a second retirement, they exuded an aura of yesteryear. Jim Rook, tall and broad with thinning hair plastered back, had the bearing of a superannuated policeman. His face was weathered to the colour of a well-oiled cricket bat and sported a drinker's spongy nose. Having been a bowler he was known to sympathise with the bowler rather than the batter when it came to marginal decisions. In contrast, the man standing alongside him, Len Chambers, was a former batsman and a renowned 'not outer' as an umpire. Once, after suffering a barrage of over-optimistic LBW appeals from Tony Crick, he had turned to the bowler and reminded him that the batsman was defending a regulation set of stumps 'not a five-bar bloody gate'. Chambers was a slight boney character given to nervous twitches and acid stomachs. Whereas

Rook sought to impose no-nonsense authority in the middle, Chambers was all fuss and bother. Neither would claim to be infallible, but of the two, Chambers' judgement was the more astute. Perhaps this was because Chambers had maintained his love of the game whereas Rook dearly wanted to draw stumps on his career and put his feet up.

As he waited for their view on Badel's suspect action, Slingsby marvelled at how often pairs of umpires appeared as versions of the 'Odd Couple'. And, like ex pros of any sport, they invariably carried a limp. Crocked ankles, wicketkeeper's knees, bowler's hips – the bill for years of athletic excess came keen and spiteful.

'Well I reckon it's too soon for any of us to say. The lad's first game, isn't it?' As Slingsby had anticipated, Rook took the Walter Matthau part to Chambers' Jack Lemmon. 'I know Paul Pywell was making a song and dance about it even with three figures on the board. He's such a mard-arse. What do you say Len? The point is,' continued Rook before Chambers could speak, 'Lord's is looking for some mug to do the dirty work.'

'I think they're only asking for your opinion,' said Slingsby.

'And what if we haven't got one? I say we do nothing. What do you say Len? It's always bowlers in the dock in this game. How many ex-bowlers are pulling strings at HQ? They're all candy-arse batters.'

'I think he throws,' said Chambers quietly.

'Oh,' said Rook, the rug pulled from under him.

'Perhaps not every ball,' added Chambers.

'Ah. Well there you are then,' said Rook as if vindicated, 'that's what I said. We need time to look. It's not fair on the lad otherwise.'

'Lord's want him filmed if either of you have doubts about his action.'

'Well it'll have to be done, I suppose. But I'm not calling him.

Not this match anyway. They're not getting my name first on the charge sheet. What do you say Len?' But Chambers had said quite enough.

6

The haze obscuring the City skyline for much of the morning had finally melted in the pale sun, but there was no feeling of dryness in the air. By the back-end of the season, the outfield would normally have been scorched brown but it looked as lush as June. The team had enjoyed a relatively successful campaign and Jephcott was eager to gee everyone up for a last push into the place money. He did not need the bonus himself but a share-out went down well in the changing room and he was always keen to establish common cause with his men. He joined Richard and Ibbo who were waiting outside the changing room for the umpires and opposition to go out after lunch. Five bowling points had been won and Jephcott's day would be made if the two openers could establish a solid platform for the reply.

'I thought you two had sorted out your running between the wickets?'

'My fault,' offered Richard. 'I should have sent Ibbo back. I was lucky.'

'Well don't waste it.' Ibbo stayed tight-lipped still convinced he had judged the run perfectly. 'Gil Atkins says he'd like to see you turn your arm over a bit more. Interesting.'

'Is it?'

'Well it seems you and your brother are both in the frame for the last place on the boat.'

'He said that?'

'Not in so many words, but reading between the lines . . .'

'He hasn't said anything about last night?' said Richard tentatively. Jephcott raised a quizzical eyebrow.

'Last night?'

'About Tony having his wallet stolen?'

'What about it?'

'We were with him at the club – for a short time.'

'So KC told me. I know Tony likes a flutter but why were you there?' probed Jephcott.

'We went there for a drink.'

'Expensive way to get a drink?' said Jephcott sceptically. 'Is there something I should know about last night?'

'No. It's just that the local rag might dig up some rubbish and put one or two of us on the spot.'

'And you'd like me to reassure Atkins that you're a man of moderation and early nights?'

'Something like that.'

'Well I could try,' said Jephcott with a conspiratorial smile that left Richard feeling he had more to hide than was the case. 'I doubt if Gil is interested in what you get up to. If you're under consideration you'll have been vetted already.'

'Oh,' said Richard intrigued.

'The only doubt they're likely to have is whether to take a batter who can bowl or a bowler who can bat. So if the opportunity is there to put you on, I'll lob you the ball.'

'Ahead of Mal?'

'Well let's see shall we? It would be galling if your brother got there ahead of you. He can't really bat for toffee.' Not entirely true, thought Richard. Speedy was a more than useful Number Seven. He had a good eye and quick feet for a tall man. Just as important he read the game well and could adapt to circumstances. He had certainly proved himself a better batsman than

114

Richard was a bowler. Even so, Jephcott's warmly partisan words lifted his hopes.

In this respect Jephcott was only demonstrating the sort of support expected of a county captain. A good one was sensitive to individual aspirations and willing to encourage them to the mutual benefit of player and club. Without being intrusive, Jephcott had made himself aware of every player's domestic baggage. Births, weddings and serious illnesses in the family were marked, not necessarily by Jephcott's attendance, but often with a thoughtful note. On one occasion he heard that Tessa was immobilised by a dire back complaint and sent immediately for the consultant who had treated his wife after a riding accident. The remedy came quickly and no bill followed, so both Tessa and Richard had reason to be grateful. Such ingratiation brought its rewards in terms of player loyalty. Equally important, it won over wives and girlfriends and made them more sympathetic to the demands and absences he and the club asked of their partners. And though some might have said Robin Jephcott's courtesy was calculating, it also served to conceal his ruthlessly competitive nature, something unwary opponents learned belatedly to their cost.

The kamikaze single that had left Richard eating dust, meant Ibbo was facing Hills on the resumption of play. A meal break of forty minutes was quite enough time for a bowler's muscles to stiffen, but Hills' body was more elastic than most, especially with a coaxing if pallid sun on his back. His first delivery pitched middle and leg and speared away to the off, the perfect line to a left-hander. Without any discernible movement of his feet, Ibbo reacted with an involuntary twitch. The ball took the edge of his bat and whistled at knee height, perfectly bisecting Pywell and Chatterway at first and second slip. Either fielder could have caught it but neither moved a muscle for fear, so they would claim, of obstructing the other. As the ball raced to the boundary for four, Hills stuck his crucifix between his teeth in frustration, put his hands on his head, and glared at the shamefaced duo. If the chance had been offered at any other time it might well have been snaffled, but first ball of the session was just too soon after the break for their reactions to have shifted out of idling.

'Bad luck, Hilly,' shouted Gledhill to break the embarrassed silence. Hills finally spun round to go back to his mark still biting his crucifix, while Pywell and Chatterway held a whispered post mortem to establish blame.

For a time the batsmen set out their stalls in contrasting styles. Confirming his good form, Richard flicked a delivery off his toes to the square leg boundary. His first three scoring shots had gone for four and he had to beware an excess of confidence. Experience had taught him that a scratchy start to an innings was a more reliable harbinger of a big score. If that was the case for all players, Ibbo was destined for a ton. Time and again he played and missed. When Talbot slipped him a bouncer Ibbo shaped too late for the hook and top-edged it. The ball parted his hair, soared over Gledhill's despairing star-jump behind the wicket and careered for four runs.

'Is that a bat or a white stick you're using?' sneered Talbot, following through expansively and coming to a halt a few feet from Ibbo. Knowing that Talbot was more dangerous when riled, Richard shot Ibbo a glance to warn him not to respond. But Ibbo had had enough taunting for one day.

'Just belt up dickhead and bowl.' Talbot's sneer curdled into something more menacing. Without taking his eyes off Ibbo he thrust out an arm and pointed to the square leg boundary.

'I want a man out deep, Skip,' he demanded, thereby serving notice that he was about to test the effectiveness of Ibbo's hook shot. Gledhill's shoulders slumped. He could see the ball was beginning to swing and he did not want Talbot wasting time and effort peppering the batsman with short-pitched deliveries. Knowing better than to argue publicly with him, he put a man on the edge to catch any miscues and resolved to make Talbot see sense at the end of the over.

Gledhill should have given his bowler more credit. Talbot's ire was more synthetic than real. As Ibbo shuffled distractedly onto the back-foot in anticipation of the threatened bouncer, Talbot bowled him three snaking deliveries of full length, the last of which induced an edge to be caught at daisy-height by Pywell at first slip. Talbot hitched up his flannels as if it was a routine dismissal, and greeted the plaudits of team-mates with a laconic shrug of his shoulders.

Ibbo's face was thunderous as he headed for the pavilion. Talbot's play-acting had stolen his concentration as if he were a novice. In fact the fatal delivery had swung into the left-hander then moved away off the seam. Ibbo had done well to get any wood on it at all. Not that anyone in the dressing room would dare mention it until Ibbo's bag-kicking, glove-throwing paddy had blown itself out.

Now that the lacquer had gone from the surface of the ball, the bowlers could work with spit and polish to produce an effective contrast between its two halves. The sun had never fully broken through and in the muggy atmosphere the ball wobbled more and more. While Talbot maintained a relentless off stump line at one end, Hills steamed in from the other, trapping Picken LBW and next ball bowling Jephcott neck and crop, to leave the innings sagging badly at 45 for three.

It was not the most opportune time to have Rod Brennan striding to the middle. Ever since Jephcott had removed him as Richard's opening partner, the Tasmanian had alternated between four and five in the order depending on the state of play. By keeping him away from the new ball, Jephcott hoped to use Brennan's destructive powers to maximum advantage. However, the rapid loss of early wickets had brought him to the crease when conditions were least favourable to his style of boom-boom batting.

Brennan took guard and hammered the toe of his bat into the pitch to make a mark. The reverberations echoed round the ground and immediately plugged the spectators into an unaccustomed source of energy. In the Press Box, Richard could actually see the hacks shift forward in their seats. The fielders too knew that an hour of Brennan's batting could change the tenor of the game and leave their hands stinging well into winter. The situation required both batsmen to dig in and risk nothing while they tried to put the innings on an even keel, but Gledhill had brought fielders around the bat to give Hills the maximum number of catchers for his hat-trick ball. Richard could sense Brennan's hackles rise at this affront to his explosive reputation. He observed him eyeing the untenanted spaces in the outfield but did not think seriously about urging caution. He doubted if mere words could curb such an unyielding force of nature.

The fielders tensed as Hills ran in. Instead of the fast leg-stump yorker he had intended to bowl, he delivered a succulent half volley. Brennan latched on and with a metronomic swing of the blade straight drove it. At the bowler's end, Richard had to jump hurriedly to avoid losing a foot as the ball screamed under him and tore to the fence where the impact embossed on it a blotch of eggshell blue paint.

'Alright lads,' said Gledhill, pragmatically, 'back to where you were.' Dismissively adjusting his box, Brennan tucked his ample tackle more snugly into his crotch and watched the field retreat. He felt no compulsion to join Richard for a tête-à-tête at the end of the over. To do so would have suggested there was something worth discussing – an opposition tactic to counter perhaps? Such a consideration would have been foreign to Brennan's thinking. Whatever the circumstances, he alone called the tune and Richard was content to play second fiddle while it lasted. It was fun to watch the bowling flayed and fielders scattered like beaten remnants of a retreating army. Where Richard's bat was an extension of his hands and arms, Brennan's was a weapon of destruction. It was not enough to hit the ball clear of the boundary rope, it had to be dispatched into the stands. Better still, out of the ground. He enjoyed emptying the club bars and hearing woozy veterans rate this or that blow as the longest carry they had seen there since World War II.

Having captured three wickets in rapid succession Hills and Talbot might have been expected to keep up the pressure but Brennan had made them apprehensive. While Richard nudged and pottered, he smacked balls directly at fielders as if handing out discipline. Then, frustrated at not finding the gaps, he opened his shoulders and took the aerial route, depositing a Talbot delivery first bounce into the car park.

During the next over, Richard saw Speedy rotating his arms and touching his toes in preparation for entering the attack. There were few bowlers in the country better able to take advantage of the buttery atmosphere. Now the greenness of the pitch, so evident on the first morning, had begun to show its hand, every ball pitching seam-up was leaving a dark green bruise on the surface. Richard doubted if his partner had even noticed the increased movement. Nor would it be wise to burden him with the information. Given a large slice of luck, he mused, it might just be Rod Brennan's day.

After bowling unchanged for nine overs, Hills concentrated on bowling a tight over to end his spell. Sensing he had spiked the guns of the opposition's spearhead, Brennan fatally eased off the accelerator. Playing the only authentically defensive stroke of his innings, he got a thin edge to a perfectly straight ball. His stroke-play had been so commanding since coming to the wicket that he seemed unwilling to believe the umpire's raised finger even when fielders gathered to congratulate Hills. He lifted his bat and inspected the outside edge like a suspicious wife looking for a lipstick smudge on an errant husband's collar. Though the crowd was sparse, it transmitted a wave of disappointment. Cheated of their entertainment, the hacks in the Press Box leaned back in their seats. 'Caught Gledhill, Bowled Hills, 23', hardly merited a mention even as a vignette.

'Played inside a straight one, didn't he?' said one reporter to nobody in particular.

'Where was he last night then?' said another, searching for a sleazy explanation for Brennan's dozy dismissal. The pack was unforgiving when a favourite failed them.

'Knob-slinging was he, Ron?' Grimley kept his eyes down on his notes, shook his head and shrugged. 'Was he with Tony Crick?'

'No, he's not staying in Brum.'

'Why's that?'

'I don't know,' chuntered Grimley, impatiently. 'You think they tell me every time they fart?'

'I just assumed you'd know, being such a nosey bugger.' Grimley accepted that a certain quid pro quo was in order when passing information to reporters on the regional papers. In his view being a nosey bugger was part of his job description and he did what he could to keep abreast of the daily doings of his home team players. This often involved booking into the team's hotel, the better to garner any snippets. It was amazing how time spent watching the comings and goings in a hotel foyer illuminated the alliances and conflicts that ran through a team. But the closeness he sought to cultivate could only be maintained with the trust of the players. The sort of complicity in other words that hobbled his capacity to provide objective reporting.

For years Grimley had been able to satisfy the demands of his local readership without disturbing his cosy relationship with the players. The home supporters were gluttons for good-news stories about their heroes and scandal was not a staple of the back page. But a new editor some twenty years his junior had parked his backside behind the sports desk and was determined to make his mark.

'I want stories that fizz off the page,' he enthused. 'Don't describe the scorecard, Ron. I can read that for myself. I want the story behind the scorecard, the men behind the figures. Give me personalities and bad boys, clashes, rows and walk-outs. I want jokes and puns, Ron. I want a column that rocks.'

It had shaken Ron, he did not mind admitting it. He was not sure if the new editor knew anything at all about sport. He was a football sort of chap at best for whom the cricket season was an inconvenient blip in the calendar. Grimley, aka 'The Sports Supremo', suddenly felt like a fish out of water. Panicking, he had even debated the pros and cons of becoming a teacher. It was not simply a case of unpicking his carefully woven relationship with the players, there was now a fundamental mismatch in journalistic philosophy. Through his columns he believed he spoke to fellow sports lovers not to a slavering rabble made up of the prurient and the puerile. With a sickening feeling in his belly he wondered what would happen if the sports editor got wind of Tony Crick's current misadventure. Grimley's ability to control the story had already been ceded to the local stringers. He could hardly be seen to be the only one out of the loop should the story sprout legs. Neither did the scoreboard bring him any succour. At seventy one for four, his last filing before the afternoon deadline would be a muted affair that played down the mediocre batting and magnified Richard Hastie's continued good form under the eye of an England selector.

Stunned though he was, Rod Brennan was not one to dwell on misfortune. By the time he was half way to the pavilion the chagrin was gone and his sunny disposition reinstated by the thought that there would always be another day. 'Good luck, mate,' he said to Crick as they passed.

Cometh the hour, cometh the man?

Richard watched Tony Crick striding to the wicket. The mishap to Murfin on the previous morning and Jephcott's decision to play Shanks instead of a replacement batsman had meant promoting Crick in the batting order. From the way he was carving air-shots to all parts of the arena, he was intent on proving the elevation to be no more than his due.

Richard read the scoreboard. He knew the loss of the upper-order demanded absolute caution from the last recognised batsmen. It was not the most auspicious moment for either man to be facing his brother. He had hoped Brennan's dismissal might have persuaded Gledhill to keep the wilting Hills in the attack, but having bowled nine incisive overs either side of lunch, the West Indian paceman took his sweater. Speedy measured out his run-up, furiously polishing the ball on his backside. On a typical Wilf Bristow pitch, Speedy was invariably introduced as first change when the batsmen were in the ascendancy and the innings was well established. Now, with the opposition in retreat, he could hardly have hoped for a better moment to show Gil Atkins what he could do. Trusted by Gledhill to set his own field, Speedy moved players hither and thither to block Richard's favourite channels of run getting, strokes that had remained in his repertoire ever since his brother was running in to bowl past the bay window and the begonias at Number Twenty Two.

Knowing one another's game inside out, the duels between Richard and Speedy had never been less than hard fought. Though sibling rivalry was common enough, it went to a whole new level when the protagonists were seriously involved in sport. The brothers' parents had always tried to promote feelings of generosity between them and an acceptance that each dog would have his day. But it was an uphill struggle. The boys did not loathe one another exactly, they just hated coming second in a two-man contest. Hastie Senior's claim to strict neutrality had not stopped them accusing him of favouring one over the other. He had hoped in vain that one day the bat hurling tantrums would give way to mature good grace. And though the childishness was more hidden now, memories of squabbles and injustices were deeply etched into their relationship.

Once his field was inch-perfectly in place, Speedy ran in. A familiar straight approach to the crease, knees high, head textbook still, ball at the end of his fingers like an apple picked at a stretch. Richard resolved to push well forward if possible to reduce the risk of an LBW dismissal should a delivery nip back to hit his front pad. The first delivery swung in from the off to confirm his fears. Propping so far forward he was in danger of splitting his flannels, the ball struck his inside edge and cannoned into his pad. Encouraged, Speedy sniffed the air and rolled up his sleeves another notch.

The second delivery swung in and broke back again. This time Richard failed to get even an edge as his front pad took all the impact. Behind him, Gledhill offered a stifled appeal but the ball was clearly bound wide of the leg stump.

'You should linseed oil that pad,' Speedy smirked. Richard

did not respond. He needed to maintain maximum focus both to survive and to dig the team out of a deepening hole. By altering the position of his fingers on the seam and the angle of his wrist at delivery, Speedy could produce a number of variations, some of them unpredictable even to himself. In helpful conditions he had learned to reduce his pace and concentrate simply on landing the ball seam-up on the track. Accordingly, instead of moving into Richard as the previous two balls had done, the third nipped away sharply to the off to beat the bat as he groped for a connection. Gledhill was so busy admiring the delivery he failed to take the ball cleanly and it escaped far enough to concede a bye and brought Crick to the receiving end. Speedy had made his brother look ordinary and won a small moral victory. Not wishing to concede this, Richard refused to make eye contact as he jogged up the pitch towards him. Somehow Crick survived the rest of Speedy's over and came up the pitch to confer with Richard. 'What's it doing?' he asked. Unless Crick had had his eyes closed it was a stupid question.

'Nothing very nice,' answered Richard. Crick nodded and leaned on his bat.

'I'd better stick my left dog down the wicket and hope for the best,' he said. It was an unusual comment by someone not known for scaling back his ambition, but Richard could not have put it better himself.

More comfortable against Talbot, the pair scratched and scrambled three singles before Speedy took off his sweater again. Richard glanced towards the pavilion in the hope of seeing Gil Atkins asleep. He could not have asked for a better venue to make a good impression, but circumstances were conspiring against him. Jephcott's decision to field on the first day and the vagaries of the weather since then had given his team the trickiest of the conditions.

Speedy paused at the start of his run-up and visualised Richard's destruction. A rip-snorting delivery would be ideal – one that pitched, jagged and speared through his defences to leave the timbers shattered. But what Speedy delivered was not a wrecking ball, even though the result was much the same. It was an insidious delivery that snaked silently between Richard's bat and pad and picked a single bail off the stumps as deftly as a child sneaking a cherry off an iced fancy.

'Well bowled, Speedy,' shouted Gledhill, clapping his gloved hands like a performing seal. Richard looked back at the stumps, perfectly intact but for the missing bail. Even in his state of mortification he had the nous not to linger slack-jawed at the crease. As Speedy walked triumphantly down the track, he turned quickly and made for the pavilion. For one who prided himself on leaving no gate between bat and pad, Richard felt non-plussed. It was as if he had been undone by sleight of hand rather than a failure of technique. As he walked off the field, he could hear the numerals on the scoreboard flicking over like a battery of camera shutters. 'HASTIE BOWLED HASTIE 34' it proclaimed below a total of 74 for 5 wickets.

The door to the coop was open and a rout was in prospect. Richard's dismissal had caused panic in the dressing room. Bowlers who had been relaxing in stockinged-feet, hauled themselves from behind newspapers and out of chairs to put on boots and pad up. KC could barely contain his fury. Having bowled unchanged throughout the morning to pull the team's fat out of the fire the least he expected was to put his feet up for the rest of the day. Jephcott was equally dismayed but with a 'nought' against his name he was in no position to upbraid others for their lack of application.

With his usual gift for tact and timing, KC chose Richard's return to the pavilion to complain about the hotel accommodation. 'I'm not surprised he missed a straight one. He can't have slept a wink last night.' Jephcott was in no mood to bandy words but KC gave him no choice. 'He had to sleep on a bloody camp bed.'

'Oh? Why was that?'

'It was either that or get into a double with me. No contest.'

'No,' agreed Jephcott.

'I've told the office time and again to book me a single.'

'I thought that was understood.'

'When they know you're staying private, Robin, they stick us in anywhere.'

'I'll have a word when we get back.'

'It looked a good 'un,' offered Ibbo as Richard sat down with a heavy sigh and began to unbuckle his pads.

'Good enough for me,' said Richard still stunned. From outside they heard a sudden agitation of voices and scattered clapping. Ibbo stood on a bench to peer above the frosted half of the window onto the field.

'Mal's out.' Even in the most propitious circumstances Mal Shanks was less than brave against pace. Knowing this and sensing a capitulation, Gledhill had brought Hills back in place of Talbot to finish the job. It was Speedy, however, who delivered the coup de grace, accounting for Crick, Badel and Topsy Turner in quick succession to finish with four wickets for sixteen. A last ditch frolic by 'Doc' Holliday had saved some dignity, but a score of 115 all out reduced the dressing room to embarrassed silence.

Richard glanced at KC. He had not spoken since the fall of the sixth wicket but his disgust could be gauged from the throbbing blue vein in his temple and the stamp of his boots on the floor. The team's submissive performance was unforgiveable against a side he regarded as 'a bunch of big city candy-arses'.

126

Even Jephcott knew it was best to puff on a cigarette in the corner rather than provoke the eruption of Mount Colclough with a superfluous comment.

In the midst of the shame and humiliation, Alvar Badel sat bemused, like a guest at a family meal where the patriarch frowns on conversation while eating.

Chapter Seven

1

Though it was six years since they had last met and her hair seemed redder than she remembered it, Tessa had no difficulty in recognising Maggie as she entered the café. 'Well hello,' she said smiling broadly before embracing Tessa. 'What a lovely surprise to hear from you.' Tessa had called her old conveyancing office knowing Maggie still worked there.

'This is Sarah and Jessica,' said Tessa.

'Hello Sarah and Jessica.' The two girls smiled shyly as required before focusing on their buttered teacakes, nipping tiny bites out of the circumference to see who could make it last longest.

'Two little angels?' smiled Maggie sotto voce.

'Sometimes – when asleep.'

'Lovely,' said Maggie, a hint of longing in her voice, the girls nibbling, sure in the knowledge that they were objects of admiration.

'And you?' asked Tessa, tentatively. 'Children?'

'No. Bruce and I haven't clicked. A shame, I suppose. I think he wanted a family more than me.'

'Still time, isn't there?' Maggie shrugged.

'Que sera, sera. To be honest I like working.'

'This is work, believe me,' said Tessa glancing ruefully at the girls.

'I mean for money, dear, and independence.'

'Well you look good on it.'

'If I was half a stone lighter I would agree with you. You're looking rather wonderful yourself. The same fabulous figure — infuriating.'

'Are you having something to eat?' said Tessa catching a waitresses eye.

'What are the tea-cakes like, Sarah?' asked Maggie.

'Scrummy.'

'Then I'll have one.'

'Two more tea-cakes, please,' said Tessa to the waitress, 'and a pot of tea for two.'

'So how's your famous husband?'

'Oh fine, I think.'

'I don't pay much attention to sport but Bruce keeps up with it. He says Richard is doing rather well?'

'Yes. They say he's a possible for England's tour of the West Indies.'

'Really? That's fantastic. Though hard for you, I expect?'

'Well I've sort of got used to not having him around.'

'Serious grass widow stuff,' said Maggie appreciating Tessa's situation with a little more acuity.

'I'm winning,' shouted Jessica.

'No you're not, stupid,' said her sister.

'Tell her, Mummy.'

'I think you're both about level,' said Tessa, brokering a truce.

'Smashing to see you again but quite a surprise,' said Maggie, gently inviting an explanation.

'I was thinking of going back to work,' lied Tessa. 'Two or three days a week.'

'With us?'

'Just a thought.'

'It would be great to have you back. There's certainly enough work but I'm not sure the partners would be happy with a part-timer – other than James Egan of course. He'd be thrilled.'

'What makes you say that?'

'Well I thought you two were still quite pally. Don't you bump into one another at the cricket club?'

'Very occasionally.' Deflectively, Tessa turned to push Jessica's plate away from the edge of the table, but Maggie's suggestive expression was still there when she looked up again.

'Anyway I wouldn't blame you for wanting to come back to work. The job is the only thing that keeps me sane. How else would I meet any men?' Tessa giggled then realised Maggie was not being frivolous.

'Isn't one man enough for you these days?' said Tessa, trying to keep it light.

'What do you think?' Tessa saw the quizzical expression on Sarah's face as she tried to make sense of her mother's old acquaintance.

'Is Bruce away a lot?'

'No. I only wish he was. It would make things easier.' Maggie lowered her eyelids as she took a sip of tea. Tessa realised it had been naïve of her to imagine other people's lives were any less complicated than her own. Certainly the alibi she had come to request from Maggie was unlikely to disconcert someone who was clearly in the throes of marital disenchantment herself.

'Children might have made a difference, I suppose.'

'I wouldn't be so sure about that,' said Tessa in a tone that implied they were singing from the same song sheet. 'It just makes things harder to resolve.'

'Well it's blindly optimistic for someone to commit to one other person for life. Sooner or later it's boring. And if it isn't, you must be boring.'

'A lot of people seem happy that way.'

'Well not me. And not you, I'm guessing. But perhaps I'm wrong?' Tessa made no reply. She recalled that Maggie had openly envied her the match she had made six years previously. It had been a source of pride as well as celebration and she suddenly felt reluctant to admit to things going flat. Maggie had reminded her of her younger, fashionable, happier self. Humdrum domesticity had made her feel plain, bored and unappreciated. Her fault, perhaps, for believing she could compete with Richard's first love, the game by which he earned his living and their family's keep.

'I won,' shouted Jessica. 'I won, Mummy, I won.' Sarah did not contest the claim. She had tuned into Maggie's disillusionment and gone quiet.

'I suppose we expect too much. Once the novelty wore off I'm afraid marriage has been a bit of a let down. Auto-pilot in the bedroom, taken for granted out of it. No fun at all. Bruce isn't a bad sort really, but after a while you become their sister, or worse their mother.'

'So where does that leave you?' asked Tessa.

'I have a friend.'

'Ah.'

'More than one actually. They're not hard to find once you make it clear you're available. But that's enough of me. What about you?'

'Oh you know...' muttered Tessa enigmatically.

'Leave the nitty-gritty 'til we have a girl's night out, shall we?'

'Yes we'd better,' said Tessa, happy to abort her mission for the time being. 'These two have been amazingly good but best not to push my luck.' Maggie took another sip of tea and looked searchingly into Tessa's eyes.

'You know I never did think it would be all wine and roses for you either. We owe it to ourselves to be happy. What else is there?'

Chapter Eight

1

CRICKET STARS IN NIGHTCLUB ENQUIRY

County cricket all-rounder, Tony Crick, was today helping Police with their enquiries regarding the theft of money after spending the evening at a Birmingham night spot. Fellow clubbers at Billy Bigtime's reported seeing Crick and team-mates, Ibbotson, Hastie, Picken, and Turner in party mood before the theft of Crick's wallet was discovered.

The dance and gaming venue successfully defended itself in court recently after moves to rescind its liquor and gaming licence. William Devereux, the owner, is still awaiting trial on a charge of living off immoral earnings.

A spokesman for Derbyshire County Cricket Club said any disciplinary issues arising from the incident would be an internal matter for the captain and cricket committee.

Grimley read the front page of the local *Post* and felt a hot prickly sensation under his shirt collar. It was a Press Agency piece and as such available to any regional paper willing to pay a few quid. He did not have to wait long before a call came from the office.

'What the fuck's going on, Ron?'

'What d'you mean . . .?' Agitated, Grimley could not recall the sports editor's first name.

'This story about your lot boozing and chasing tarts.'

'My lot?'

'Don't fuck with me, Ron. You're paid to bring in stories like this.'

'I thought I was the cricket correspondent?'

'What?'

'I cover the day's play not after-hours antics.'

'Who says?'

'A few of the lads had one or two drinks that's all. Nothing would have been said if one of them hadn't had his pocket picked. Everything else is nonsense.'

'Listen, this landed on the news desk and got stuck on the front page without any reference to me. D'you know how that makes me look when I've got my own man on the bloody spot?'

Grimley had quite forgotten what it felt like to be under a ton of bricks when it came down. As a cub reporter he had, on occasions, arrived at the wrong venue and received similar bollockings, but experience it seemed had not thickened his skin. He should have realised from the outset that there was no chance of him being able to suppress the story once it was subject to journalistic manipulation. The only thing he could do was to proclaim his innocence and hope Crick and the others believed him.

The rapid decline in the visitor's batting meant tea was taken between innings. It gave Grimley the chance to grab Crick before he went back onto the field. When he got to the rear of the pavilion he found him talking to a uniformed officer.

'Sixty five pounds?' said Crick, counting money from a brown envelope.

'Yes,' said the copper. 'We had a word at Billy's and they had a whip round.'

'A whip round?'

'Not a bad result.'

'I lost a hundred pounds.'

'I think that's near enough in the circumstances, don't you?'

'Yes. Well, thanks,' said Crick not wishing to push his luck.

'We'll be in touch if there's anything further to report. We know where to find you.'

'Fine,' said Crick, not entirely chuffed to be in such easy reach of the Law. Once the officer had climbed into his squad car, Grimley button-holed Crick, a copy of the local evening paper clenched in his fist.

'Tony. Thought you should see this.' Crick frowned at the news story.

'Shit.'

'Yeh.'

'Will it be in the paper at home?'

'Yes. The news desk got hold of it. I'd appreciate it if you'd tell the lads it was nothing to do with me.'

'Looks like I could be in the back bedroom for a while.'

'Sorry. If you think it might do any good I could call and see your missus tonight? Put her straight about what happened?' Crick was tempted to accept Grimley's offer but only for a second. Grimley might deflect some of the lightning, but there was a good chance he could make matters worse. Grimley may have been a journalist but, as a skilled dissembler, he ran Crick a very poor second. Crick looked at the paper again.

'Can I keep this to show the lads?'

'Course. And remember my offer. It wouldn't be any trouble.'

Crick listened to the ring tones and braced himself for his wife to answer. He saw Richard exit the dining room and passed the *Evening Post* for him to read.

'Hello, love. I thought I'd better call . . . You've seen it? It's rubbish, love. I had my pocket picked in a crowded bar . . . I was having a drink with the lads, what else would I be doing? Look I didn't know the place had a reputation.' Crick grimaced at Richard and decided to widen his terms of reference. 'None of us did. It was Topsy who got us to go with him . . . Yes, we should've checked . . . It looks bad, yes, I know, love. We're all pissed off about it . . . I can't help what your mother says . . . Then don't listen. It's rumour and gossip, love. You know I wouldn't do anything like that.'

Richard got out of earshot before he became bilious. Given his own situation perhaps he should have stayed to hear how an expert got himself out of the guano. Instead he went into the changing room and laid the newspaper face up for Ibbo to read.

'Fuck.'

'Yeh.'

'There may be Questions in the House.'

'Just a few.'

'Cheeky bastards,' exclaimed Crick, entering the dressing room, buoyed but not entirely unbowed, after the phone call to his better-half. 'The police got Billy's to cough up my money.'

'How?' said Ibbo.

'You tell me. They said the club had a whip round. Sixty five quid they've given me. Case closed.'

'That's sixty five for you, thirty five for them?'

'You've got it. They're on the take. Grimley says he was

hoping to keep the story out of the local rag, but the news desk got it from the Press Association.'

'Front page, the same?' Richard asked pessimistically. Crick nodded.

'But as long as we all stick to the same story.'

'Remind me,' said Ibbo.

'Topsy suckered us into going.'

'You what?' protested Topsy.

'You got us all into the club, didn't you?'

'Yeh and you jumped in happy as frogs up a drainpipe.'

'Dicky and me only stayed for one drink,' countered Ibbo.

'Only because Tony and Barry nabbed those tarts you were trying to chat up.'

'Bollocks,' said Ibbo. As the tone deteriorated, Richard glanced uneasily at Jephcott who was pretending not to listen. KC meanwhile was all ears, scowling like nanny at bath-time. Rod Brennan simply sat back, arms folded, and enjoyed the bickering.

'You're the only single bloke,' argued Crick.

'So what?' said Topsy.

'You won't have to explain yourself to anybody.'

'What about my mother?' Topsy's response produced a gust of laughter that finally blew the plug out of Mount Colclough.

'Belt up you lot and look at the bloody scoreboard,' he thundered. After a chastened pause, Jephcott broke the silence.

'Thank you, KC. I don't normally do immediate post mortems but I suggest you all think hard about your contributions to this match. KC and Alvar put us back in the game this morning and we've pissed their efforts up against a wall. We've handed the opposition eight points already. If they get another ten for a win they'll be above us in the table. That's money we're talking about. So let's get a grip.'

Jephcott's rallying cry fell someway short of the Agincourt model, but by emphasising the bunce rather than the glory, at least he showed an understanding of his audience.

Knowing the paper would be delivered at home, Richard thought about calling Tessa again, then resisted the urge. Too much kowtowing might suggest he had something to hide. Besides, hearing of Grimley's offer to smooth things over with Crick's wife, he decided to call in a favour.

2

The pimply youth, dispatched at short notice from Fine Film Features, explained to Slingsby that their 'main man' was 'shooting a company promo' at a dye-cast foundry in Smethwick. Slingsby was not interested in the 'whys' and 'wherefores'. He just wanted the job done, dusted, and off his plate. 'I know it will be tricky, but I want you to be as hush hush as possible.'

'Yes, so the office said. That's why I'm wearing this.' Slingsby blinked at the youth's olive green parka. 'Camouflage see. Very good for wild life shoots.'

'To start with, I suggest you set your camera up in the lee of the grandstand, keeping to the shadows.'

'In the shadows, right,' said the youth, warming to the clandestine nature of the job.

Gledhill nominated the light roller to be used between innings. Like Jephcott before him, he had no wish to squeeze any more moisture to the surface of the pitch. The sun was playing peek-a-boo as it had all day, and the atmosphere was warm and close. In theory, conditions would be just as helpful to Jephcott's bowlers as they had been to the home side. However, it took an optimist to believe his team could win the game from the position in which they now found themselves. Realistically a draw was the most they could hope for unless the bowlers repeated their heroics of the morning session.

In fact, an early wicket apiece for KC and Topsy immediately reduced Gledhill's team to 13 for 2 before Pywell and Short steadied the ship. Jephcott had brought Badel into the attack after Topsy's opening burst in the hope of unsettling Pywell. A couple of days with the First XI and a three-wicket haul in the first innings had bolstered the young man's confidence. Gone were the quivering flannels and the sweaty palms. He even thought about asking the skipper for Mal Shanks to be moved a yard deeper at mid-off but then lost his nerve and said nothing.

After dragooning Badel into the Bordesley Green 'do' the night before, 'Doc' Holliday had taken it upon himself to instruct the new boy in the rituals of dressing room life. There was the daily collection of players' valuables into a shoe bag to be deposited in the club safe; the after-play drinks order which ensured a trayful of beer at close of play; the boots to be left accessible for whitening by the dressing room attendant; the weekly collection of grass-stained flannels for dry cleaning. All in all, it was a steep learning curve for the lad off the field as well as on. Most shaming of all, Badel noticed he was alone in wearing white socks whereas his team-mates wore thick woollen ones – blue marl in colour, spun, carded and dyed in deepest dankest Yorkshire.

'Blue socks for cricket?' exclaimed his mother when he reported back home. 'I've never heard the like.'

For a time Slingsby avoided checking on the whereabouts of the would-be wild life cameraman lurking inside the ground. He had an agenda to finalise for a committee meeting, cheques to sign, accounts to approve. From the expression on Wilf Bristow's face as he entered the office, he also had a groundsman to placate.

'What's this Denis?' Wilf Bristow held a small piece of note paper which Slingsby recognised as his.

'Yes, sorry about that, Wilf. You weren't in your den when I called.'

'A new fixture this late in the season? Can't be done, Denis.'

'I know, I know, it's an imposition, but the Banker's Association have been badly let down and they've asked us for help.'

'Stick 'em on the practice ground then 'cause they're not coming on my square. Not likely.'

'We can't put them on the practice ground. They need a hospitality suite during the match.'

'Can't be done, Denis. I've no more pitches left.'

'I'm sure they're not averse to playing on an old one.'

'There's not a single inch on the square that doesn't need a rest.'

'It's only a forty-overs jolly,' said Slingsby, wheedling for a more gracious response.

'Exactly. They could do untold damage in that time. Last time they played here, one of 'em was sick on a length. You can still see the stain.' It was doubtful if this was true, but the image was burnt for ever on Wilf's retina.

'The fact is the bank have asked for this favour, Wilf. It would be wise to oblige.' Wilf clamped his lips tight shut and snorted. He looked past Slingsby onto the field. Spotting something in the distance, his eyes narrowed.

'What's that bugger in the green anorak doing by the score-board?' Slingsby's heart sank. When he turned to look, Brum's answer to Alfred Hitchcock was less conspicuous than he had feared, though not inconspicuous enough to escape Bristow who had the eyesight of a buzzard over his terrain.

'He's making a film. I've cleared him to do it.'

'Huh.'

'Though I'd prefer it if you kept it to yourself. Players can get a bit self-conscious when the camera's on them.'

'Play up to it, you mean? Oh yes, a bunch of show ponies right enough.' That was not what Slingsby had meant, but having struck a harmonious chord he was reluctant to pluck another.

Alvar Badel's introduction into the attack had created a measure of anxiety for Pywell and Short, but he was nothing like as threatening as he had been earlier in the day. After confirming with 'Doc' Holliday that Badel's pace was much reduced, Jephcott ambled up the track to have a word with him.

'Everything okay?' he asked.

'I don't know,' said Badel haplessly.

'Why's that?'

'I can hear something when I'm running in.'

'Your footsteps?' Jephcott ventured.

'No, something whirring behind me.' Jephcott frowned and scoped the boundary boards for a possible source. 'It's putting me off.'

'Then shut it out. I need you firing on all four.' Jephcott jogged back to first slip and retailed the conversation to Richard and 'Doc', his tone implying some-mothers-do-have-'em. But Richard also thought he had heard something. Scanning the expanse of empty stands behind the bowler's arm, he spotted the olive green parka on manoeuvres near the scoreboard. At a distance of a hundred and fifty yards he could not readily identify what the figure was up to. But when Badel ran into bowl, he heard a faint metallic chatter in the air.

'It's a camera,' concluded Richard after Pywell had blocked Badel's delivery. 'A cine camera.' Jephcott moved across to share Richard's viewpoint. 'At the side of the scoreboard.' The olive green parka dodged in front of the tripod as Badel walked back, obscuring Jephcott's view.

'You sure?'

'Positive. See what happens when Alvar turns to bowl.'

'Oh,' said Jephcott affirmatively when Badel ran in again and the parka nipped back behind his camera. Although the scoreboard offered a modicum of concealment, the camera was in a poor position to film Badel's right-arm action. The purist would have sited it in a slightly elevated spot in the stands beyond mid-off. Rankled by the discourtesy of having one of his players secretly filmed, Jephcott took Badel off and switched him to the pavilion end, making the camera's location even more ineffectual. Jephcott did not explain the reason for the switch to Badel. He believed the witch-hunt against bowlers with suspect actions had gone too far. Umpires were being strong-armed into making hasty judgements, and injustices were bound to occur. There was certainly something different about Badel's action but he felt he should be given time at least to mount the scaffold before the axe came down.

The distraction caused by the presence of the cameraman had contributed to a slackening of concentration by the fielding side and Pywell and Short survived and prospered to push their team's lead to 197. With eight wickets still in hand, a run dash was in prospect for the following morning prior to a declaration. That would enable Gledhill to set a stiffish target while giving his bowlers plenty of time to capture the ten wickets needed to win the game.

Those sensitive to the mood of a dressing room could detect an unmistakable whiff of resignation in the air as players took their beers from the team tray. They had spent most of the first two days on the backfoot and the third day promised more of the same. In KC's view the rearguard action now demanded of them was a direct result of Jephcott's hare-brained gamble to field after winning the toss. The skip could be a 'bugger' once he got something into his head, he opined, and now the chickens had come home to roost.

Jephcott had taken Badel aside as they walked from the field and told him not to worry about the filming. It was, he suggested, a movie for the home club's archives. He knew he would have to spend longer with the lad at some stage and explain to him the more likely scenario, but he wanted to be away from the ground as soon as possible, so it would have to wait for another time.

3

'I've got to dash,' Jephcott shouted above the hubbub in the showers. KC turned his scowl towards a showerhead's spray. 'KC, will you organize a round on my bar tab?'

'Yes, Skip,' said KC, having uncharitably thought Jephcott was leaving with the captain's expenses in his pocket. 'Soft drinks all round after that display.'

'Whatever you say, Senior, you're in charge.' Jephcott smiled and edged towards the door.

'If only,' said KC mutinously, as the captain disappeared beyond the thickening curtain of steam and exited.

During the season KC had captained the side on two occasions when Jephcott had been missing and both matches had been won. He did not have Jephcott's tactical skill, but he commanded respect through his experience and achievements. Anyone tempted to question his right to call the shots would be invited to 'look in the book' and peruse his record. Unlike Jephcott, there was no waiting for the right moment to voice a criticism of a player. If a thing needed saying it was said – tersely and often crudely but the admonition was rarely unfair or resented. In truth, a whole season of KC's tough-love captaincy would have worn thin in the face of a daily barrage of problems needing solutions. As a stand-in, however, he had novelty value and the team ethos ensured for him the unwavering support of the players. Some suspected it was their way of telling Jephcott he was not indispensable.

The morose mood evident in the changing room had begun to dissipate under the balm of hot water. Now that Jephcott had gone, Topsy felt free to belt out his rendition of 'My Way', accompanied by a ragged barber's shop quartet of Shanks, Holliday, Crick and Ibbotson. KC ignored them with the benign tolerance of one well versed in the intimacies of pithead ablutions. Under a battery of showers they stood shoulder to shoulder, buttock to buttock. After hours spent outdoors, their necks, faces and forearms below the elbow, had been weathered to Apache Brown on the Dulux colour chart, sharply contrasting with the pallid lily tones of their legs and torsos.

'... the record shows, I took the blows, I did it my waaayyy.' They were athletes to a man but their physical differences never failed to surprise Richard Hastie. Mal Shanks, short and square, his hips swaying suggestively to the song as he soaped his white hairless chest. His hams were shaped like small beer kegs between which his cock popped out of a nest of curly ginger pubes like a misshapen tuber. Alongside him was the elongated figure of Topsy. His chest and coat-hanger shoulders boasted little in the way of muscle or flesh. Below the waist his stomach was flat and taut, his shaft straight and proportionate, his thighs and calves as shapely and lithe as a Sadlers Wells dancer. Ample evidence to a bulldog like KC that Topsy was a whippet bred for speed not stamina.

Richard had drawn the short straw in a very obvious way by showering next to thirteen and a half stones of Tasmanian beefcake, a hefty joint of which he carried between his legs. 'You stopping for one?' Richard asked as Rod Brennan skipped out of the showers and onto the coarse concrete floor like a man treading on hot coals.

'Yeh, just a swift one for the road.' Richard was hoping the drinks 'do' for the two teams, customary at the end of the second day, would prove an extended affair thereby shortening his evening with Speedy and Sheila. When Ibbo persuaded his fellow songbirds to join in for a blast of 'Ferry 'Cross The Mersey', KC wrapped a towel round his middle and escaped through the drizzle into the changing room where he found Badel sitting disconsolately under his changing peg.

'Has the Skipper had a word with you about that filming?'

'He said he'd see me tomorrow.'

'Tomorrow?'

'Said not to worry.'

'Oh, did he,' muttered KC. Loyalty to the cause inhibited KC from voicing his disapproval of Jephcott to a junior player, but clearly the young man needed more reassurance than he was getting. He glanced at 'Doc' Holliday who was thinking the same thing. 'What're you up to tonight?'

'I don't know,' shrugged Badel. 'Topsy said something about a place to eat.'

'Oh yes, then what?' said KC suspiciously. 'What you need tonight is a good kip.' 'Doc' hid a smile. He knew better than to try and channel a young player's energies into sleepy backwaters. 'Mal and me will be eating at the hotel. Do yourself a favour and join us.' Badel blinked up at Mount Colclough. The bath towel wrapped around KC had lost its pile through daily laundering and was bobbled like a sheet of Braille. It was fastened just below his nipples and sheathed an ample mid-section containing no discernible waist. The day before, Badel would have treated his invitation as an ultimatum, but a few hours acquaintance with the 'lads' had already made him leery of closing his options. He liked 'Doc' and had been grateful for his company the previous evening, but he would much rather have been named and shamed on the front-page of his local newspaper along with the others. Dinner with KC and Shanks, he imagined, would be like spending the evening with his dad.

'How about it?' KC persisted.

'Yeh, probably will.'

'You have to learn that there's us and them.' KC saw the incomprehension in Badel's face. 'There's South and North, batters and bowlers, gentlemen and players, right? And what you've got at Lord's is Southern batters. They think they own the bloody game. Us and them. D'you get me?' But Badel was lost, aware only of a sudden lack of oxygen in a confined space. 'We don't let the bastards grind us down.'

KC whipped his towel from round his middle and turned his broad porcine rear to Badel. As far as KC was concerned the young bowler was innocent until proved guilty, and if he had his way that would be decided by wiser men than they could lay their hands on at HQ. 'If brains were gunpowder they couldn't blow their hats off.' On the other hand, nobody who had respect for the game could condone a cheat, and in the end that was what a thrower was judged to be. But whatever the rights or wrongs, Badel was one of the team and entitled to the support of every other member. Unity, solidarity, mateship, these were words drummed into KC's consciousness well before his times tables. With his own modest England record a sour memory, KC had no fear of sticking up for the little man against the battalions of well-fed faces. He rather doubted if Jephcott would do likewise. After all, he was more one of 'them' than 'us'.

Chapter Nine

1

'One, then we'll go,' said Speedy as he and Richard went into the club lounge bar.

'Just one?'

'You know Sheila – we're scheduled.' As the brothers made their way to the bar, Rod Brennan drank up and passed them on the way out.

'Going already?' asked Richard.

'Yeh. See you boys.'

'See you, Rod.'

'Must be on a promise?' suggested Speedy.

A small number of members remained in the bar after close of play, but mostly it was a gathering of players, umpires, scorers and committeemen. Richard noted how players chose to socialise with their opposite numbers – bowlers with bowlers, batsmen with batsmen, even to subsets of spinners with spinners. Richard and Ibbo found themselves talking to Pywell and Weetman, opening batsmen all.

'Your kid did himself no harm today,' said Pywell gesturing in the direction of Speedy. 'Right time, right place.' There was a pregnant pause during which Richard imagined the others thinking how his own chances of recognition had been dealt a corresponding blow. He realised this was well wide of the mark when he saw their eyes were trained on Curtis Short's wife entering the bar. She had long blonde hair and wore a strappy mini dress that showed off her slim arms and shoulders honeyed by the sun. Looking like a Swedish film star but with an accent acquired in Perry Barr, she was an object of much binocular focus wherever her husband was playing.

'Jeez', said Weetman, 'what wouldn't you pay to give her one?' Richard inwardly cringed at Weetman's crassness while agreeing with the sentiment. He believed, somewhat unscientifically, that lust was an inevitable by-product of a drawn-out game like cricket. Though competitiveness was integral to every ball bowled, it had to be sustained and held in check for the duration. For testosterone-fuelled young men, this tension had a sexual dimension, and the temptation to let off steam was hard to deflect. Despite this, or perhaps because of it, his fellow cricketers had tended to marry young, their readiness to settle down apparently as keen as their desire to play the field. The misadventures and deceptions involved in squaring this circle could play havoc with a player's form, especially if the player in question was intent on concealing a liaison from his team-mates as well as his wife.

In this respect Richard was fortunate that Laura Kyle was the model of discretion. Ten years his senior and the wife of Geoffrey Kyle, a member of the cricket club committee, she selected her lovers and planned her assignations with the utmost care. At least Richard assumed there were others, though she never spoke about them. Even her husband, whom she claimed to love 'dearly', remained off-limits during their pre and post coital conversations.

Laura's husband had inherited a small family hosiery business and had transformed it into a market leader. For a successful businessman he was surprisingly modest and retiring, admirable traits but a frustration for his wife both in and out of bed. The Kyles had two boys at boarding school and she, with too much time on her hands, had grown restive. She was an attractive woman and about to hit forty. Once her season's clothes shopping had been accomplished, another room redecorated, and her do-gooding quota satisfied, she felt there was something missing. Her husband was a good and generous man but he seemed blind to a new dress or hairstyle. New interior design features that she had agonised over went unnoticed. She accepted it was shallow but she needed greater appreciation of her talents.

Geoffrey Kyle's interest in cricket was negligible but in the county club treasurer's opinion, he had the sort of collateral to stiffen the club's loan guarantees and he cannily invited Kyle's two sons to junior net sessions. Urged on by Laura, who thought he should widen his sporting interests for the benefit of the boys, Kyle was persuaded to accept co-option onto the committee. Her own involvement was thus seamlessly achieved as she dropped them off at the county ground or accompanied her husband for match-day refreshments in the committee box. Later, she would tease Richard that she had picked his name from the scoreboard like a novice punter might stick a pin in a race card. In reality, more cautious reconnoitering had preceded their liaison.

'Hastie by name, hasty by nature?' she had enquired in the club bar after play had finished one day.

'I like to take my time, but if I have to I can get a move on.'

'That's good to know,' she said, her brown eyes brazen and sparkly as she took a sip of wine. She was less in control than she affected to be. Although she had worn a wide-brimmed hat, the day had been hot and she had consumed too much alcohol. Surrounded now by two teams of tanned young men, their hair still wet from bathing, she felt a tingle in her thighs and a touch light headed.

'Has Geoffrey talked to you about us getting a net built in the garden for the boys?'

'No.'

'Do you think it would be a good idea?'

'Of course. Nothing better,' said Richard. 'It kept me and my brother out of trouble for years.'

'It's just that we'd like some advice. What sort of pitch to lay down – that sort of thing. You're the boys' favourite player so I told them I'd ask you to take a look.'

But the boys were not there when Richard turned up at the Kyle residence, only a housekeeper who watched them suspiciously from the drawing room window as he and Laura disappeared behind shrubs and into a glade. A weathered shed stood in one corner, its corrugated roof abundant with moss. 'We thought here would be good?' Richard scanned the stretch of grass for a patch of level ground and assessed the potential hazards from stray and mis-hit cricket balls. He stood on the prospect and mimed a straight drive with the back of his hand.

'Is that your boundary fence?'

'Yes.'

'The boys can't hit that far just yet, but in a couple of years it could be a nuisance.' Laura came to his shoulder as if the debate relied on her sharing his viewpoint. She was wearing a denim-blue cotton sundress with inch-wide straps above a bodice fitted to the waist and falling in a fuller, knee-length, skirt. She leaned over touching his upper arm with her breast. From the raised outline of her nipples he could tell she was wearing no bra.

'Nuisance?'

'To the neighbours.'

'Oh, they won't mind. It's just an orchard over there.'

'In that case here seems fine. Away from the shed and the windows.'

'And parents. They can get up to any mischief down here.' She smiled, her weight still biased against his arm. Feeling compromised, he turned to the house to make sure the housekeeper had not maintained her vigilance, but only the high-pitched roof and chimneystacks were visible above the rhododendrons. 'Didn't you believe me?' she said playfully.

There was no mistaking her intent or his own susceptibility. Their previous flirtatious exchanges, he realised, had led him inexorably to this fork in the road. Six months had gone since the arrival of baby Jessica Hastie and as had happened with their first born, Tessa's libido had sailed into the post partum Doldrums. Richard was not unresponsive to his wife's need for comfort and support. He had read his share of self-help books. He knew that after a while the family would absorb its additional member and find a new equilibrium. In the meantime he would have to accept his demotion in the order of things.

'Come and have a look at the pavilion.' As Laura Kyle made for the dilapidated shed, the declining angle of the sun made her dress translucent, silhouetting her legs beneath it and the pudendal mound between. 'Come on,' she repeated without turning, knowing he would follow.

The shed was a depository for rusting garden tools, redundant tins of paint and demised crawlies. It smelt of earth and hessian sacks. Without preamble she took his face in both hands and kissed him with a wide consuming mouth, so confident of his complicity it alarmed him. Detaching one of her hands, she reached behind her back and unzipped the top of her dress.

Gently hugging him, her shoulders narrowed, inviting him to release the shoulder straps and lower the top to expose her breasts. As he bowed his head to kiss them, he felt one hand reach down to stroke his stiffening cock while the other unhitched his belt. For a moment he was at a loss to imagine what next step he could possibly make when his trousers fell.

'The chair,' she said, as if reading his thoughts. He spied a dark-stained bentwood chair beneath a cluttered work-bench. He grabbed its arched back support and dragged it clear of the bench. His hand left its print on the dusty frame and he was conscious of the accumulated grime on the seat itself.

'Sit,' she instructed after sliding his Y-fronts down to join the trousers at his ankles. The chair creaked perilously as he sat. His erection was so rigid that when he looked down it was staring straight back at him. As she straddled his legs, he ran his hands up the outside of each of her thighs and found only nakedness beneath the dress.

'Would you like some tongue?' he said, trying belatedly to take the initiative.

'Another time.' Placing her sandalled feet either side of him, she took hold of his shaft and after teasing the tip for a moment, she lowered her weight onto his lap and impaled herself to the hilt.

Richard had been aware since first sitting that the chair was unlikely to bear their combined weight without capsizing. However it was low enough for Laura to support most of her weight on the balls of her feet. Gripping the chair frame behind Richard's shoulders and levering herself off her toes, she was able to dictate both the rhythm and depth of their coupling.

When it was over they slumped, breathing heavily, head on one another's shoulders. She had planned and choreographed the whole episode and he felt stunned and exhilarated. At her request he reached down to rummage a handkerchief from his trouser pocket. She put it between her legs as a swab and backed off his lap. She scooped herself into the bodice of her dress, zipped up and made to go. Richard was surprised that her dress showed so little sign of dust and grime. He suspected his backside offered a more squalid picture. Without meeting his eye she pushed open the door to go.

'Call me,' she said crisply. 'Early afternoon is best.'

2

It took barely five minutes for Speedy to drive Richard from the ground to his home. The 1950s semi off the Harborne Road was in mid-refurbishment under Sheila Hastie's taut project control. A pallet, freighted with building rubble, compressed Speedy's parking space and Richard had some difficulty squeezing out of the car.

Sheila's face dodged into view at the sitting room window then reappeared smiling at the door. She reached out to kiss him on each cheek as she would one of her small sons. Her hands looked red and sore through over zealous housework. 'Come in, come in, my love,' she trilled. 'We're in a terrible state here and the boys won't go to sleep without seeing you.'

'I'll go up.'

'Tell them I'll be up in a minute,' added Speedy. Richard climbed the stairs. Behind him he heard Sheila cooing congratulations.

'Four wickets.'

'Yeh, for sixteen.'

''Clinical', the radio report said.'

'I wouldn't argue with that,' said Speedy self-mockingly.

'My hero,' she said, kissing him. Richard felt his spirits dip again. At least the boys were small enough to cuff if the taunts became too much to bear. Yes, their Dad was a fantastic bowler. Yes, he had got their Uncle out. But remember, Richard warned them, the match was not over yet and he might just have something up his sleeve. He tapped the side of his nose. 'Never count your chickens, boys.' They guffawed mockingly. Six and eight years old and already reading the game as well as him.

'Give me girls any day,' Sheila said whenever her sons had been unusually taxing. Richard sometimes suspected it was her way of commiserating with him for not having a son to follow in his footsteps. Hitherto that thought had not intruded to any great extent. He loved his girls deeply and looked forward to seeing their beauty and intelligence blossom to be the equal of their mother's. Yet the events of the day had made him reflective. Whatever personal reservations he might have about Sheila, no one could doubt her commitment to his brother. It seemed sometimes that she had borne him sons by sheer act of will to cement, not only their marriage, but also their way of life. The boys' precocious ball skills echoed those of Speedy and Richard at a similar age. With Sheila clucking at its centre, the household possessed a collective muscularity that rowed them powerfully in one direction.

At supper Richard had no doubt his sister-in-law would bandy cricketing gossip as readily as any fervent fan. How different it was with Tessa, for which blessing he was generally grateful. The friction he had experienced between his sporting career and his domestic life, however, could not be dismissed lightly. Compared to Speedy, he felt any success he had achieved in the game had been accomplished against the undertow of Tessa's antipathy.

'I really am surprised at you.'

'Oh?'

'Nightclubbing at your age – during a game – without your partner.'

'I was with Neil Ibbotson – he's my opening partner.'

'Ha ha, very funny. When I spoke to Tessa on the phone she pretended not to be bothered.'

'She isn't.'

'Well I know different. She'll feel humiliated when she reads about it. When her folks read about it.'

'I called her. She knows it's bollocks. We had one drink.'

'Even one drink in that place is bad enough. I have a friend – well, more of an acquaintance – who goes there. She says she has to chase the tarts off before she can grab a bloke.'

'Does it for free herself, does she?'

'Well yes, she is a bit of a goer, but that isn't the point. It's a well-known dive and you should have known better. You'll have to buy Tessa something nice.'

'Is there much more of this?' Richard asked wearily.

'No, I've had my say. But take it from me, she isn't happy with you.'

'Well that's probably nothing to do with any newspaper story.'

'Oh?' Sheila turned quizzically from the sink and he immediately regretted his flip rejoinder. 'Problems?'

'No, not really. The usual – kids and cricket.'

'Kids and cricket? That's your life, Richard,' she said pointedly before turning back to the sink to de-starch a colander of rice with boiling water. It was a refurbished kitchen with space enough for a refectory table, but with Sheila on the footplate it seemed claustrophobic. 'Kids and cricket, what would we do without them?' Richard stayed silent and sought refuge in a bottle of beer, courtesy of Ansell's, a club sponsor.

'Suppose they pick you for the West Indies? What would Tessa say then?'

'I've no chance of selection.' From Sheila's lack of dissent, he gathered his chances were not rated highly round her kitchen table.

'If Speedy got the call I couldn't wait.'

'Couldn't wait for what?' said Speedy, entering the kitchen and grabbing a bottle.

'To see the back of you. If you were gone for five months, I could get this place finished.'

'Charming,' said Speedy, feigning offence. 'What difference do I make?'

'You're always sticking your oar in.' Speedy grinned in response to her rebuff, clasped her round the waist and nibbled the lobe of her ear. She would not have been Richard's pick from the retinue of young women once at Speedy's beck and call, but he had been wrong. His brother clearly loved the way she exercised control over the household, allied as it was to her tenacious support for his ambitions. It was touching how much of a buzz she got from being married to someone in the public eye. Despite the prospect of being a lone parent, Richard believed there was nothing she would not do to get her husband on the boat. 'Speedy says he did you through the gate?' Richard took a swig of beer. He had no intention of talking cricket technicalities with Sheila. 'He says it was a jaffa?'

'It must have hit a pebble,' said Richard sarcastically.

'That ball would've done for better batters than you,' Speedy jeered.

'Wasted on him was it, love?' giggled Sheila. The evening was proceeding very much as Richard had feared. He took the top off another Ansell's Pale Ale and hunkered down for more two-on-one banter to go with his chilli con carne. 'Only joking,' she said as she laid a plate in front of him and gave his shoulder a patronising squeeze. 'Whatever happens, you've had a wonderful season.' She took off her pinny and joined them at the table. 'Now who's this chucker you've got playing for you?'

'Nobody I know,' Richard replied, glancing accusingly at Speedy.

'I said they were filming him, love, that's all.'

'You said he should be playing darts,' she persisted.

'Just a joke, Sheila. The umpires haven't called him.'

'Is he quick?'

'Quickish,' answered Speedy.

'You know he really shouldn't be playing if he throws, Richard. Someone could get hurt.'

'Leave it to the umpires eh, love?'

'And when did they last do anything unless they were told?'

'Just leave it, Sheila.' Speedy shot a warning look that pierced even Sheila's boiler-plated hide. She shook her shoulders and took another direction.

'So, tell us what are your lot up to at home?'

3

Crumbs from Grimley's individually-boxed fruit pie snagged like confetti in the folds of his pullover. There they joined debris from a sausage roll similarly consumed as he drove the Hillman eastward via Spaghetti Junction. He had been the last to leave the Press Box after phoning in his copy to the London office under his broadsheet pseudonym, J.P. Dawlish. Prior to that he had filed a report on the full day's play to his local evening paper. The two reports may not have been distinguishable to the average reader, but to Grimley they were like chalk and cheese. J.P. Dawlish was commissioned when one of the regular broadsheet correspondents was indisposed and it represented Grimley's perk on the side. It was not only the pecuniary advantage that motivated him but the opportunity to scatter the odd literary allusion or apposite epigram. The reportage of J.P. Dawlish, he liked to think, was caviar to the general.

HILLS AND HASTIE ON TOP
J.P. Dawlish at Edgbaston

Although wickets fell with similar regularity to both sides at Edgbaston it could hardly be called Derbyshire's day. Dismissing the visitors in under three hours, Warwickshire led by 121 on the first innings, before widening the gap to 197 by the close.

Hills bowling with pace, fire and fluency – the sort of form that must gladden the hearts of West Indian selectors – sliced through Derbyshire's early batting with a return of four for 42, paving the way for an inspired spell from Philip Hastie of four for 16 to finish off the visitors for 115.

Of course the trick was to make it look effortless. The reader should be assured that he or she was in good hands. Grimley as Grimley had the hands of a competent plumber whose lagging would not let the customer down. J.P. Dawlish, in comparison, had fingers that might pluck lightly on a harp. Using a minimum of words he would capture the mood of a match as well as the state of play. Even so, moronic sub-editors were quick to seize on any perceived prolixity and cut him and his columns down to size, so he was careful not to push his luck by striving for effect. Grimley glanced at the half-eaten fruit pie. He had loosened it from its crimped silver tray while waiting at traffic lights at

Newhall Street. He assessed the highway ahead as trouble-free and took a bite.

Hills' return to form was an ominous feature for England supporters. Bowling with steadily increasing hostility, yet with an easy rhythm which suggested an end to his injury problems, he trapped Picken LBW then uprooted Jephcott's middle stump before the batsman had completed his stroke.

Richard Hastie, whose first scoring shots included five boundaries, found an enterprising partner in Brennan, but after some trade-mark power play during which he gave no hint of permanence, he was caught behind to become Hills' third victim. A shrewd bowling change by Gledhill brought Philip Hastie into the attack and almost immediately he bowled his brother, Richard, to expose the visitors' tail. With Upton sealing up one end with his looping left arm spin, and Hills and Hastie continuing to make inroads at the other, Derbyshire could make little headway and only a gritty 28 from Holliday enabled them to stagger beyond three figures.

Grimley patted the front of his pullover and pastry flakes and fag ash fluttered into the foot-well. J.P. Dawlish would have dined somewhat differently, he mused. Perhaps lemon sole on the bone accompanied by a nicely balanced Sancerre; the repast served in a wayside hotel run by a husband and wife team who had learned their trade in one of London's finest?

Maybe he would try and find such a place the following evening. After all he was likely to need cheering up. His team was in for a towelling and he would have to present it to his local readers as a blip, an aberration, a god-awful misalliance of the planets over which the players had no control. For most of the season they had performed well as a combine and on the whole they were a decent set of blokes so he did not begrudge some blatant massaging of the truth. Nor did he mind, as now, doing a favour for someone as influential to the team as Richard Hastie, the odds-on captain-in-waiting.

Grimley had played no part in inflating the nightclub story but he felt the team would tar him with the same brush as those who had. Certain members of the side, he thought, had played with fire often enough for the current unpleasantness to be inevitable. In his view others, like Richard, did not deserve the domestic opprobrium and suspicion it was bound to cause. Accordingly, he was more than agreeable when Richard had asked him to drop in on Tessa and explain the wicked ways of the Press, lest she jump to the wrong conclusion. She had always seemed to Grimley well able to work such things out for herself, but perhaps the relationship was no more immune to doubt than the next. Long-since divorced, Grimley found himself rehearsing anew the basic moves of the matrimonial ring – jab and retreat, clinch and hold, dodge and sway – in the hope that he would not prove a liability in Richard's corner.

Derbyshire's struggle had been foreshadowed in the morning session. Pywell glowed momentarily, taking just four minutes to complete his century, but soon subsided after which the innings dissolved unhappily as the total stuttered from 192 to 236.

The debutant, Badel, started Warwickshire's collapse in the morning when Pywell played back when he should have been forward and was adjudged LBW. Badel, who generates surprising pace from his jerky delivery, then clean bowled Philip Hastie and Stinton. Colclough, as ever, was impeccable at the other end taking four for 33 in a nine over spell, and only the doggedness of Ledbrook enabled the home side to collect their third batting point.

Days were shortening noticeably in anticipation of autumn and it was almost dark by the time Grimley steered the Hillman off the ring road and towards the suburb where Richard and Tessa Hastie lived. The former hamlet was the last wave in a ribbon of residential development that joined it to the city. In fact Grimley had lived there as a boy and knew the farmer whose parcel of farmland was now the location for eight newly-built detached houses off the main street. A pleasing lack of symmetry to the development had given the Hasties a corner plot not overlooked at the front by their nearest neighbours, and a small lay-by to one side in which a couple of visitors could park.

As Grimley nosed his car towards the house, he saw the Hasties' car in the drive and a vacant spot for the Hillman behind another car parked in the adjacent lay-by. He switched off the engine and prepared his patter. A straight-forward assurance of Richard's innocence was more likely to arouse suspicion than quell it, so he had contrived a line about wanting to do an interview with Tessa if or when Richard got an England call-up – 'the loyal little wife left at home' type of dross for the week-end section.

He climbed out of the Hillman, smacked his pullover free of remaining crumbs, and reached for his jacket. Just as he was about to slam the door, a penny dropped in his brain and spun drunkenly for a moment. Staring at the car he had parked behind, he realised he recognised it. He scanned the registration plate for confirmation. Then, for reasons he could not immediately explain, he looked round to check if anybody had seen him arrive and climbed back into the Hillman. Deadened by end-of-day fatigue, his alertness now sprang instantly back to life. What? Why? How? When? He went through the cub reporter's interrogatory checklist in an effort to come up with an innocent explanation for the car's presence. However, his gut instinct told him something was out of joint; or maybe his journalistic opportunism was resurfacing like a long-repressed spark of sexual desire. Either way, until he knew for sure, knocking at Tessa Hastie's door was not an option.

He started the Hillman, pulled out of the lay-by and found another more distant parking spot from where he would carry out surveillance on foot. His meal-on-wheels had barely quelled the rumblings in his belly and he badly wanted a drink, but first his curiosity needed to be satisfied.

Having watched from behind a neighbouring ornamental tree for twenty minutes, Grimley saw Tessa switch on a bedside lamp and draw curtains across an upstairs window. He willed his eyes to penetrate the material but he could discern no movement beyond the drapes. Half an hour later, the bedside light went off. Grimley waited for a few minutes in case someone left the house, but all remained quiet. He had not resolved in his mind what he might do with his suspicions. He had seen no clear evidence of inappropriate behaviour and there could still be an innocent explanation. He decided to call again in the morning when daylight might compel less lurid thoughts.

4

After slipping down more bottles of Ansell's during the evening, Speedy was in no position to give Richard a lift to his hotel. Even when Sheila offered to drive him, Richard declined. It was a twenty minutes stroll at most to the hotel and the night was fine. He could walk off their hospitality and feel better for a little solitude after a gruelling evening inside Sheila's force-field.

'Take care now and give my love to Tessa and the girls. See you all soon, I hope.'

Although Richard was loath to admit it, exchanging banalities with Sheila had helped to mask his melancholic mood. Out on the street, however, it washed back over him. One part of him was convinced the day had been pivotal to his future and he had blown it, another part that his chances of tour selection had been exaggerated by well-meaning mates and deranged commentators. Acceptance of either scenario was unlikely to lift his mood.

Two-tone Fleetline buses cruised past like ghost ships in the night, the faces of passengers jaundiced by the yellow interior lights. He wondered if it was too late to call Tessa and imagined how it might play out:

'It's me,' he would say. 'Did I wake you?'

'What's happened?' she would reply anxiously.

'I think I've screwed up my chances.'

'What?' she would say in baffled irritation.

'Nothing. Forget it. I love you, Tess.'

'That's nice but couldn't it have waited.'

'Do you love me?'

'Have you been drinking?'

'Do you?'

'Of course but it's late and the girls have been hell.'

'I'm sorry. I just felt so . . .'

'Sorry for yourself? Tomorrow's another day, isn't that what you always say?'

It was true. It was what he always said, but his prospects for the next day were dire. At best it was likely to involve an ugly last-ditch stand that would please neither the spectators nor an England selector. Perhaps, Richard mused, Mrs Kyle might offer more solace? He checked in his wallet to confirm her phone number was still there.

Laura Kyle had continued to plan their infrequent meetings

with care and discretion. He still found them exciting but a sympathy screw was not her style and neither party was wont to bring day-to-day baggage to their assignations. But if he could lose himself for an hour between her breasts and thighs, he thought dreamily, he could steal refreshment without arousing her suspicion. But a telephone call? That really would take the biscuit. 'This isn't the Samaritans,' he imagined her saying with the waspishness that both repelled and turned him on.

Somewhat belatedly, he became conscious of walking with a limp. Six weeks previously he had been hit on the little toe while batting. It was a painful blow greeted with hilarity by his fellow professionals as he hobbled around the crease. Any hard knock below the neck was considered good for a laugh, especially one warranting only a blast of freeze spray.

Finding himself outside the Berni Inn where he had eaten the night before, he sat on the perimeter wall and took off his shoe. Massaging his toe, he tallied his current inventory of knocks, sprains, and bruises. In spite of his protective padding, the outside of his left thigh was constantly discoloured. A yellow and purple stain under his left nipple marked the spot where a ball had reared up to rattle his rib cage. The knock had impeded his breathing for days after. A blow had swollen his knuckles, temporarily preventing him from wearing his wedding ring. A ball had burst a vein to the side of his right calf, and his clumsy fielding the day before had left him with an aching knee. Together with the graze currently burning the underside of his elbow, it amounted to nothing unusual for a cricketer at the back end of the season.

Richard stared mordantly at the lights of the Berni and recalled the waitress who had served him the previous night – her too-tight black and white uniform and her bootlace bow tied coquettishly at the collar. After she had endured Crick's tawdry chat-up routine, Richard had shown her more respect and received smiles and laughter in return. His tip was generous, not only reflecting his satisfaction but also a desire to disassociate himself from the likes of Crick.

As he put his shoe back on, a man got out of a parked car, slammed the door and went into the Berni. The aggression in the man's stride suggested he had been waiting some time and grown impatient. A few moments later, he reappeared and returned to lean against the car, hands thrust deep into his pockets. Richard saw the door of the steak house open and heard the shrill farewells of a female voice. Then, half running, half wriggling to slip into her coat, the waitress emerged from the Berni. Illumination from the highway stretched too dimly into the car park for Richard to see clearly but he guessed the man to be in his late twenties. The girl stood in front of him, her narrow shoulders knotted in tension. Richard could barely hear the start of the altercation but that changed when the man's tone became more threatening and her protestations more defensive.

'Liar! There's not been a customer in there for twenty minutes!'

'I had to clear up.'

'In the back with him?'

'Don't be stupid. It's my job.' Enraged, the man grabbed the girl by the throat one-handed, squeezing her jaw between his fingers.

'Don't call me stupid! I know what you get up to in there.' His grip was so tight the girl could not respond. He swung her round, backing her up against the car and seemed about to hit her with his other hand.

'Leave her alone.' The man froze. Richard had the feeling his voice had come from someone else.

166

'Who the fuck are you?'

'Leave her alone.'

'This is private, piss off.'

'Let her go.'

'Just keep your fuckin' nose out of it.' As if to affirm his alpha male status, he banged the back of the girl's head against the roofline of the car. Richard jumped forward, grabbed the man by his jacket collar and yanked him away. The man released the girl and fell back. Richard stood above him hoping it was finished but the man got up on one knee and like a sprinter out of the blocks, catapulted forward to butt Richard in the groin. A bolt of pain shot through Richard's body. His hands gripped his testicles as he sank to his knees then rolled into a foetal position on the ground.

'No Danny!' he heard her scream before a kick speared into the back of Richard's head at a point where the boney skull gives way to the softer tissues of the neck. The shattering starburst in his field of vision mimicked the zap drawn round the fist of a comic book hero. That, and the taste of blood in his mouth, recalled the time he had been hit on the head by five and a half ounces of fast-travelling leather.

'No!' he heard her shriek again. Instinctively he put both hands up to protect his head and left his balls to fend for themselves. He wondered if he should attempt to crawl under the car. He could hear the girl trying to pull the man away.

'Get the fuck off me!'

'Leave it, Danny.'

'Stickin' his face in.'

'Come away, Danny.' For a moment it seemed it was over, but after withdrawing a few steps the man turned back to take a running kick, puncturing Richard's protecting arms and smashing into his face between his eyebrow and temple.

Absurdly, in the moment before he passed out, it triggered in Richard's mind a replay of Speedy snaking the ball between bat and pad to dismiss him.

5

It had gone sorely against the grain for two doyens of the taproom like KC and Mal Shanks to order a pot of tea for two as their nightcap. Two pots in fact since the Senior Pro was minded to stay up until at least a majority of the crew were safely aboard. The day's play had already been dissected in detail over a grisly hotel dinner consisting of food coloured either grey or brown. At first Shanks had matched KC grumble for grumble, but as each moment of woeful incompetence was revisited, even he had decided to put a sock in it. The reluctance of Badel to join them was the last straw in KC's opinion. It was a symptom of that same malaise he was banging on about.

'You can't play at county cricket, Mal. It's a job. Show ponies most of these youngsters. And this lad won't be any different if he listens to the wrong people.' Shanks nodded, his hand holding a strainer over a cup decorated with roses.

'More tea, Ken?'

'He had chance to listen to some sense tonight and turned it down. He needs to have his card marked because Lord's is looking to make an example of someone.'

'If he throws, he throws.'

'It's not as cut and dried as that. I could name half a dozen bowlers who've played for years with dodgy actions.'

'Spinners though most of 'em.'

'Maybe so, but if it's a scapegoat they're after, the Skipper should make damn sure it's not one of ours.'

'Well I reckon he'll be out on the lash now,' said Shanks, leaning back and examining his spinning finger for wear and tear.

As it happened Badel was no more than thirty yards away in the hotel car park, shivering in the back of Topsy's Cortina Mark II Twin Cam. From the driving seat Topsy watched Ibbo exit the hotel and get in beside him.

'They're still there.'

'Doing what?' said Topsy, exasperated.

'Drinking tea.'

'Don't be bloody daft.'

'Tea, I'm telling you.'

'If we could get Mal on his own we could persuade him to create a diversion?'

'No chance. Him and KC are as thick as thieves.'

'Well we've got to do something, the stink's ruining my motor.' Topsy looked over his shoulder at the sodden figure hunched in the back, teeth chattering, water draining out of him into the Cortina's aptly-named bucket seats. The situation was severely testing Topsy's infatuation with his vehicle, boasting as it did a dash-top auxiliary dial pod, aluminium sports steering wheel and leather gearshift gaiter. The swish interior trim was somewhat at odds with a cargo that had been dragged from a canal, especially one as murky and malodorous as the one running through Brum's Gas Street Basin.

Topsy had taken Badel under his wing as an apprentice recruit to the 'fast bowlers' union' rather than leave him to endure an evening with KC and Shanks, two of cricket's mightiest wiseacres. On reflection, Badel's capacity to hold his beer should have been established prior to sampling the pubs around the wharfs and basins of the 'Venice of the North'. It had been part of Topsy's own rite of passage as an uncapped novice and he remembered it fondly despite spending the night thereafter embracing a lavatory bowl. He and Ibbo had no idea how their predicament had come about. One moment Badel was skipping alongside them, the next they were dragging him out of the drink with a bargee's bill-hook. The good news was that the shock, plus the diluting effect of swallowed canal water, had rendered Badel stone-cold sober. The bad news was that he had only one set of civilian clothes. The Corby trouser press in their rooms might after all have its uses.

'Go back and open a fire door.'

'You go. They'll know something's up if I keep nipping in and out.'

'It's my car he's stinking out.'

'It was your idea to take him on a pub crawl.'

'He's only had three pints!'

'Are you alright, Alvar?' asked Ibbo. It seemed only polite to include him in the conversation. Badel's nod set his teeth chattering again. Topsy made to get out of the car then paused.

'I'm not taking the blame for this, Ibbo.'

'Why not?'

'You were nearest to him when he fell in.'

'Piss off.'

'Listen, if he isn't fit to bowl tomorrow, I'll have to carry the can and I'll have to bowl his overs.'

'Too bloody right,' said Ibbo, unsympathetically.

In spite of his often-successful imitation of a man in control of his own destiny, Topsy was not a good conman. Not rushing, not dawdling, just acting normally, or so he believed, he walked into the hotel trying to look like a man who was not searching for a fire door.

'What's he up to?' said the Senior Pro, immediately clocking

Topsy's false front as he passed the open door to the lounge. Like a loyal batman, Shanks got up and went to the door to look out. 'Is Alvar with him?' Shanks stepped out to get a better view of the lobby.

'Doesn't look like it.'

'What's happened to him then?' KC got up stiffly and rubbed his back. Ideally he wanted to go to bed and leave his charges to their own stupid devices, but the unfamiliar injection of caffeine at the end of the day had set his mind racing.

Ibbo, Badel, and Topsy made their way to the rear of the building. Though canal water had stopped draining from Badel's upper parts, it was still tugging at his trousers and pooling in his shoes. As they rounded the building, Topsy's confidence began to fade. Having released a fire door, he realised the piecemeal building sprouted several fire escapes. In the dark he was at a loss to know which door he had opened. He tried mentally to transpose his interior journey onto the hotch-potch of exterior annexes.

'Which one?' asked Ibbo. The lack of an immediate answer rang alarm bells. 'Topsy?'

'Hold on, I'm thinking.' Ibbo glanced at Badel. His hands were in his jacket pockets clasped together to stop his trousers falling to the ground. Ibbo was pretty sure he was witnessing the lowest point of someone's life so far.

'That one, I think,' said Topsy vaguely. They climbed uncertainly, hands on the rail, up the unlit metal staircase. When they came to the door at the top, it appeared to be shut. Topsy pinkled at the jamb with his finger tips, regretting he had not wedged it open.

'It must have blown to.'

'Try a car key.' Topsy groped in his pocket.

'I left it in the car.'

'Are you sure this is the right door?'

'I think so.' He sounded even less certain.

'Why don't we just take him in the front and take our chances?' said Ibbo, resignedly.

'After the fuss last night? You're joking.'

'It's only KC not the Skipper.'

'Give me the Skipper any day. I told KC I'd look after him, so I am.'

'Yeah, sure.'

In the upstairs hotel corridor, KC could hear indistinct mutterings from the other side of the fire door. Having observed Topsy's attempt at subterfuge, he had battened down the safety bar and was waiting on events with malign anticipation. What was the contraband this time? Birds, booze, or both? In his experience he had no need to consider other options. Such unfettered behaviour was unacceptable at any time, but with a match to save the next day, he was determined to curtail any dereliction of duty on his watch. As he reached forward to lift the bar and release the door, Shank's voice made him stop and turn.

'KC. Phone for you. It's the hospital.'

6

Under the sodium strip lights the hospital walls loomed neither blue nor green but something 'duck egg' in between. KC hated hospitals. The endless melamine floor muffling his footsteps as he padded along corridors to rooms leading to other rooms and on morbidly to the final room, the ante-room to death.

'Sorry, KC. I said I could take a taxi but they insisted.' Richard was sitting on a trolley bed, legs dangling, drinking a glass of water.

'They did right to call,' said KC, examining the swelling around Richard's eye and a four-stitch repair to a cut on the brow. 'Who stitched that – not a woman?'

'No.'

'I thought not. Your missus won't fancy you with that bugger on your face.' Richard did not need a mirror to confirm KC's assessment of the duty doctor's needlework. KC took a closer interest in the black nylon stitches spiking through the congealed blood and yellow iodine stains.

'Will you be able to bat tomorrow?'

'Yes, sure.'

'What were you doing?'

'Just walking back from Speedy's. I saw this bloke beating up his girlfriend. He was better with his feet than me.'

'Any other injuries?'

'Sore balls and a crack on the back of the head.'

'Oh?'

'They've done an X-ray. It seems okay.'

'Right Sir Galahad, let's get you back. You'd best have the big bed tonight.'

'No need for that.' But as Richard's feet touched the floor, his legs wobbled and various bruised bits of his body complained in unison. It was obvious that the camp bed would be a trial.

'No arguments,' insisted KC.

Chapter Ten

1

Though they had met many times before, when she opened the door Grimley realised he had never before made true eye contact. She wore no make-up and her smooth pink skin and barely dried hair suggested she had freshly bathed. 'Hello?' Tessa's expression changed quickly from startled to quizzical. Her indulging smile made him feel like the fat and frayed small boy he had been of yore. He was in love with her and he was sure she knew it. 'What are you doing here?'

'I'm door-stepping. It's what we do.'

'Well you'd better come in.' Grimley followed Tessa into the hall then into a sunlit through-lounge. The car in the lay-by had gone as expected but he thought he caught her eyes sweeping the room for anything out of place.

'Has Richard said anything about me writing a feature about you.'

'No?'

'Well, since he's been touted as a candidate for the winter tour, I thought it might be a nice idea. The wife left at home knitting comforts, sort of thing.'

'Is that how you see me, Ron?'

'Not exactly.'

'I'm pleased to hear it. I'm sorry to sound negative but wouldn't an article like that be a bit dull? Lots of husbands have to go away from home to work. It's not that unusual is it?'

'No, I suppose not, but the Features Editor seemed quite taken with the idea,' he lied.

'Have you time for a coffee?'

'Well . . .'

'Kettle's boiled.' She moved off into the kitchen, her hips swinging in tight-fitting jeans. He pushed his specs tighter to the bridge of his nose and tried to suppress shameful thoughts. It was a titanic struggle between the decency of J.P. Dawlish and the prurience of a Peeping Tom from 'The News of the Screws'. The light sweet fragrance of shampoo that wafted in Tessa's wake had masked, he believed, a heavier note of musk. It took the nose of a Peeping Tom to detect the unmistakable aroma of a recent sexual encounter.

'Where are the girls?'

'They've stayed over at friends. White?' she called from the kitchen.

'Please. One sugar.' Grimley's mind felt hot as hell. No kids? Convenient. He breathed in deeply to resuscitate Dawlish, to get him up off the canvas and boxing his weight. If what he thought he had discovered got out, it would cause mayhem in the club. How could it not come out? Dawlish could be relied on, but what of Peeping Tom? He had no loyalty to anything or anyone. Not to the Championship, the John Player League, or the noble game itself. He saw nothing beyond a Sunday 'splash'. So who else might be greasing the axle of that sleek body, Grimley found himself thinking? 'Just ask her straight out,' screamed Peeping Tom, pushing Dawlish back onto the ropes.

'One sugar?' Tessa handed him a mug with a cricket bat motif

— a gift a child might choose for a dad. 'Are you alright?' she asked.

'Yes?'

'You look worried.'

'No, I just spotted last night's paper.' He gestured to the evening edition lying on a side table, the nightclub story face-up on the front page.

'Ah,' she responded, her tone giving no pointer to her feelings.

'None of my doing, I hasten to add.'

'Not your scene, Ron?'

'Absolutely not,' he harrumphed, coming over all Dawlish. 'The lads were misinformed about what sort of place it was.'

'Really.'

'And then some little sod stitched them up.'

'Snitched, did you say?'

'No, stitched. Made it up'.

'Ah.'

'I could weep quite honestly at the quality of person now working in my business.' Tessa was wearing a fine cotton blouse above her belted jeans. Beneath it, her breasts were pertly lifted by a bra trimmed with lace. Grimley felt Peeping Tom stir in his shorts. 'One of the perils of being in the public eye, I suppose. Still, I'm sure you're not the sort who believes everything you read.'

'Richard phoned me about it.'

'Did he? Good.'

'He said he had one drink then left.'

'Exactly.'

'I didn't think you were there?'

'No, I wasn't, but I know Richard.' Fearing this line in casual exoneration would begin to whiff, Grimley changed tack.

'Anyway about this article?'

'Do you think he'll be selected?'

'Hard to say. He's certainly in contention.' She smiled.

'Well if it happens, it happens. And if it does, I'll get knitting.'

'It would round off a wonderful season.'

'Yes.' Her response was imbued with an unmistakable note of ambivalence. A car pulled up outside and Grimley saw the Hastie girls tumble out of it dragging with them comfort blankets, teddies and carrier bags.

A few minutes in the company of Tessa Hastie would normally have been a pick-me-up for Grimley, but as he pointed the Hillman in the direction of the ring road, he was overcome by a feeling of gloom. He liked Richard. He adored Tessa. He admired them as a couple and the family they had made. But at the very moment Richard seemed likely to achieve his ambition, he felt a crisis was unfolding that would reverberate well beyond the confines of the marital home. How would Dawlish deal with it? Grimley had half a mind to go back and confront Tessa with the prima facie evidence. It was her choice, of course, but in God's name had she no appreciation of the consequences? She must see that she was making a terrible mistake. Stop it immediately and nothing more would be said.

Just as he was contemplating a U-turn, another voice slithered from the shadows. What was he, a bloody Agony Uncle? Fine mess he had made of his own marriage. Did he really think he was qualified to interfere in someone else's? Get a grip Grimley! He slid the Hillman onto the by-pass and put his foot down for Brum.

2

No doubt to spur Richard into getting out of bed, KC had pulled back one half of the bedroom curtain before going down to breakfast. The abundance of space in the double bed and a more forgiving mattress had proved no panderer to sleep. Richard's head had ached throughout a restless night. The blood had clotted around the stitches in his eyebrow and stiffened his entire forehead, giving him few options of where he could bearably lay his head.

KC's selfless offer to take the camp bed had resulted in a continuous soundtrack of creaks and groans the equal of a derelict barn in a crosswind. Using his arm to shield his eyes from the morning sun, Richard assessed his ability to make it through the day. At times during the night he had not been sure if he was awake or hallucinating, but he seemed to remember leaving the room to take a pee in the early hours. Emerging from the lavatory he had seen Tony Crick, shirt hanging loose over his trousers, letting a girl out of the fire door at the end of the corridor. Confused as he may have been through broken sleep, he was convinced she was the waitress from the Berni steak house.

Richard's arrival at breakfast was greeted with a ragged round of clapping in ironic recognition of his heroics. In no mood for piss taking, he waved a bored hand in acknowledgement, noticing the way Crick's lips twitched in a wry smile as he buttered his toast.

Having failed to hi-jack Badel the previous evening, KC made a point of sitting next to him at breakfast. He wanted the lad to fully comprehend his offer of solidarity. One or two of the morning's match reports had commended Badel's figures while slyly drawing attention to his 'idiosyncratic' bowling action. KC thought this had made the lad retreat into his shell again. Whatever the reason, he seemed more monosyllabic than ever. And there was an odd drainy smell that KC could not get out of his nose. He had smelled something like it on a weekend package trip to Venice. He sniffed at his cup and then his cutlery without locating the source. One way or another he would be glad to get away from the place. When he got back to County HQ his first job would be to make known his displeasure about the accommodation.

KC cast a critical eye over his fellow players. The eager momentum of Spring had carried them into the balmier days of the Summer campaign, but now they were fading fast, out on their legs and jaded. They had reached the stage where a bad season could not be retrieved and a good one barely improved. The imminent publication of the retained list served to concentrate the minds of those players on the fringe of the side but if pressed, others would admit to being heartily sick of the game. KC, for one, would not countenance any end–of–term slacking. There was prize money at stake as well as self-respect. If he had to leave Birmingham as one of a defeated team, he was determined it would not be with his tail between his legs.

Chapter Eleven

1

En route to the players' changing rooms, Jephcott popped into Slingsby's office and learned for the first time of Richard's visit to hospital.

'A Mrs Kyle telephoned me just before midnight.'

'Kyle?' Jephcott sounded surprised.

'Do you know her?

'Well yes, but how was she involved?'

'I have no idea. Anyway she said one of your players had gone to Casualty after being injured in a fight – did I know where you were staying? I told her you weren't at the hotel but I'd call there and tell Ken Colclough.'

'Is Richard alright?'

'I think so. They didn't keep him in anyway.'

'Right,' said Jephcott, his mind befuddled by the mention of Laura Kyle.

'Was there something you wanted me for?' prompted Slingsby.

'Yes, sorry. I wanted to ask you about the cameraman.'

'Ah, yes. I'm sorry about that, Robin. The request came from Lord's.'

'You might have had a word with me?'

'Of course, but they weren't sure you'd be willing to co-operate.'

'What d'you mean?'

'They thought you might not bowl Badel if you knew.'

'So you stuck him up by the scoreboard where we wouldn't notice?' Jephcott did not normally resort to sarcasm but he was furious that the debate had been conducted over his head. Not for the first time he felt a lack of respect had been shown to the smaller less prestigious county. 'Is he here again?'

'No. Apparently he got enough footage yesterday.'

'Have Lord's leaned on the umpires?'

'They've been asked to make a detailed report. Neither is keen to call him until they have photographic evidence. Between you and me, Rook won't call him whatever the evidence. Chambers thinks he throws but not every ball.' Slingsby knew this information would help Jephcott in deciding from which end it was safe to bowl Badel. He hoped the tip-off might atone for his perceived duplicity in the covert filming. After a pause Jephcott nodded his appreciation.

'Thank you, Denis.'

Jephcott had not yet formulated a plan for Badel. Given the state of the match it would have been easy to exclude him from the attack and consign him to Second XI duties for the remainder of the season. If, as seemed likely, the witch-hunt lost its fervour after the winter tour, Badel could be brought out of his wrapper for a new season in a less critical environment. On the other hand, after his useful first innings figures, not to bowl him might be seen as a vote of no confidence in his legitimacy. Opponents and the M.C.C. would draw the obvious conclusion.

Standing at first slip as he did, Jephcott was not in the best position to judge a bowler's action. Nor had members of the team voiced any misgivings. Whatever their views, he was aware they would be looking to him to handle the problem in a staunchly partisan manner. But as he stood in Slingsby's office, hand in pocket, jiggling change, the last thing he wanted at this stage of the season was a crisis. Like the majority of his players he felt physically drained. More importantly, he was mentally jiggered. Unlike any other sport, a cricket captain was required to give on the spot answers to an unceasing number of questions. Every fall of a wicket or over bowled demanded a new decision. It was like being pecked to death by a thousand sparrows. By mid-August the rolling permutations of runs and wickets, overs and minutes, had become a blur, and he found himself more and more switching to auto-pilot to direct bowling changes, field settings and declarations.

He had captained the side for six seasons and his resilience to the ups and downs was dwindling. This was true not only of the team's performance but of his own playing contribution. It had not helped that his personal life had intruded more than in the past. He was fortunate in having Pamela to keep the home running while he was on active service. As a public couple they appeared as solid as a rock, but behind the scenes there had been hints of growing disquiet and resentment.

Having married the bosses wife, Jephcott was both her husband and her business partner. It was high time, she had suggested, that he assumed the permanent post of managing director and allowed her father to retire. Although Jephcott enjoyed the change of scene when he rejoined the family firm in the close season, he was doubtful if he would relish the job as a year round slog. In any case he rated himself still good enough to play First-class cricket – 'in his prime' he would insist after a drink or two. He had promised Pamela he would not linger when the time came. But not now, not for another season at least. In response, her shoulders had sagged, her lips had zipped disobligingly, and there had been a chill silence in the house for a day or two.

Jephcott exited Slingsby's office and straightened his posture. The thought of retirement had put a tiger in his stride and stiffened his resolve not to let the day drift into spineless surrender. In the corridor he spotted Rod Brennan trying to pass unobserved into the dressing room. Brennan's contrite expression discounted any need for Jephcott to look at his watch. 'Sorry, Skip, there was a bastard of a tail-back into town.' Jephcott observed Brennan's stubble-chinned impersonation of a small boy caught apple scrumping and felt weary again. The Tasmanian knew well enough the dangers of taking on the morning rush-hour traffic, especially on the third day when the game started thirty minutes earlier. It was precisely why players stayed in hotels rather than risk a no-show for the beginning of play. Earlier in the season Jephcott might have been moved to censure, but his capacity even to maintain discipline had waned. Instead he composed a severe expression and left the team's fines-keeper to hit Brennan in the pocket.

'You'd better find 'Doc' and pay up. A quid, I'd say.'

'Shit, that's a bit steep, Skip.'

'A quid,' insisted Jephcott. 'I hope she was worth it.' Brennan thought better of debating the matter further and moved off.

'First Murf, now you. We're keeping Casualty busy.' The skipper leaned in for a closer inspection of Richard's right brow. Richard had not appreciated before the blueness of Jephcott's eyes nor the extended sweep of his lashes. He became conscious of his breath on his cheek.

'That's what you get when you play the gentleman,' said KC, unsympathetically.

'Do you feel fit enough to play?' asked Jephcott.

'Yes, I'm fine,' said Richard, still suppressing intermittent bouts of nausea.

'We could arrange for the opposition's twelfth man to field for you?' The offer was hughly tempting but dressing room machismo required a stoic refusal.

'A couple of aspirins will do the job.'

'Let's go and see if their Physio can oblige.' At first Richard thought Jephcott was accompanying him to the Physio's room to get a second opinion as to his fitness to play, but his solicitousness proved to be for another reason. 'Apparently the hospital phoned Laura Kyle?' Richard's frown sent a fresh stab of pain across his forehead.

'About what?'

'They were trying to identify you and must have found her phone number on you.' His tone was too insinuating for Richard's liking.

'I coach her boys occasionally.' Jephcott's nod was barely discernible. 'That's why I keep her phone number in my wallet.'

'But not your own?'

'I know my own number.'

'I suppose so,' said Jephcott equivocally.

2

Forewarned by his skipper's inquisition, Richard feared the worst when he was called to the phone in the dressing room corridor. 'You stupid prick.' Laura Kyle was not pleased.

'They must have found the number in my wallet.'

'Don't tell me, the one you keep in the inside pocket closest to your heart?'

'God you can be a sardonic bitch. Aren't you even going to ask how I am?'

'At this moment I couldn't care less.'

'How did you explain it to Geoffrey?'

'I said I'd asked you about giving the boys some more coaching. You were due to call back with some dates.'

'Did he believe you?'

'Cricket coaching at the end of August, when all the boys can think about is the new football season? What do you think?'

'What did he say?'

'He said nothing very loudly.'

'Suspicion doesn't prove anything, does it?'

'Oh shut up, shut up.' For a moment he thought she was going to cry. It had never occurred to him that she was capable of breaking down. 'I expected you to be careful not to act like a bungling novice.'

'Careful'? Well yes she was entitled to be angry on that score, but the 'novice' was a role for which she herself had enjoyed casting him. The ten years difference in their ages had been a key element in their mutual attraction. If anything he thought she would like him to have been even younger and more authentically biddable than his play-acting had affected. He guessed Geoffrey Kyle was eight years or so older than his wife. His squat, round-shouldered physique was well short of the athleticism his wife craved. For his part, Richard enjoyed the delight she took in his body. Whether he was lying or standing naked at a window, she would work her hands over his back and down his spine to his buttocks, squeezing firm wads of flesh and muscle as she went. Then, pressing her cheek against a shoulder blade, one arm would encircle his chest as the other reached down to tease him to a new erection.

Just as their first sexual encounter had suggested pre-planning, subsequent meetings had confirmed her eye for detail and a talent for invention. It was not love-making as such but a sensory exploration with lips, fingertips, and tongues. And he would turn, push wisps of fringe from her eyes and hold her face in his hands. Her make-up would all but vanish in the initial coupling and expose shiny skin, pinch-pink on her cheek bones, the tip of her nose and her chin. Her mouth declined more on one side than the other and gave her a rueful look. Her eyes, softer and more vulnerable when she was naked, were creased at the corners as befitted her years, but the youthful upturned nose hinted at the head girl she had once been. As his tumescence grew she would pull him back to the bed, and he could tell by the way she grasped his buttocks that once he was inside she would not easily release her hold.

At first he expected a rush of guilt to overtake him and when it did not come he adopted duality to justify his behaviour. He loved Tessa, he loved his home and children. He could never imagine a life without them. But his encounters with Laura Kyle were nothing to do with that life. Self-servingly, he believed he had broken no genuine emotional bond. The possibility of discovery, however, considerably quickened his pulse. Laura was such a quick-thinking and resourceful woman, Richard felt sure she could convince Geoffrey Kyle of her fidelity.

'Is the fact that I had your phone number such a big deal?'

'He's not a fool.'

'I never thought he was.'

'He'll delve. Hire someone even.'

'A detective?'

'Who knows, but make sure you haven't left any more loose ends.'

'Is that it then? For you and me?

'What do you think?' she snapped. He was about to offer words of regret and consolation when the phone went dead.

When Richard shuffled back into the dressing room, Ibbo was collecting his gear for net practice in the hope of re-tuning his mis-firing strokeplay. 'You look like crap.'

'Cheers,' said Richard, thankful that nets were regarded as optional on the third day of a match. 'Tell me something. I may have been hallucinating but did I see the waitress from the Berni in the hotel last night?'

'Yes.'

'With Tony?'

'Yes.'

'Why?' said Richard, unwilling to believe the obvious.

'What d'you mean 'why'? Tony was doing what Tony does best.' A fresh surge of nausea washed up into Richard's throat. 'He dropped in at the Berni not long after you'd been taken to hospital and found her waiting for a taxi.' Richard was thunderstruck.

'You saw how she was with him. She loathed him.'

'Women,' sighed Ibbo, equally baffled.

'I get a kicking and he gets his end away.'

'Tony's got what birds want, mate. If you could fathom it you wouldn't want it because it would make you as big a plonker as him.'

3

Grimley had chewed over his dilemma all the way to Edgbaston. At first he had tried to swallow it straight down as not his problem, but it had stuck in his gullet like a piece of gristle he could neither consume nor spit out in polite company. It was possible but unlikely that what he knew was already common currency in the dressing room. Desperate to rid himself of the responsibility, he thought of sending Richard a warning note from an anonymous 'well-wisher', only to balk at the risk of being discovered or betrayed in the process. Perhaps there was nothing for it but to keep his head down and let the protagonists play with fire?

Just as the matter was beginning to settle in Grimley's digestive system, it experienced a fresh jolt. After retrieving his satchel and typewriter from the back seat of the Hillman, he straightened and spotted a figure heading for the practice nets – a heavy-set man in his sixties with an ample girth and ponderous tread. He had a cream linen blazer folded over one arm and wore a Panama hat sporting the same club colours as his tie. His capacious flannels, belted well above the waist, wafted like a pair of curtains above his basket-weave shoes. Broadsheet correspondent, Julian Lycett, regarded Oxford as the northern-most outpost of his bailiwick and his appearance in Birmingham therefore put all other considerations out of Grimley's mind. A Julian Lycett match report almost certainly meant the decommissioning of J.P. Dawlish for the day. But the loss of his perk did not distract Grimley half as much as the question of why such a big beast was roaming in his part of the jungle.

In search of an answer, Grimley followed Lycett to the rear of the nets where despite their distinct sartorial styles they displayed the same prominent silhouettes. Rod Brennan was busy launching balls into the stratosphere with gratuitous violence as a way of showing serious intent after his late arrival.

'Grimmers,' chortled Lycett. 'How are you, dear chap?'

'Fair to moderate, thank you, Julian,' said Grimley, flattered to be hailed so heartily. Unless reporters covered games in the capital or in the southern Wealds and Downs, exchanges with Lycett were infrequent. News of his arrival at a ground would cause a ripple of alarm among the Press pack and a shuffling of feet and paperwork to clear a space for him. Even as they spoke, Grimley assumed his PA cum chauffeuse would be making things commodious for him in the Box – checking typewriter ribbons, sharpening pencils, and commandeering a phone.

'Is this business or pleasure?'

'Always a pleasure to get out of Town,' said Lycett, disingenuously. 'Wally used to strike the ball like this chap,' he continued smoothly as Brennan savaged another delivery. 'Puts bat to ball. Good to see. Pity he's from Downunder. Who's the boy bowling to him?' Badel was again bowling at half pace for fear of causing injury.

'Badel. Alvar Badel.'

'In the wickets, I read?'

'Yes.'

'Your report, very readable. Good man, old Dawlish. You must be disappointed to see me?'

'Always a delight, Julian,' said Grimley, through clenched teeth. 'I'm only surprised you think it worth your while? The match looks over as a contest.'

'Fie, fie, Grimmers. Never say die.'

'Of course, some players are still hoping to make a favourable impression on the selectors.'

'I imagine so,' said Lycett, giving nothing away.

'Assuming Pywell and Topsy Turner have booked their tour places, what about the Hastie brothers?'

'Ah yes, an intriguing little contest. One brother could go but no room for both. Sticky time for the Hastie clan.'

'Is that the story you've come for?'

'That would be telling, dear chap.' Typical of him to keep

things close, thought Grimley. Mere acquaintance would not admit him to the inner workings of Lycett's mind any more than to his coterie.

In fairness, Lycett had shown a willingness to canvass opinions from all quarters when the debate about the England captaincy was at its height two years previously. Richard Hastie had recounted to Grimley how, during a three-day match at the Oval, he had been invited along with Jephcott and KC to dine at Lycett's club in St. James's. Ostensibly it was a goodwill gesture meant to reassure them of his continued interest in teams not indigenous to his home patch. The world of button-backed leather chairs and the taking of port in the library was one as alien to KC as it was Jephcott's natural habitat. For Richard it was an invitation to mix in a social milieu to which he was unlikely to gain regular admission.

Before the soup course was finished, Lycett was pressing the trio for feedback on a possible change of England captain. The incumbent was Mike Sayward, a fine batsman with a stupendous run scoring record for Surrey and England. From the outset, Lycett had championed his selection as captain and urged patience on detractors who questioned his ability to take hold of a game at key moments. On a deeper level, Lycett believed cricket was about more than winning or losing. It was a game of rules and manners and aesthetics. In Sayward, England had the man who came closest to personifying that view. Yet if Lycett was honest, the incumbent had been a disappointment. The burden of the England captaincy had affected his batting and his introspective disposition put a damper on team morale. Potential victories had slipped too easily out of England's grasp. Traction lost for want of some grit.

'Tell me then,' said Lycett, dabbing his napkin daintily across fleshy lips. 'If you had a man who was a very good captain but a bit of a shit, and another who was not quite such a good captain but a thoroughly nice chap – who would you choose?'

'The shit, of course,' said KC, as if the answer was self-evident. 'If you want to win matches that is.'

'What do you say, Robin?' Jephcott's lips twitched into the ghost of a smile. It was obvious Lycett was drawing a comparison between the Surrey man and Foxton of Lancashire who was being widely touted as his replacement.

'We're talking about the England job, I assume?'

'Maybe.'

'Then KC's right. Foxton's a winner.'

'Of limited-overs games maybe, but not in the Championship.'

'That's because Lancashire are short of bowlers. However good you are as a captain you can't win a campaign without bowlers. Besides Surrey haven't come that close either.'

'I believe Foxton would be divisive.'

'Only in the committee room. He's a tough nut, Julian. Players respect him and that's what counts.'

'He's a man's man, Mr Lycett,' added KC. 'He's not a headboy who does what the headmaster tells him.' It was a typically blunt observation and Lycett's pendulous double chin sank further for a moment before reshaping under a forbearing smile. Over the years he had been right to cast doubts on KC's suitability as an overseas ambassador for the M.C.C. The man was a superb bowler but he was also a diplomatic incident waiting to happen. Lycett leaned back to give the waiter more elbowroom to serve his Barnsley chop. It was a Northern themed night to be sure.

Brennan continued to smash the net bowling to smithereens until Jephcott called a ceasefire. As the team's overseas player,

Rod Brennan had enjoyed a successful first season and though his captain would have liked more discrimination in his batting, he was chary of reining in Rod's natural aggression. Almost without exception, his fellow batters had moved up a gear in response to the Tasmanian's example. Richard Hastie especially was a different player to the solid accumulator of runs he had been. Without Brennan's influence, it was doubtful if he would have made the leap to become a legitimate England contender. It worried Jephcott that Rod's contract for the following season remained unsigned. 'Sure I'll get round to it,' he had said in his lazy Tassie twang. But that was a month back and still the Club had not nailed him down.

Despite his adolescent-like proclamations of devotion to his fiancée, a former Miss Hobart, Rod had led a frantic social life. Possessing no great organisational skills, he often conspired to invite rival groupies to the same day's play. And though Crick and Picken, hovering like seagulls over a ketch, were ever eager to dive on any 'spare', Rod's cast-offs would be inconsolable. It seemed unlikely that Miss Hobart had got wind of Rod's heroic attempt to satisfy a sizeable swathe of Blighty's womenfolk, but Jephcott suspected she had insisted on naming The Day. Brennan's return for another season could therefore hinge more on Miss Hobart's inclinations than his. In short, he thought the Club would be well advised to line up another overseas player to fill the large hole that might open up in the middle order.

As Brennan and Jephcott exchanged places, Rod gestured over his shoulder in the direction of the two men behind the rear netting. 'Pinky and Perky.' The sight of Lycett alongside Grimley immediately sent the skipper's curiosity into overdrive.

'Good morning, Robin,' boomed Lycett.

'Hello, Julian? What are you doing here?

'Malingering, as usual, dear chap.'

'Pull the other.'

'Well if you must know, my chauffeuse desired an outing in the Shires, so she put a pin in the map.'

'I see,' said Jephcott, dismissing the notion. Barring a Test match, he doubted if Lycett had covered a game at Edgbaston since the outbreak of war. Fishy. Very fishy.

'Will Richard be netting?' piped up Grimley.

'Don't think so, Ron.'

'Is he not minded to practise?' said Lycett.

'He's a bit under the weather.'

'Ah, then he should take more water with it.'

4

By the time he arrived at the backdoor of the pavilion, Grimley had heard all about Richard's perceived act of gallantry and subsequent hospitalisation. Nevertheless, it was a shock to see his condition when he appeared wearing flip-flops on his feet but otherwise dressed to take the field.

'Impressive shiner. I trust you landed one or two yourself?'

''Fraid not, Ron. Never laid a glove on him.'

'Huh, too bad. I thought you'd like to know I called and had a word with Tessa.'

'How was she?'

'Reassured, I think. Naturally I apologised for the riff raff who peddled the rubbish, but she didn't strike me as being too bothered about it.' Bothered or not there was a nervous vibrato in Grimley's voice that Richard found disconcerting. For a moment the two men stood in a silence filled with unspoken anxieties. 'Will you be able to bat?'

'Yes,' said Richard, his head still thumping. 'All hands will be needed on deck. It won't be pretty but it doesn't matter, Gil Atkins isn't here. I blew my chance to impress yesterday.'

'Don't give up just yet. Atkins might not be here, but Julian Lycett is.'

'What's he doing here?

'He's not saying. Spying mission, I reckon.' Grimley took Richard by the elbow and squeezed it in the manner of a father encouraging his son. 'Get your head down. You could do yourself some good.' Richard nodded uncertainly. There was an air of sincerity about Grimley that went beyond his usual old chum's act. An intimation of pity even.

After years spent in a business that was often grubbier upstairs in the editorial offices than down in the print room, Grimley counted himself lucky to have kept his hands relatively clean. Doing the 'right thing' had never really been an issue. Nor would it be now had he kept a prudent distance from those who provided his source material. Instead he had embedded himself to the point where he believed he was almost part of the team. As a boy he had ached to have some modest co-ordination of hand and eye, but astigmatism and an ungainly body condemned him to the role of non-combatant and dumped him into the company of the similarly afflicted and other weird kids at the back of the class.

Though Grimley suspected the taunts of his boyhood still found an echo in the team's dressing room banter, his daily review of players' performances guaranteed him a certain measure of respect as well as trust. He kept to himself the dejection he felt when in autumn he swopped the camaradarie of the county circuit for a twice-a-week kickabout at Carlisle, Hull, or Bury F.C. There, where the floodlights struggled to penetrate the gloom and the brainless bellicosity of the fans supplied the soundtrack, he was just another hack vying for enough space in the Press Box to lodge a small typewriter and a fat arse.

Having identified himself so closely with the team, it was natural for Grimley to take a grave view of the Hastie problem. The potential fallout, he decided, would affect him as much as anyone, but he still had no idea what to do about it. He had rejected the anonymous note solution as one that risked being mistaken for a malign prank. His face-to-face exchange with Richard had convinced him that he had neither the nerve nor the finesse to convey his information without making matters worse. He had rehearsed in his mind the role of a family solicitor – kindly, wise, and trusted. But try as he might, he could not see himself as that man. Nor was Neil Ibbotson if he chose to pass his worrisome parcel to Richard's closest team-mate. Of course he could go to Jephcott with what he knew and risk being bracketed ever after as a poisonous meddler. Such a reputation would stymie his access to the players and make it harder for him to do his job.

Just as he was preparing to dig a hole in the sand to put his head in, Grimley pointed his binoculars at the pavilion and brought into focus the solution to his problem. It was so blindingly obvious, so sweetly devoid of risk, that only his proximity to the Big Beast stopped him jumping up from his seat and punching the air.

Chapter Twelve

1

Speedy poked his head out of the opposition dressing room to find Richard sitting with his feet up in the players' viewing enclosure. The rest of the team were in the nets or still changing and he had been left alone and grateful for it. 'What's this our kid? What you been up to this time?' Speedy's tone turned from joshing to concerned the closer he got to inspecting his brother's scarred face. 'When did that happen?'

'After I left your place. I tried to stop a bloke beating up a girl.'

'And got done over yourself? Sounds to me like a case of too many Ansell's?'

'Probably.'

'Well I'm sorry, mate. You look ropey.' The two had fought like cat and dog down the years, but they quickly stuck together to repel outside aggressors. Anything less than brotherly solidarity would earn the sternest of rebukes from Ma Hastie, and threats to Richard from his peers at the school gates, soon evaporated at the mention of his older brother. 'Not fielding, are you?'

'Yup.'

'A shiner like that's got to be worth a morning off?'

'I'll be fine.'

'Right,' said Speedy. He was not going to waste the time knocking sense into his brother. It had never worked in the past.

2

The highly polished Bentley would normally have caught Tessa's eye, but a neighbour had called together with her clutch of kids and she was otherwise engaged pouring pop and dispensing biscuits in the kitchen. The din was such that only Sarah heard the doorbell. 'Mummy, there's a man.' Her shrill voice from the hall was drowned out by the competition. Leaving Geoffrey Kyle at the door, she went to make herself heard. 'Mummy, there's a man at the door.'

The sight of a small child greeting him had induced an unpleasant fluttering sensation in Geoffrey Kyle's stomach. It was as though he had stepped onto a stage after rehearsing his grimly earnest lines only to be met with a rabble of children expecting a panto. He was on the verge of making a run for it when Tessa came to the door looking attractively harassed, her hands held out in front of her as if wet or sticky. For a moment she failed to recognise the caller with his sheepish smile, hand-made charcoal grey suit and silk tie.

'Hello,' he said, softly. 'Geoffrey Kyle.'

'Of course. I'm so sorry, Mr Kyle. I'm not with it this morning.' If she had spotted his car there would have been no hesitation. For Tessa, that alone, distinguished Kyle from the many suited professionals she had met in her time as a solicitor's conveyancing clerk.

'It's me who should be sorry, Mrs Hastie. I can hear that you're busy.' A half step backwards betrayed his desire to go.

Jessica had wrapped herself around Tessa's legs and was staring at the visitor.

'No, no, it's fine. If you can stand the racket, come in.' Kyle could see the kitchen door being yanked open and shut by a boisterous boy of about five. Beyond the door a baby was crying.

'No, really. I just came to tell you about your husband.'

'Richard?' she said, surprised he had not used his name.

'Richard, yes. You may have heard already?' Tessa frowned and shook her head, picking up the gravity in his tone. 'He was injured in a fight late last night.'

'A fight?'

'You didn't know?'

'No.'

'He had to go to hospital for treatment.'

'A fight?' she repeated disbelievingly.

'The hospital called us just before midnight.' Tessa held Jessica's head, stroking the child's hair with her thumb.

'Go and see what the others are doing, darling. Go on or they'll have eaten all the biscuits.' Jessica disappeared.

'I gather he's alright and fit to play today.'

'Oh. Well I can't think why he hasn't called to tell me himself, but I'm very grateful to you for taking the trouble.' She was still trying to work out how and why he had become involved. 'Did you say the hospital called you?'

'Yes, they called the house.'

'Why was that?'

'He was out cold. They found our phone number in his wallet.' Kyle's voice had lowered as he strained for a suitably severe expression.

'I'm sorry. Did it wake you up?'

'Me more than my wife.' Rightly or wrongly Tessa felt she was being reprimanded for a crime in which she had played no part. He seemed on the point of divulging something when Jessica slid back beside her mother. Kyle glanced down at the child, smiled perfunctorily and fixed his eyes again on Tessa. 'You've met my wife?'

'Yes.'

'Laura means a lot to me. She's the centre of our home. The mother of our boys. I love her dearly.' Tessa looked at him in polite bewilderment as she would at a drop-by evangelist whose sincerity she admired but had no wish to share. 'I'd rather she didn't see your husband anymore. Goodbye.' He turned and walked away leaving her rooted to the spot, eyes unblinking, a wave of nausea breaking in her chest.

'Who was that, Mummy?'

'Just a man, darling.'

Chapter Thirteen

1

A sudden sprinkling of rain delayed the start of play for fifteen minutes and condemned Jephcott's bowlers to bowling the first overs of the day with a wet ball. The promise of a home side victory had not excited a rush through the turnstiles. If anything the ground was less inhabited than on the previous two days. Faced with such indifference, a travelling circus might well have rolled up its tent and moved on, but county cricketers were an obdurate bunch. A crowd may have lifted their spirits, but a deserted arena made scant difference to the stubborn competitiveness with which they played the game.

When finally the umpires walked out to the middle, they received a weather forecast courtesy of Wilf Bristow. 'More juice in an hour. I'll put money on it.' His prediction was borne out by flecks of rain still spitting in the breeze. Jephcott led his men onto the field knowing that an extended interruption would improve his team's chances of forcing a draw. On the other hand, light showers would simply freshen the wicket for the bowlers without eating into the allotted time. With a lead of 197 runs and plenty of wickets in hand, the opposition were in a strong position. Unless their top order committed hara-kiri, containment was all Jephcott could hope for before Gledhill declared.

'Take the first over, Alvar,' called out Jephcott. 'No cameras to upset you today, so don't hold back.' Then to reassure Topsy he was still Strike Force One, 'You can give me a blast when the ball's drier.' Even though he was changed into his whites, Eau de Gas Street Basin still clung to Badel's nostrils and encrusted his tongue. The taste was a continuous reminder to him of coming up for air and breaking through a surface iridescent with foul-smelling diesel oil.

With 49 runs already against his name, Pywell was nicely set to go to the races. However, he would rather have restarted his innings against the usual opening attack of KC and Topsy. Aged thirty two, Pywell was in the prime of life as a batsman, but his difficulty in picking up Badel's deliveries had given him an inkling of what batting would be like when his eyesight was less than 20/20.

From the Press Box, Lycett watched Badel's first over through binoculars. More intrigued by the Big Beast than the game itself, Grimley observed his lips pouting pensively as though he had sipped wine of doubtful provenance. Then, without explanation, Lycett got up from his seat and left the Box. A voice from the back row crassly suggested he had found his seat too hard and had gone to get a rubber ring to ease the pressure on his piles. Grimley, however, caught sight of him climbing the steps to an adjacent stand before parking his bulk on one of a multitude of available seats.

Lycett's absence from the Box bemused his chauffeuse when she appeared carrying the cup of coffee she had been detailed to fetch. She was a well-scrubbed Home Counties gal in her twenties. Without any evidence to prove or disprove the notion, Grimley imagined her to be the daughter of a Lycett family friend. 'He's over there,' he said, pointing to the stand from where her boss was observing Badel's second over through binoculars.

'Is this the bowler he's come to see?'

'Bowler?'

'Bedlam, is it?'

'Badel.'

'That's him. The chucker.' Grimley's eyes popped open wide enough to threaten the repair on his spectacles.

Pywell nurdled a streaky single to escape to the other end where he could lean on his bat and watch Curtis Short take on Badel. The run had brought up his fifty and a smattering of melancholy clapping echoed under the covered stands. Short was normally an adept player of the short-pitched ball, getting his hands high and hooking with precision. Badel's fast skidding bouncer, however, came onto him like a bolt out of the blue to leave him half-hooking and half-ducking. The ball smacked Short on the glove, crushed his hand against the bat handle, and looped over Ibbo's head at short leg. 'Run,' shouted Pywell, followed even more urgently by 'two!'

Short completed a hurried second run before taking off his glove and flexing his fingers. The trauma to his hand had produced a feeling of cramp. Badel wiped his wrist across his mouth and returned to his mark without glancing in Short's direction. A seasoned bowler would have paused in the middle of the pitch to enjoy the batsman's discomfort but as yet Badel had not been inducted into the fast bowler's fellowship of muggers, gurners, and ham actors. His run up was a quiet undemonstrative affair without recourse to visual or audible distractions. More experienced hands would let their shirtsleeves unwind and waft like torn flags in a stiff wind. Others wore boots with steel toecaps, the rivets loose so they jangled disconcertingly with each stride.

Watching from second slip, Richard thought Badel's lack of theatricality made him, if anything, more chilling. So when the baby-faced assassin ran in again and bowled a ball that tore through Short's foot-tied defence to rip the middle stump out of the ground, it seemed like nothing personal.

2

At 82 for three, the opposition had to be careful not to squander their advantage. Pywell and Ledbrook, the incoming batsman, would have to play sensibly for a few overs to avoid a collapse that might give their opponents an easily achievable fourth innings target. For a time the teams played cat and mouse with Ledbrook finding himself facing more than his share of Badel's bowling as a result of his partner's manipulation of the strike. Jephcott gave short spells to KC, Topsy, and Crick, at the other end and the score drifted past 150 without either batsman opening their shoulders in pursuit of quick runs. In the event, it was Jephcott who chose to change the tempo by throwing the ball to Richard.

'Okay, give us a twirl.' The request was so much at odds with the passage of play, Richard was tempted to question its wisdom. He had not bowled in the last four matches, and though Jephcott had agreed to put him on if an opportunity arose, it did not seem to be the moment for experimentation. If nothing else, the seam bowlers were using up time with their extended run-ups. The batsmen's reluctance to chance their arm had allowed the game to meander usefully, a situation that would quickly be reversed by a couple of untidy overs of off-spin from a rusty bowler.

Irked by his demotion to second spinner, Shanks turned his back on the proceedings and did a 'teapot', truculently planting his fists high on his hips. 'The field for Dick,' shouted the skipper. 'Just scatter.' Richard wiped the palm of his right hand in the bowler's dusty footmarks to dry the sweat. Regular spinners had a pad of toughened skin at the point where the finger imparted traction onto the ball, but his was soft from underuse. It was too late now, not to say importunate, to adopt the time-honoured remedy of pissing uric acid onto his spinning finger to harden it up. In any case, though it was always useful to give the ball an early tweak to plant suspicion in a batsman's mind, his immediate concern was to find his range rather than strive for turn. A flattish trajectory and a gentle rolling of the index finger across the seam would get him through the first tentative deliveries. He could try ripping it later. He inhaled deeply, hoping a slug of oxygen would subdue the jitters.

Out of his first four balls only one offered to deviate off a straight line. If he wanted it to turn he would have to bowl slower with more loop and put more work on the ball. Instead, he pulled the ball down short giving Pywell, on the backfoot, time to pick a gap and rifle the ball between cover point and Shanks slightly behind square. Shanks dived, or more accurately reclined, to his right. He measured at least four feet too short to stop it and a fair few ticks too late. He stayed flat out on his belly until Picken volunteered to jog to the boundary to retrieve the ball. When he finally got to his feet, there was not a blemish on his flannels. Clearly if he was to be discarded as a bowler, he was damned if he was incurring a dry cleaning bill as well.

Pywell perused the scoreboard and assessed the possibility of his second hundred in the match. His score stood at 69 and if he could farm the strike to take the lion's share of the bowling, he reckoned he could just make it before a declaration intervened. Reassured that Richard's off-breaks posed no threat, he reviewed the disposition of the field before facing the last ball of the over. This time, however, instead of imparting spin on the ball with the tip of his index finger, Richard kept the seam and wrist vertical. As the 'arm' ball looked destined to go down the leg-side, Pywell went down on one knee to sweep. But having committed himself to the shot, the ball drifted in flight to the off. Pywell's elegant sweep failed to make contact and the ball hit his front pad. Richard and 'Doc' Holliday both went up in a loud appeal. Pywell's stride was so far down the track his gusset was popping at the seams. He stayed down on his right knee, certain the umpire would give him the benefit of the doubt. 'That's out,' said Jim Rook raising his finger. Pywell glared up the pitch in disgust but his indignation was wasted on Rook. 'And over,' said the umpire, quietly cherishing the life and death power residing in his first digit.

'He didn't like that,' commented KC as he passed Jim Rook.

'Bad shot,' replied Rook, as if that alone justified his decision. Ibbo slapped Richard on the back.

'Well bowled, maestro. Was it out?'

'Look in the book,' suggested Richard, his pleasure in dismissing Pywell overriding any qualms he might have felt about the decision. Pain was still gathering in his eyeballs but for the moment the narcotic of success had banished the pounding in his head.

Gledhill arrived at the wicket bristling with purpose and muttered instructions to Ledbrook. Aware that rain could cut into the day and make a nonsense of any declaration target, it could be assumed he was telling his Number Five to get a move on. Ledbrook duly obliged by nurdling a single to give his captain ample opportunity to put Badel to the sword.

Gledhill groped forward and failed to make contact with any of the next three deliveries. 'Bowl at the blasted stumps,' mumbled Jephcott to nobody in particular. As if he had heard the imprecation, Badel's next ball was almost a yorker and bang on target. It took the inside edge of the bat and scuttled between the batsman's back leg and the leg stump. Gledhill had the grace to grin sheepishly at the keeper and slips, only for the last ball of the over to wipe it off again when Badel reverted to pinging the ball at the batsman's ribs. Gledhill's desperate flailing hook shot in response, caught a top-edge and sent the ball steepling into the sky. Ibbo, who was directly beneath it, and Badel, following through, could have comfortably caught it, but it was 'Doc' charging in from behind the stumps who bellowed 'Mine!' It was always safest to let the man with the gloves do the necessary, so both backed off and watched him snaffle it to make the score 126 for five.

For a captain there was no greater joy in life than to have a shock bowler at his command whose pace could be held at the opposition's throat like a bandit's knife. With KC and Topsy to call on, Jephcott had been luckier than most skippers in that regard. But though KC was still a model of control, the fire that used to instill fear in the opposition had gone.

From what little Jephcott had seen of him, Badel had the potential to step into KC's shoes, not in terms of accuracy, but in his ability to spread panic. In thinking this he was conveniently ignoring the issue of Badel's action, which to most observers was the chief source of the opposition's agitation. Unless and until the 'Powers That Be' ruled his action illegal, Jephcott it seemed, had no intention of foregoing a match-winning asset. This ambivalence in a man widely regarded as a beacon of decency was a trait roundly approved of by his players. They saw rule-bending and gamesmanship as an inevitable part of the job, and they would not have appreciated a captain whose scruples might leave them at a competitive disadvantage.

Hollick's dismissal brought Speedy to the wicket uncomfortably aware he was on a 'pair' and that his brother was bowling. After Richard had said farewell the previous evening, Speedy and Sheila had continued to speculate on his possible selection for the winter tour. Their shared excitement had provoked a restless night. Sheila, ever eager to inflate her husband's self-belief, agreed that another good bowling performance in the second innings could clinch the prize. His immediate problem however was negotiating the period up to a declaration without making a pig's ear of it.

Speedy knew his brother's bowling inside out; knew he was short of match-practice; knew he had nothing in the way of spin or flight to bother him; and yet... As Speedy took guard, Richard tossed the ball from hand to hand just as he had done as a boy on summer evenings at Number Twenty Two, the swifts screaming and jagging above the rooftops. The fear now of succumbing to a dumb stroke or a freak delivery tightened the knot in Speedy's stomach, and the normally sinewy connections had stiffened in his arms, hands and wrists.

Speedy would reflect how often he had wanted to kill his brother. He had come close to doing so once, dunking Richard's head in a water butt and holding him under for so long his body had gone limp. Quite soon after, he had carried that same body for almost a mile when Richard injured himself falling from a tree. There was conflict but no contradiction in the two scenarios. Their sibling rivalry involved such genetic affinity it felt as if they were conducting a love-hate relationship with themselves.

Aiming for consistency, Richard bowled successive balls on off stump. Propping forward, Speedy played almost identical defensive pushes to each one. Seeing the nervous rigidity in his brother's batting, Richard threw the last ball above Speedy's eyeline, luring him out of his crease like a trout tempted by a gaily-feathered fly. Belatedly, Speedy realised he had been deceived in the flight and aborted the stroke, scratching desperately to put bat or pad into the path of the ball. From an inside edge the ball cannoned off his left boot and squirted out onto the leg side for a face-saving run.

'How did you get on to bowl?' said Speedy, covering his embarrassment with an insult. 'Normally you couldn't get a bowl in a Chinese restaurant.' Richard was not to be drawn. He had made Speedy look lame but that was to be the extent of his success. Without taking undue risks, Ledbrook and Speedy advanced the total to 177, before rain again drove the players into the pavilion for an early lunch, during which Gledhill declared the innings closed.

Chapter Fourteen

1

In the visitors' dressing room a whiff of submission mingled with the swampy smell of damp wool pullovers. Their target to win was 299 runs. In dry conditions a typical Wilf Bristow pitch, mown on the third morning, tended to yield substantial fourth innings totals. But the weather remained uncertain and intermittent showers had refreshed the track and given encouragement to the bowlers throughout. They would have to bat their boots off and take risks if they wanted to overhaul the target.

It would be up to Jephcott to decide how many wickets to sacrifice before the team gave up the chase and dug in for a draw. None of this needed to be articulated. Richard and Ibbo knew by heart the fatuous instructions they would be given. 'Play normally and see how it goes.' 'If it's there to be hit, hit it, otherwise don't.'

The dressing room attendant had pinned a note from Grimley onto Jephcott's jacket hanging on his changing peg. Jephcott read the message and decided there was time to take lunch before responding to its contents.

Speedy also found a note from the same source waiting for him when he returned to the pavilion. He was conscious of the need to keep on good terms with the Press, but he drew the line at Grimley who, as a hack from another parish, was in no position to further his career. By the time Speedy had taken his pads off, swilled his face, and found his flip–flops, Grimley had taken a soaking by the door at the rear of the pavilion. He had tried in vain to persuade the dressing room attendant to let him stand inside to wait out of the rain. 'Players only, pal', the attendant had snorted. 'The public are verboten in here. Pressmen very verboten.'

'No brolly?' said Speedy, unsympathetically. Grimley forced a smile. 'What's with the note?'

'It's delicate.' The word seemed incongruous coming from behind Grimley's nicotine-stained teeth. 'Sensitive, you know.' He paused, perhaps hoping that mental telepathy would obviate the need for further explanation.

'Sorry, Ron, I don't know.'

'It's about Richard.'

'Oh?'

'I hope this is confidential – for Richard's sake, and Tessa's.' The introduction of Tessa cut deeper creases into Speedy's brow. 'I don't want anyone thinking I'm a snooper. I look after my local team. That's my main concern. And I think they trust me. I value that.' Although it was wet it was also warm and it was difficult to distinguish between sweat and rain on Grimley's forehead and upper lip.

'What is it, Ron?' said Speedy, becoming more irritable.

'I was doing him a favour. I said I'd call on Tessa to pour oil on troubled water. Explain to her how the nightclub story was a Press set-up. So last night, on the way home, I went to their place intending to see her.'

'And?'

'I didn't. I couldn't. She had a visitor.'

'Visitor?' Speedy's eyes narrowed at Grimley's insinuating tone. 'What d'you mean?'

'If I saw what I think I saw, it would cause mayhem in the dressing room. I mean major, major, trouble.'

'Why are you telling me and not him?'

'Because it's not my place. It's personal. You're family and I'm sure you can keep it that way.'

2

THROWING CONTROVERSY RUMBLES ON
By Julian Lycett

The controversy surrounding the issue of throwing shows no sign of abating. A number of bowlers in First-class cricket have been referred to the M.C.C.'s Special Sub Committee set up to adjudicate on those who have been called or reported. Already two players have been suspended pending corrective work on their actions.

Loath though I am to thwart the chances of a young man standing on the threshold of a career in cricket, I would have to add the name Alvar Badel to the list of those already under scrutiny.

My first sighting of Badel revealed a player of pallid features and slender physique who is capable of generating enough pace to hurry, not to say harry, that most accomplished of batsmen, Paul Pywell. This in itself might be sufficient to arouse curiosity if not downright suspicion.

Lycett's thumb-sucker article for his weekend column could be something of a chore. Over a season, repetition was inevitable. In this respect the issue of throwing had been somewhat of a boon since there was no easy resolution to the problem. In addition, because there was a frisson of scandal attached, it seemed to capture the interest of those who were not otherwise drawn to cricket. It smacked of the underhanded flouting of rules so beloved by slur merchants at the tackier end of Fleet Street. Not that he associated himself with that school, but new adherents to his column were always welcome. Loyal readers, he knew, looked to him to tell them what to think. An arrogant assumption no doubt, but one from which he refused to fight shy. He had earned their trust over many years and took seriously his responsibilities as the game's oracle. After all, only the most senior cricket administrators had his breadth of experience. He had never played the game, but he was pleased to regard himself as the embodiment of it.

'Mr Colclough would like a word if possible.' Lycett swept his spectacles off his face, leaned back in his chair and cocked an eyebrow at his PA.

'Ken Colclough?'

'I was reading in the car and he tapped on the window.'

'Did he indeed.'

'If you could meet him by the car, he'll be there in five minutes.'

'Well, when the Master calls,' said Lycett feigning compliance. He believed an occasional show of humility never went amiss.

Even with his buttocks wedged snugly into the driving seat of his Mercedes 250 SE, Lycett felt out of his comfort zone. His jaundiced opinion of the ground and its environs had been fully rekindled. It was not just the utilitarian nature of the concrete amphitheatre that ran against the grain, the air itself tasted to him of iron filings. Sitting beside him was KC, his stone profile on a furrowed-frown setting.

'It's not like you to bother about what I write?'

'I read your stuff now and again,' admitted KC gruffly.

'Well I'm flattered, but that isn't what I said.'

'Why didn't you tell the Skipper you were here to watch Badel?'

'I thought it might dissuade him from bowling the young man. Then I would have had a wasted journey.'

'Did Lord's ask you to come?'

'What makes you think that?

'How else would you have known about him?'

'I read match reports too.'

'M.C.C. can try as hard as it likes to show it's putting its own house in order, the Windies will still pick Chester Deeds.'

'I daresay you're right.'

'So why do you want to be part of a hanging party?'

'I'm my own man, KC. You should know that by now.' Lycett tried to sound hurt. 'People are confused about this issue. Bowlers have been getting away with suspect actions for years. Even if you're right about Deeds, something still needs to be done to clean up our domestic game. Chuckers derive an unfair advantage from their infraction. They should either bowl according to the laws of the game or take up darts.'

'So you think he throws?'

'Don't you?'

'He hasn't been called or officially reported.'

'Yet.'

'I reckon it's up to the umpires to do the job not the newspapers.'

'From my observations, umpires have shown a marked reluctance to make judgements.'

'Who can blame 'em? It's not easy with the naked eye. Not cut and dried – not enough to finish a man's livelihood anyway.'

'Who told you the reason for my visit?'

'The Skipper got a note from Ron Grimley.'

'Ah.'

'And the Skip showed it to me.'

'And he sent you to see me?' KC shook his head.

'Jephcott should be sat here himself but he reckons talking to the Press usually makes things worse.'

'He has a point.'

'The lad was only filmed yesterday. Isn't there a committee at Lord's that's set up to do the dirty work?'

'Yes, a Special Sub Committee.'

'Right, so there's no need for others to act as judge and jury, is there?'

'Me, you mean? My dear KC you make it sound as if my columns are handed down on tablets of stone. I'm a hack, nothing more, nothing less.'

'That's bollocks.' The sudden sourness in KC's voice took Lycett a little by surprise though on reflection he realised something had been brewing for a long time. For years even.

'Is this about Badel or about you?'

'What d'you mean?'

'Have I been judge and jury to you?'

'That's for others to say.'

'You were a fine bowler, Ken, but there were other fine bowlers. It was nothing personal.'

'If you say so. But that's in the past, this is now. I don't want this lad taken apart by the Press. If his action's not legal, that's for others to decide, and I don't reckon you should be making their minds up for them.'

KC exited the car. Though the rain had stopped, beaded droplets on the windscreen distorted Lycett's view of KC's receding frame. He had once faced down a mob of machete-waving plantation workers in Malaya but he was hard-pressed to imagine a more implacable adversary than KC. He gripped the leather-strapped steering wheel with both hands and felt a faint arrhythmia tripping in his chest. Discretion, he mused, would be no bad thing.

3

For reasons Ibbo could never explain, the second 'dig' was always a less stressful affair than the first innings and consequently his bowels remained unmoved. Instead he took the sink next to Richard and gargled water for a while.

'We can get these,' he said, matter-of-factly.

'Yeh?'

'Easy peasy. We might not even have to bother the others.' Richard enjoyed Ibbo's flights of fancy. As far as he could recall there had never been a target that Ibbo considered taxing. He was a Jekyll and Hyde performer. An obdurate opener who transformed himself into a batsman of giddy abandon whenever a run chase was in the offing. In such circumstances Jephcott would state, somewhat superfluously, that if either batsman was still at the crease at the close with a hundred against his name, the match would be won.

It was a valid enough prediction. For a lengthy run chase to succeed, a sheet-anchor innings that prevented a haemorrhaging of wickets at both ends was usually required. The sages in the dressing room would pointlessly advise Richard and Ibbo to see 'how it goes' before doing anything impetuous. What that usually meant in practice was Ibbo making a dash, while Richard sat on his splice.

Speedy saw Richard exit the shower room and turned his back to shield the phone and mute his voice. 'I want you to call Tessa,' he whispered into the receiver.

'When?'

'Now.'

'I'm cleaning the cooker.'

'Soon as you can then.'

'What's happened?'

'Richard got into a scrap last night after he left our place.'

'Scrap?' Sheila Hastie had answered the phone call wearing rubber gloves.

'He had to have stitches in a facial wound.'

'Is he alright?'

'Yes, but I'm not sure Tessa knows about it. Anyway it gives you an excuse to call her.' Sheila twigged something was wrong.

'Is there some sort of trouble?'

'Possibly. Just see how she is. See if she'll confide in you. Any worries, that sort of thing.'

'What is it you're not telling me?'

'We'll talk when I get home.' Sheila heard the anxiety in Speedy's voice. She began to peel off her Marigolds. Despite the protection, her hands emerged chapped and lobster-red.

4

Relieved to have passed the toxic baton of 'truth' to Speedy, Grimley sat down in a lighter mood to pen his piece for the afternoon edition. As a work-in-progress, the match had assumed a clear shape and direction. A languid three-day game had in effect become a limited-over contest. In the three hours plus twenty overs left to play, the run target set by Gledhill was perfectly attainable. With Richard Hastie to play the mainstay and Rod Brennan to produce the propulsion, there was every reason to be positive.

Yet in tune with the misadventures both on and off the field, Grimley was less than sanguine about the probable result of the match. The local hacks had already pencilled-in a home win, and though their smugness narked him, Grimley had to admit their premature triumphalism was not unjustified. Nevertheless, he would stir his readers with an optimistic assessment of their chances and leave the outcome for his report in the following day's edition.

5

Once Tessa's neighbour and her clamorous kids had left the house she had been able to reflect on Geoffrey Kyle's visit. After the unholy racket of the previous hour even Sarah and Jessica were relieved to sit drawing and colouring in silence at the kitchen table.

Tessa tried to remain still, hoping the swirl of thoughts in her head would settle like liquids of different densities in a bottle. But then another stab of emotion churned everything up and confusion returned. Her own affair, for weeks at the forefront of her mind, had been displaced by the shock of Kyle's disclosure. Banal questions tumbled through her head. Why, when, and where had it all happened? The psychodrama of her own transgressions had consumed her. She had been so busy covering her own tracks it had made her blind to any signs there might have been. In all conscience, her duplicity should have removed her right to feel hurt and betrayed, yet those feelings welled up inside her.

She had met Laura Kyle on only two occasions and

remembered her as an attractive woman who had both the style and the means to indulge it. She was clearly a bosses wife with a gift for charming the shop floor, whether hosiery workers or professional cricketers. She was friendly without being familiar, dispensing a smile here, a lightly patted arm there.

Tessa began piecing together the events of the past weeks and months, or could it have been years? Her stomach lurched at the thought of the endless possibilities. Where had they been meeting? How often? Who was the seducer, who the seduced? Tears of rage and humiliation blurred her vision, mingling with those of her own shame and guilt.

'Are you alright, Mummy?' said Sarah, sensing the changed atmosphere.

'Yes, darling. I must have a cold coming on.' Tessa dried her eyes under the subterfuge of blowing her nose. The sight of her daughter's gaze and Jess's frown of concentration brought more tears.

It was ironic that she had ended her affair that morning. Her relationship with Richard having wound down to a dutiful routine, the excitement of being desired had made her feel alive again. At first the clandestine meetings and urgent fumblings surprised her with their intensity. Though she had not entirely lost her bearings – coming back to the girls had made certain of that – the illicitness had become a high.

'Where's the harm,' he had whispered. 'Be careful and nobody need get hurt.' She had tried to justify her actions by making herself a victim of Richard's negligence, even convincing herself he would not care if he discovered her infidelity. But the situation had become overheated and the task of juggling a husband, two children and a lover, unpleasantly fraught and risky. Somehow, somewhere, a mistake would betray her and the consequences would be too dire to contemplate.

Whether the clean break she had demanded would hold she was not sure. She had lain on her side staring at the bedroom clock realising she could put it off no longer. She turned and watched him fasten his belt and button his cuffs. He paused, seemingly anticipating what she was about to say. He had been discreet and considerate, now she hoped he would see the necessity of ending it.

She had loved Richard passionately before the onrush of family commitments had blunted her responses. Deep down she felt she could rediscover that passion. The affair had given her new momentum and she was resolved to direct that energy into making things right between them. But her relief at kicking the habit before lies corrupted her further was tempered by the revelation that Laura Kyle had stuck her elegant stiletto heels into her lawn.

Chapter Fifteen

1

BRIGHT START TO RUN CHASE
By Ron Grimley

Set a target of 299 runs to win by Warwickshire at Edgbaston, Derbyshire made a promising start. Despite playing second best to the opposition for the majority of the match, Derbyshire sought to redeem their early failings through an enterprising stand of 46 between Hastie and Ibbotson for the first wicket, but whenever they looked likely to gain the ascendancy, the loss of a wicket snatched it back for the opposition.

Gledhill's declaration had been astutely pitched to keep the opposition in the hunt and interested. If they lost wickets, he would simply feed them runs to keep the target teasingly achievable – sufficiently so for the remaining batsmen to take chances rather than dig in for a draw.

The sages in the dressing room who had advised Richard and Ibbo to see 'how it goes' before doing anything stupid, had been forced to avert their eyes as Ibbo darted and flirted at every delivery within reach. In this, his Mr Hyde mode, Ibbo could be

220

seen as the selfless team man willing to sacrifice his wicket for the cause rather than someone with just two gears – regular and reckless.

Despite his more staid approach, Richard Hastie progressed almost run for run with his more fired-up friend. Their opening stand of 46 ended when Ibbo was out to a caught-and-bowled dismissal that would have decapitated Talbot had he not stuck up a defending hand as he followed through.

According to Grimley, Barry Picken at Number Three had been a consummate professional all season. That is he had never done more than the minimum required to stay in the team and under contract. Grimley admired his pragmatism while lamenting the waste of his talent. A gifted ball player, he joined the county staff from school and also signed forms for Sheffield United Football Club, one of a dwindling number of players good enough to earn a living at both trades. A chronic knee condition shortened his soccer career and took some of the ginger out of his footwork, but his eye and reflexes had secured for him the pivotal Number Three berth.

As a run chaser Picken was busy without being brutal and for a time seemed to be auditioning for the role of anchor-man already taken by Richard Hastie. After surviving a confident appeal for LBW, Picken sketched the outline of an innings with some deft strokes but then failed to capitalise on it when another LBW appeal went the bowler's way.

It was hard for Grimley to look at Picken without a degree of contempt. If he had been given a fraction of Picken's ability he would have treasured it. He could not comprehend the profligacy of a man who seemed to get more satisfaction from an opportunistic leg-over than the magical talent bestowed upon him. When he was on song he was probably the best timer of a ball in the team, leaning into his strokes and dispatching balls with silky wrists through the leg-side as if he were caressing a baby's head.

The scoreboard read 70 for two. It represented a respectable if not compelling start to the run chase. Grimley observed Jephcott closely as he walked to join Richard Hastie. The captain's batting form had been patchy and indicative of a mind not fully on the game. He had been a good school rackets player and this showed in the dominance of his bottom hand and his partiality for the carve and the cut. However, when bowlers kept the ball well up to him outside the off-stump, the bottom hand became a false friend and he was apt to provide catching practice to the slips.

At the beginning of the season it would have been absurd to question Jephcott's position. He had proved himself an adept leader but now Grimley feared the team was about to lose its way. There was still quality to be found in its working components, but the sum added up to less than its parts. In essence this was down to Jephcott to reverse, but for reasons both on and off the field, his authority seemed to be waning. If the information he had passed to Speedy became common knowledge, Grimley believed Jephcott would be unable to hold the team together.

A streaky four and an edged single was all Jephcott could contribute before he took his leave. Flashing at Hills without getting his foot to the pitch of the ball, he feathered a chance to Pywell at first slip, who made the fast-travelling catch look as easy as a hawk taking a bird on the wing. It had not been Jephcott's match, reflected Grimley, and it was far from over.

Richard Hastie, not out on 43, was playing a tactically astute innings and Julian Lycett had nodded approvingly when the opener punished a couple of wayward deliveries without fuss, one of them from his brother who had taken over from Talbot.

'He looks in goodish nick.'

'Are you a fan?' enquired Grimley.

'Not really seen enough of him.' It was noticeable that Lycett had stopped typing and was watching the game instead. Grimley wondered if he had finished the Badel piece, shelved it, or was simply allowing it to marinate in the juices of his punctilious prose. Lycett trained his binoculars on Rod Brennan slashing at the air on his way to the wicket like a frontiersman clearing a path through brush. 'This the Kiwi?'

'Tasmanian.'

'Fireworks now, d'you think?

'Possibly,' said Grimley who had seen too many short-lived Brennan cameos to be more effusive. The score was 91 for 3 with an hour to go before tea. Sixty minutes of Brennan would certainly put them ahead of the clock, but he was just as likely to hit the first ball straight up into the air. If he was dismissed quickly, Jephcott would probably favour hanging on for a draw rather than persisting with the chase. The loss of Murfin to injury on the first morning had left him with a longer tail than was ideal in the circumstances.

Gledhill needed no warning about Brennan's potential to make his declaration look foolish, but in Speedy he had a steady hand to keep one end tight. At the other he brought on lolloping Les Upton, a slow left-arm bowler with a philosophical attitude to operating on Bristow's pitches. A beanpole of a man, his shirt sleeves buttoned to the wrist, he wheeled away more in hope than expectation. No big spinner of the ball, his only encouragement came from bowling at the City End where the slope nagged the occasional delivery away from the right-hander's outside edge. Fielding on the boundary he would often encounter a West Indian veteran wearing a suit, a loud kipper tie, and a trilby. 'Does it take spin today, Mr Upton, or is it slightly straight?' the old-timer would ask, suppressing a snicker for barely a moment before the tee-hees burst forth from behind a gold-spangled grin.

By introducing Upton, Gledhill aimed to deprive Brennan of the pace that he was apt to harness and return with additional rockets attached. Upton, he thought, had the nous and the control to flight successive deliveries higher and a little wider, making the batsman leave his crease to fetch the ball. Persuaded to hit on the move like this, a batsman risked jiggling his vision enough to induce errors. Stumpings were possible though rare given Upton's lack of turn, but Gledhill's offside field was set in the hope of a catch from a mis-timed drive. Brennan took the bait straight away and drilled a low stinging catch to Talbot, at short mid-off, who dropped it. He wrung his hands in pain then examined his fingers for breakages. 'You only catching your own today?' chuntered Upton to Talbot.

Most batsmen given a 'life' would have gone chastened into their shell but Brennan took a step down the track and bludgeoned Upton's next ball back over his head, one bounce into the advertising boards. Richard sensed an immediate note of agitation in Gledhill's voice as he fiddled with his field. If Brennan got going, the opposition skipper would have to put his men half way back in the stands, and Richard resolved to give his partner as much of the strike as possible.

First though, he had to get away from Speedy who had started well, bowling a tight line and cramping him for room. He could tell from the set of his brother's mouth that their current confrontation dwarfed all previous encounters in significance. If it really was the case that they were competing for the same place on the winter tour, the match in progress placed Speedy ahead of him by a long neck. If passion and determination were the criteria for selection, Richard would in all honesty have to defer to his brother. Speedy wanted the recognition so much it oozed from his pores. Yet rivalry was too hard-wired into Richard's psyche for him to simply stand aside and let his brother take the prize. He would not break until he was broken.

Speedy bowled two balls of immaculate line and length. Surmising Brennan's power would disturb his brother's metronomic efficiency, Richard dabbed a quick single. 'Run!' he shouted, catching Hills back on his heels and a couple of yards too deep at mid-on.

The sun had made another appearance and Wilf Bristow's lads stripped off their shirts and lay behind the covers away from his disapproving eye. The desultory atmosphere around the ground, the sparseness of the crowd, and the quiet ticking movements of the scoreboard, belied the steadily building pressure on the field. Betting in the Press Box still favoured a Home win, with a draw as the next most likely result. Much to Grimley's surprise, Julian Lycett was still showing an interest in the game long after he had expected to see his 250SE nosing out of the car park and heading south.

The effect of Brennan's presence on the opposition never failed to surprise Richard. It was not uncommon for batsmen to be cowed by coruscating speed. Even spin bowlers of quality could induce trepidation, but it was rare for a batter, posing no obvious physical threat, to create such alarm. The palpable tension had been exacerbated by Talbot's missed catch and the geometry of the field had altered. Fielders in the ring were standing deeper and gaps through which runs could be scored had widened. Bowlers visibly stiffened, steeling themselves like Tommies about to go over the top. Even if their adversary perished quickly, they knew he would not go quietly.

Richard dismissed any pretence of establishing the same degree of domination. He could and probably should have spent the winter months building up his strength in the weights room. To depend so much on timing left him bereft when pitches were slow or wet and muscle rather than finesse was needed to force the ball through the infield. Even when conditions were favourable, to be 'in touch' could be a transient and elusive thing. The near silent 'tok' of a well-timed stroke could be followed inexplicably by the jarring thud of leather on a bat that suddenly seemed to possess the unyielding hardness of teak rather than the springy recoil of willow.

Such niceties by-passed Brennan. Whether off the meat of his blade or the edges, the ball seemed to disappear regardless. Where Richard tried to pick the lock with a hatpin, the Tasmanian reached for the gelignite and blew the door off its hinges.

Speedy concentrated on maintaining his control, straining neither for variety nor pace as was often the temptation when faced with aggression. Brennan sniffed at his first delivery and, deciding there was nothing to trouble him, cuffed the next to the cover boundary. To his credit and Gledhill's relief, Speedy held his line, but after ticking along steadily the score had cantered on and was threatening to gallop. Wary of allowing the momentum to go unchecked, Gledhill changed his spinners from one end to the other, interspersing them with Speedy for added variation.

Brennan's unfettered strokeplay brought purrs of delight from the Big Beast in the Press Box. 'Wally used to tap it like this fella. Have I said that before?'

'Yes,' said Grimley.

'Fine player, Wally. Len could hit the ball hard as well. Not everyone appreciates that. Quite a find though, this man. Will he be back next year?'

'I'm not sure. He hasn't signed a contract yet.'

'A matter of money, I suppose?'

'Possibly,' said Grimley, suggesting he was more in the know than was the case.

'Oh, good shot, sir!' Brennan had dispatched Speedy scornfully on the up through wide mid-off. Such was the speed of the ball, the fielder on the extra cover boundary had barely moved before it jumped the rope. 'Exhilarating stuff.'

Speedy blew his cheeks out in frustration. He was not bowling badly yet the ball was rocketing off the bat. Since Talbot's drop, Brennan had showed no sign of fallibility. Even more infuriating to him was Richard's smug performance as he manoeuvred to give his partner the strike. Not for the first time he cursed himself for not holding the little shit underwater for another thirty seconds all those years ago.

The pair had put on 71 in twelve overs of which Brennan had scored 50 to Richard's 21. When Speedy bowled again, Brennan punched the ball back down the track. Like most bowlers, Speedy was quick to react to save runs off his own bowling. However, unable to arrest his follow-through to the offside, he could only dangle his trailing leg in the hope of blocking the shot with his foot. It was an instinctive reaction that came at a price. The ball hit him on the inside of his boot near the arch of his foot and ricocheted onto the stumps at the bowler's end. Backing up in readiness to take a run, Richard had seen the danger and spun round to scrape his bat through the crease at the non-striker's end. 'Owzat!' came a pained cry from Speedy.

'Not out,' pronounced Jim Rook, impassive behind the

stumps and in no position to judge the possible freak run-out. Denied the balm of Richard's dismissal, Speedy felt the bones in his foot register ten on the trauma scale.

'Bollocks,' he groaned, hobbling around the square like a winged wildebeest. Richard patted the face of his bat with one hand to applaud a stroke so unjustly denied a boundary by his brother's foot.

'Hard luck, Rod,' he shouted up the pitch. Taking this as a taunt, Speedy fired a warning glare at his brother. Painful though it must have been, Richard knew Speedy would brush off the injury and charge in faster, madder, and hopefully with a little less control. While it was haemorrhaging blood internally, Speedy's foot would be warm and still flexible. Later when the bruising had time to clot around the bone, walking would become an agony.

With what was almost a carbon copy of the previous stroke, Brennan rewarded Speedy for his pluck by drilling the next delivery straight back down the pitch again. This time Speedy did not make the mistake of using his foot as a last line of resistance. Humiliated and bruised, he watched the ball streak unimpeded to the boundary.

'Shot!' shouted Richard. Well aware that a big score by his brother could damage his own prospects in the months to come, Speedy turned on Richard.

'Why don't you give your mate a hand, or are you playing for a draw?' he snapped, taking his sweater from Rook.

'Look at the board,' said Richard, welcoming his brother's loss of self-control. Speedy's lip curled in malice. This, he thought, was a chance to turn the tables too good to miss.

'I know the score, smart-arse. So does Tessa. She scores at home while you're away.' Richard stopped tapping blemishes in the pitch.

'What?'

'You heard.'

'What're you on about?'

'Ask her.'

'Ask her what?'

'Whose car was outside your place last night.'

'Car?'

'At least she keeps it in the club.'

'What is this crap?' said Richard.

'I'm only the messenger.'

'Whose car?'

'Who wasn't staying at the hotel? Work it out.' Speedy put on his sleeveless pullover and turned, leaving Richard calling in his wake.

'Heh!' Speedy heard the panic and confusion in his brother's voice. He was still full of rage but already wished his words could be unsaid. He had to tell him sometime but not then. Not in anger. Not in spite. He turned to face Richard.

'Sorry, mate. No easy way to tell you.'

'It's true?'

'That's what Grimley said.'

'Who is it?' said Richard, but Speedy held up both hands in contrite refusal.

'It's between you and Tessa. Ask her.' Richard felt as if he had been involved in a head-on crash and was walking dazed away from the collision. Len Chambers held out his arm to stop Upton bowling a new over.

'New guard, batsman?' he asked, hoping to capture Richard's attention. 'Are you ready, Dick?' Richard gathered enough of himself to return to his mark on the crease. He stood for a moment and pretended to survey the disposition of the field afraid he was about to vomit.

'Play,' shouted Chambers, losing patience. Richard bent into his stance out of habit and Upton bowled. The ball hung in the air for what seemed an age then dipped and hurried past to the keeper. He may have played a shot but he could not be sure. He saw his bat above his head and his front pad outstretched and assumed he had shouldered arms.

'Bowled, Les. Keep it there.' Gledhill's voice from behind the stumps came from another world. 'Work it out,' Speedy had said, but Richard could not get his brain even to accept the premise. Tessa, his wife? His Tess? Upton bowled again, this time a little straighter. Richard felt himself prop forward, wrists soft on impact the ball dropping dead off the face of the bat.

Robotically he repeated the stroke to the next delivery while rewinding Speedy's words in his head. 'Who wasn't staying at the hotel?' The answer was literally staring him in the face. He looked at Rod Brennan leaning nonchalantly on his bat at the far end of the pitch. It could not have been anyone else. Tessa had made no secret of her liking for him. It was she who suggested inviting him for supper 'to make him feel welcome' when he first arrived from Tasmania. 'The best cheesecake he had ever tasted', he claimed. The best piece of arse too?

Upton trundled in, his floaty deliveries adding to Richard's sense of disengagement. Recent events skittered through his mind. He remembered Tessa arriving to watch a Sunday League match on a hot sunny day, a breeze shaping her frock against her body. In the car park she had bumped into Brennan. Smiling broadly, he had carried the girls, one in each muscle-bound arm towards the pavilion. He recalled the laughter in Tessa's eyes, the sudden spike of jealousy at his exclusion from this tableau of domestic felicity. Now he realised he had ignored the signs and allowed complacency and trust to override his instincts.

'No,' shouted Brennan, as the ball squirted from Richard's bat

230

off the inside edge. Richard's memory worked furiously to place Brennan's whereabouts over the summer months. He had been missing from the team's hotel on a number of occasions, often travelling substantial distances each day. Only his success with the bat had stopped Jephcott from insisting on him booking in with his fellow players.

Richard's guts lurched again as he calculated the away days Brennan and Tessa could have met without fear of discovery. But where and how? And what had she done with the girls? His two bright buttons, all-seeing all hearing. How could Tessa make them disappear? She would not do that. He knew her. He loved her. She just would not do that. For a moment he let reason and hope administer a sedative to his system.

Upton bowled again. To Richard, the pitch appeared to be a long windowless tunnel and the ball a small sphere of fascination that he perceived with such acuity he could read the maker's name. He heard the ball on his bat but felt no sensation. 'No!' shouted Brennan, a rising note of urgency in his call. Previously he had been fed the strike but now five dot balls had been bowled and he was getting fidgety.

Richard stared at Brennan at the far end of the tunnel. He was prodding his protector more comfortably into his groin, an unselfconsciously lewd gesture that quickened Richard's downward spiral. By way of tasteless innuendo, he had jested to Tessa about the prodigious size of Brennan's penis and the number of admirers who had been grateful recipients. Not so amusing now he imagined his wife on the end of it.

The crude and invidious comparison brought a reflux of bile into his throat. He swallowed hard to avoid retching as Upton wheeled up to the bowling crease. The delivery of fullish length, six inches outside off-stump, demanded to be driven. Richard had no sense of what stroke he had played even after he heard the ball smack against the advertising boards to be greeted by a sprinkling of applause. 'And over,' drawled Chambers.

'Great shot, mate,' said Rod Brennan, sauntering down the pitch to confer, blind to the mental turmoil engulfing his partner.

'Don't call me 'mate'.'

'What?'

'You're no mate of mine, you bastard.' All colour had drained from Richard's face and he felt unsteady on his feet.

'What's got into you?'

'Where were you last night?'

'Last night? Why?'

'Grimley saw your car.'

'Yeah?'

'You were with Tessa.'

'What?'

'You've been sniffing around her from the off.'

'Thank you, gentlemen,' said Chambers, calling the two men to order from behind the stumps. His hackles raised, Brennan strode back to his crease and thwacked his bat into the block hole. The tremor sent shock waves rippling to the rope. Richard imagined Tessa in Brennan's arms, their writhing bodies joined by his pounding cock and his stomach heaved again.

Speedy's first ball was a perfectly respectable delivery but it was treated with unspeakable savagery by Brennan who made room for himself and belted the ball to the square cover boundary. The next delivery, he stepped outside the line and thrashed it over mid-wicket. The exchange with Richard had clearly added more powder to his ordnance. Speedy watched the ball's trajectory as it landed a yard inside the boundary and wondered how long the barrage might last. Gledhill semaphored to his fielders to move this way then that, feeling increasingly like a man with a large hole in his bucket.

Speedy's much-prized command of line and length had now become a weakness. By virtue of its predictability he had found himself in the crosshairs of Brennan's sights. Only variations of pace remained unused in his armoury.

His next delivery was a well-disguised slower ball but Brennan was only initially foxed. Early with his stroke, he made a late adjustment and succeeded in scuffing the ball off the inside edge to deep fine leg. Talbot was slow to cut the ball off, but Richard knew he had a good throwing arm. 'Two', he shouted. The batsmen crossed for one as Talbot picked up the ball. Brennan touched and turned in order to take a second run. Half way down the track he heard Richard shout. 'No!'

Talbot's throw was on its way to the keeper at Richard's end as Brennan's boot spikes failed to dig in and check his forward momentum. As his feet slid from under him, he saw Richard standing safely in his ground. The ball thumped into Gledhill's gloves as Brennan scrambled to his feet. 'Bowler's end,' shouted Speedy. But Gledhill had already weighed up the situation and was lobbing the ball to the opposite wicket. Brennan saw the ball looping over his head, outstripping him for pace as he tried to get home. Like a man arriving too late to catch a bus, he gave up and watched Speedy catch the ball and break the wicket.

Brennan was not often moved to rage, but he turned and gave his partner a glare sour enough to pucker paint on the fence in front of the pavilion.

2

In the Press Box, a collective groan attested to Grimley's view that Brennan's exit marked the end of the visitors' run chase and the start of an attritional grind to secure a draw. If they failed to save the match, the ten points conceded, would enable Gledhill's team to leapfrog them in the table.

Of more immediate concern to Grimley was the manner of Brennan's dismissal. Unlike the often-chaotic run-calling when he was partnering Ibbo, Richard had developed an almost telepathic understanding with Brennan. Therefore what Grimley had just witnessed was an aberration – or something infinitely worse.

'Pity,' drawled Lycett. 'There seemed a comfortable second run.' Grimley bit on his pen. Lycett had insisted on loaning him his binoculars in order to sample the genius of German optical engineering. He had therefore witnessed the earlier exchange between Speedy and Richard as if from a front row seat. It was obvious the content of their conversation did not abound in brotherly love.

The tightening sensation he had felt earlier had again lodged itself under his breastbone. It was absurd to think Speedy would choose the field of play to convey the sensitive information he had been given. And yet the 'run-out' seemed so contrary to Richard's customary good sense that Grimley was compelled to consider the possibility.

His fears grew apace when he now trained the same binoculars on Richard. He was squatting on his haunches while waiting for Crick to arrive at the crease. His cap was upturned on the ground between his legs and he seemed on the point of throwing up into it.

Rod Brennan's bat flew through the air and smashed into the dressing room wall. He threw himself down onto the bench below his changing peg, his head shaking from side to side in speechless rage. 'Doc' Holliday had never seen him in such a strop. 'Hard luck, mate.'

'Luck!' snorted Brennan. 'To hell with luck. The bastard ran me out.'

'Well, it happens.'

'I mean he meant to run me out.'

'No, Rod.'

'I'm telling you.' Showing respect to Brennan's fury, the dressing room had gone quiet. Jephcott entered, disgruntled by the turn of events.

'Tough luck, Rod. You were going well.'

'Luck had fuck all to do with it, Skip.'

'Rod thinks Richard ran him out on purpose.'

'On purpose?' said Jephcott, disbelievingly.

'I'm not joking. He went mental on me. Accused me of screwing his missus.'

'What?'

'He wanted to know where I was last night. Said my car was outside his place. He's gone loco.'

'You weren't there, were you?' said KC, now part of the gathering group.

'No.'

'So who says you were?'

'He said Grimley had seen my car. It's just bollocks.' A sombre mood descended. Topsy thought fleetingly of lightening things up by asking Rod who he had been pleasuring if it had not been Tessa Hastie, but he chickened out when he saw the grave expressions worn by KC and Jephcott.

One by one the players who had not been party to Brennan's outburst were brought up to date in whispered exchanges. Without a confidant inside the team, Badel was left in the dark and reluctant to ask questions. It was as if he was attending the funeral of a person with whom he had little acquaintance and was unsure about his entitlement to see the corpse.

Crick left the pavilion with instructions to bat for survival until tea when Jephcott would make an assessment of their progress. While Brennan was batting, all things had been possible but his dismissal had immediately shortened the odds in favour of the opposition. Though Richard was still occupying the crease, only a longish tail of hit-or-miss merchants would be available to offer support.

When the umpires took the bails off and called for tea to be taken, the score stood at 185 for 4 with Richard unbeaten on 72. To the outside observer, victory might have seemed like plain sailing. In reality, the Mother Ship's engine was misfiring and its hull was taking in water.

'Batted, Dick. Heh, hold on.' It was hard for Crick to keep pace with Richard as they left the field. 'What's the rush?' Richard acknowledged neither Crick nor the thin applause from the card-carrying faithful in the members' seats. The interval had come as an unwelcome interruption in his tailspin to despair. Now he would have to face his team-mates. He wondered how many of them knew, and how long they had known. He kept his head down all the way into the dressing room. Without casting aside his equipment he walked straight ahead and out of the door into the internal corridor. KC heard the door to a lavatory slam shut. 'What's up with him?' said Crick. Nobody in the room appeared to want to tell him. 'What?' persisted Crick.

Having glimpsed Richard's traumatised expression, Ibbo sat staring into his hands. If there was any truth in the rumour, he could not imagine the consequences. Yet Brennan's indignation seemed genuine. In Ibbo's opinion, he was too simple-minded to maintain such diabolical duplicity.

Ibbo had also been aware of the on-field altercation between Richard and Speedy and put it down to their inbred gamesmanship. Certainly Brennan's demolition of his bowling must have bruised Speedy's ego. At such moments of stress it was not unknown for sexual taunts to be thrown at players' mothers, wives, or girlfriends. If Speedy had slandered Tessa with the intention of regaining the initiative, he had succeeded in spades – Brennan was back in the hutch and Richard had gone out of his mind.

Ibbo rose from the bench to go in search of Richard and offer a sympathetic ear, but as he was about to exit the room KC's voice intervened. 'Leave him. And that goes for everyone else.' Since Jephcott had disappeared into the player's dining room for tea, KC had clearly taken it upon himself to establish the facts. 'Get some grub, and keep this to yourselves.' He took the door out of Ibbo's hand and exited.

Richard heard the dressing room door open and close. Still wearing his gloves, he was sitting with his bat between his legs staring blankly ahead. More than once Tessa had told him she was unhappy. He had heard but not listened and now she had found happiness with someone else. His gaze was fixed on a small inconsequential patch of marine blue paint above the lock on the lavatory door.

KC listened for signs of life within the cubicle but he could hear only the hum of traffic from the Pershore Road. 'Dick? What's going on, Dick?' There was a long pause. 'You're sure it's not somebody putting the poison in?' Opposite the battery of four lavatory cubicles was the dressing room attendant's hideout. He had left the door open and the afternoon sun slanted through the obscured windows, filling the corridor with dancing motes of dust.

3

In KC's opinion Grimley was not a bad bloke. He had chronicled his career down the years with generous praise and never been slow to castigate those boneheads at HQ who had ignored his claim to an England place. On occasion through force of circumstance the two men had even travelled to matches together, sharing a beer on the way home. Rarely did their conversation stray from cricket into the personal sphere but if it had, and in spite of Grimley's chosen profession, KC was sure a confidence would have remained just that. If Grimley really was the author of the rumour then KC feared it must contain a large dollop of truth.

He set off for the Press box as Grimley, sufficiently disturbed by Richard's running out of Brennan, came scurrying in the opposite direction. Grimley had had nothing clearer in view than to hang around the back of the pavilion and snag any player who might relieve his sense of dread. The dour expression on KC's face when he bumped into him behind the Priory Stand did not augur well.

'Just the man,' said KC. Anxiety had taken the wind out of both men's sails and they shuffled uneasily on the spot for a moment to get their breath back. 'What's this all about, Ron?'

'What d'you mean?'

'A nasty rumour said to come from you about Tessa Hastie?' Grimley groaned and sank his hands deep into his pockets. They were already bulging with notepads, biros, and his constant companion, the pocket *Playfair Annual*.

'It wasn't supposed to come out like this. I told Speedy in confidence. I assumed he'd deal with it as a private family matter.'

'It's true then?'

'I'm afraid so. I saw his car outside Richard's place.'

'Huh.' KC shook his head. 'You'd think he pulled enough skirt without nobbing the wife of a mate.'

'Who're you talking about?' said Grimley, puzzled by the response.

'Rod.'

'Rod? No, you've got it wrong. It wasn't Rod's car.'

4

Tessa heard the qualm in her caller's voice and felt her legs weaken. 'I think he knows. Or if he doesn't, he's about to find out. I'm sorry Tessa.' The receiver began to shake in her hand. In the mirror above the telephone table she glimpsed her pale shock-blasted face. 'Ron Grimley must have tried to call at the house last night and saw my car. Stupid of me to park there. Stupid.'

'Where's Richard?'

'About to go into bat.'

'What will you say?'

'No idea. It's a mess.' There was a long silence before he spoke again. 'Will you be alright?'

'I don't know.'

'I'm really sorry.'

She put the phone down without saying goodbye, struck dumb in the pitiless glare of a spotlight. Why had she not rehearsed for this moment? Why had she no excuses prepared, no exit planned? Somehow her seducer had convinced her she would never have to answer for her actions. Detecting her fallibility, he had used words to soothe and not startle – 'No one need know'.

She held her head in both hands, her eyes staring through a cradle of fingers. She could barely begin to think of the repercussions without shuddering. Questions churned randomly in her mind. Had the affair really been worth the destruction of what she and Richard had put together? Would the girls cope if they split up? She cringed at the thought of Richard's humiliation in the dressing room. What would be the effect on his career of being propelled from England hopeful to hapless cuckold? Surely he could not forgive her? Never. They were finished. The holiday needed to be cancelled; the family Christmas re-jigged; the wedding presents, given with such generosity six years previously, would have to be returned with apologies for the fraud she had perpetrated.

She imagined explaining herself to her parents, then to his parents. She wanted to weep but the shock had left her dry and empty of anything but shame.

5

Crick pushed gently at the cubicle door. It was still locked. 'The umps are on the way, Dick.' Richard had heard the five-minute bell but had not stirred. His eyes were fixed on the same swirl of brush strokes above the lock on the lavatory door. 'You coming?' The doubt in Crick's voice was genuine. Next man in, Mal Shanks, had made himself ready in case Richard did not reappear but after a brief moment Crick heard the bolt slide back and saw the door open.

Bulked out in pads and gloves, Richard did not immediately strike Crick as a changed man. Under his cap, however, his features were drawn and unfamiliar. Crick might well have pondered on those men he had rendered similarly bereft by his own philandering but he was not one to dwell on inconvenient truths. Richard followed Crick through a deserted changing room, their team-mates having delayed their return from tea out of a communal sense of embarrassment.

Unaware of the turmoil Speedy had stirred up, Gledhill's team chatted and larked while waiting for Crick and Richard to join them in the middle. 'Are you okay?' asked Crick glancing at Richard as they walked side by side. He said nothing. The only conversation he wanted was with Tessa but use of the communal payphone in the changing room corridor had been out of the question.

Now, paradoxically, the vast amphitheatre was a hiding place, and in as much as Richard knew anything, he knew he was in no hurry to leave it. Here he could be alone to chase his thoughts ragged, to whip himself into a frenzy of self-reproach. He had lost his wife to another man. How self-obsessed he must have been not to see the threat. How tractable. It was Brennan's unfettered aggression that had helped to kick-start his own season. Brennan who had showed him how to add pugnacity to his technical ability. Brennan's example that had propelled him to the verge of an England cap. Richard had taken all that was offered and not expected to pay a price.

On the resumption of play and with the match evenly poised at 185 for four, Gledhill brought on Hills to bowl at one end, Upton at the other. It was a hard-cop-soft-cop routine designed to keep the batting side interested without upping the over rate before the statutory twenty overs was imposed in the last hour.

The nature of Brennan's dismissal and Richard's zombie-like demeanour since did not instill Crick with much confidence when it came to running between the wickets. In the event he was saved the worry when Upton ghosted an arm-ball between his bat and pad. Despite hearing the death rattle of falling bails behind him, Crick's disbelief riveted him to the spot before the sight of fielders gathering to congratulate the bowler convinced him of his demise.

Richard fixed his eyes on the scoreboard not to read the score but to find a visual point that might anchor his mind. He recalled how eager Brennan had been to leave the ground after the close of play on the first and second day of the match. 'On a promise,' Speedy had suggested with a smirk. 'Left arm round,' announced Chambers from the far end of the pitch as Stinton was brought into the attack.

6

Having waited to catch Jephcott alone, KC followed him to one of four lavatory cubicles situated off the corridor and waited at the open door. For a time Jephcott seemed unaware of KC's presence but halfway through emptying his bladder he spoke. 'Everything alright, Ken?'

KC leaned back against the wall, arms folded. 'Alright?' the captain repeated. There was a long pause as Jephcott watched his stream weaken and dribble to a finish. 'Something on your mind?' He zipped his flannels and passed KC en route to the wash hand basins in the shower room.

Jephcott's former Latin master had sported beetle brows and a stare as stern as a raptor's but KC's countenance was just as forbidding. Jephcott washed his hands. He had forgotten to bring his towel and reached in his pocket for a handkerchief to dry them. 'What is it, Ken?' KC inhaled loudly through his nostrils like a diver about to take the plunge.

'It was you.'

'I'm not with you.'

'You, not Rod. Your car outside Tessa Hastie's.' Studiously calm, Jephcott dried his hands, taking his time, choosing his words.

'I did call to have a word.'

'An all night conversation?'

'You know Ken, it really isn't any of your business.'

'I daresay you think that, but not me.' Jephcott took a packet of cigarettes from his pocket and slid one out. As he put his lighter to it, he could not hide the tremor in his hands. 'How long's it been going on?'

'You're a good bloke KC, but what I do in private is my affair.'

'Not when it comes to screwing the wife of a team-mate, it isn't.'

'This isn't the time or place –'

'How long?' The door opened and Barry Picken appeared naked but for a towel draped around his waist. Alerted by KC's scowl he halted by the door.

'I was going to take a shower.'

'Later,' said KC. Picken hesitated for a moment, bewildered by the apparent shift of authority between the two men in front of him. 'I said later!' Picken retreated and Jephcott made to follow him. 'I asked you a question.'

'I don't have to answer to you, Ken, or anyone else. I'm the captain.'

'You're a cunt is what you are.' The words shook any semblance of bluster out of Jephcott's body.

'Be very careful, KC,' said Jephcott in a low admonishing voice.

'Sorry, was that lacking in respect? How about you're a cunt,

Captain?' Jephcott looked into KC's eyes. They were black and hard as pebbles. He took a drag.

'We're all adults, Ken. Things happen. Things we're not especially proud of. What's happened between Tessa and me is over, finished. Spilt milk, eh?'

'You don't get it, do you? We're a team. Day in day out we work and play, laugh and bloody cry together. We depend on each other, trust each other. We don't knife our mate in the back as soon as it's turned.'

'I admire your idealism, KC, I always have.'

'Shove your admiration, I'm not interested. My sort stick together out of necessity – to finish a shift, to last out the day. Idealism is a word for bookworms, fellow travellers like you.'

'Yes we're a team, Ken, but we're also a bunch of individuals. Flawed human beings.'

'You saying you don't know right from wrong? The lad batting out there has had a fantastic season. His career's taken off. England selection on the cards, the world at his feet. Now, thanks to you, he's like a dead man walking.'

'It takes two to tango, Ken. Dick's had a good season but he left Tessa out in the cold.'

'And you jumped in to keep her warm?'

'I'm telling you how it is.'

'Well I don't want to hear it. I trusted you to do whatever was best for the team. I gave everything I'd got whenever you wanted me to bowl. But every so often I got a nagging feeling. Something not right, something not straight about you. Like when you took those two games off. Both of 'em away games. Remember? A muscle strain, wasn't it? Convenient. Dick got a hundred in each match. He filled his boots while you were filling his missus.' Jephcott bridled.

'That's enough, Ken. I'm going.'

'Not yet.' Jephcott found himself obstructed by a large palm pressed against his chest.

'Don't be stupid. You'll be fined and sacked.'

'Better me than Dick.'

'What?'

'This is for him.' KC brought his knee up into Jephcott's groin. He let out a gasp of pain and jack-knifed forward as KC's knee repeated the action, this time to the head. The knee bone smashed into Jephcott's nose and mouth. His head jerked back, blood seeping from his nostrils and teeth.

'If you were one of the lads I might fight clean, but I never took you for one of us.' Jephcott clutched at a wash hand basin for support but KC grabbed him by the shirt collar and swung him violently over the edge of one of two baths sitting end to end.

Leanly-built though he was, Jephcott was no weakling, but he was no match for a man whose enduring strength he had hitherto relied on to win him matches. The poetic justice of this he might ponder later, for the moment there was the matter of survival. His head and shoulders hung into the bath, drops of blood splashed ever more rapidly onto the white enamel.

'For pity's sake,' he spluttered as KC's anger showed no sign of abating.

'This one's for the girls.' KC yanked Jephcott upwards and drove a punch into his midriff. He collapsed again over the rim of the bath, one arm dangling inside it, his fingers scrawling an abstract pattern in the blood. Intent on seeking justice for all, KC's hugh hands hauled him upright again as if he had no more substance than a cabbage patch doll. 'And this one's for your missus and the kids.' The blow landed behind Jephcott's ear as he shied away. Keeping his grip on Jephcott, KC lost balance and both men stumbled across the room into a tiled trough running beneath a line of showerheads.

'For God's sake.'

'Okay, this one's for the Almighty.' KC's fist crunched into the skipper's jaw causing a trauma to the throat that made him gag for air. This time he was allowed to fall in a heap, smearing a long lick of blood down the tiled wall.

KC flicked the shower control. The rose above spat a gob of cold water directly onto Jephcott's face before delivering a full-on torrent. 'If you're looking to God, you'd better get cleaned up.' He reached the door just as Slingsby poked startled eyes around it.

'What on earth's going on?'

'Family squabble,' said KC curtly.

7

On his return to the dressing room, KC affected a casual 'business as usual' manner, craning his neck for a sight of the scoreboard. Everyone else sat quietly in corners, tremulous as children after a violent parental row. Still wearing only a towel, Picken spotted blood on KC's knuckles and decided to give the showers a miss. Only Brennan with his gauche Antipodean directness was prepared to break the ice. 'Everything ripper, KC?'

'Yes, Rod, ripper.'

'Right. Only you look as if someone pissed on your swag.'

Slingsby was reportedly driving Jephcott to hospital for treatment and a bulletin was expected in due course. Far from feeling remorse, KC was full to the brim with self-righteousness. The heinous crime committed on a team-mate more than warranted the fractured jaw he suspected his clunking fist of 'justice' had inflicted.

Though he had done whatever Jephcott asked of him on the field of play, KC's forbears had taught him never to put his faith in a boss. Accordingly, when he became Senior Professional he had assumed stewardship of the men not merely by title but in his marrow. His suspicion that Jephcott was equivocal when it came to solidarity with his players had damningly been proven. The shower room ruckus had almost certainly ended KC's First-class career. Grimley would write a fulsome obituary in the Club's Year Book and he would bow out, not only justified, but free also of the temptation to play one more season below his best. Such an ending he could accept, enjoy even, but the task of confiding to Richard what he had discovered, filled him full of dread. His wife often chided him for his maladroit use of words and he doubted if he would find the right ones now.

8

A patter of applause and a flurry of movement beyond the frosted window alerted the dressing room to the dismissal of the sixth batsman. Mal Shanks, who had contributed seven runs to a stand of 20, had holed out lamely to mid-off. He had faffed and fretted for three overs, giving every impression of wishing himself back in the hutch where the heated rumour-mongering was more to his taste. During his brief stay at the crease he had tried to communicate with his partner, doubtless in pursuit of some revelation with which to regale the players on his return. But Richard had stayed well beyond Shanks's reach, retreating at the end of each over to the sanctuary of the outer corners of the 'square'.

Since Speedy's bombshell, Richard had been in a state of delirium. His innings meanwhile had proceeded on autopilot. In the past when he had been troubled by injury – a muscle strain perhaps or a damaged finger – it had appeared to help rather than hinder his batting. Physical discomfort, he had concluded, somehow diverted his performance anxiety. The pain he was experiencing now, however, was of a very different order.

His interest in the result of the match had gone, but occupation of the crease guaranteed him solitude. When Upton gave the ball more air he found his feet gliding to the pitch of the ball, the bat describing an uninterrupted arc from back-lift to follow through, its contact with the ball a split-second moment of inevitability. At first the ball ran directly towards the fielder at mid-off but Richard had turned his wrists to open the face of his bat on impact. The spin thus imparted took the ball across the turf, not in its original straight line, but in a smooth parabola that left the fielder chasing shadows as it passed five yards to his left en route to the rope.

It was a stroke the beginnings of which he had learned at elementary school using a flat piece of plywood jig-sawed into a bat shape. Along with less enthusiastic classmates he had been instructed in rank like cadet soldiers with wooden rifles. The drilled learning of the sideways-on stance, straight back lift, and left elbow well up, had been no hardship for a boy who lived and breathed cricket.

Instilled by repetition, Richard's technique became an object lesson in simplicity. Head still, weight evenly divided, one step forward or back depending on the length of the delivery. Each ball played on its merits. Sound, effective, and just a little boring, especially when mocked in the back yard by his brother for batting like a 'big girl'.

Little by little, year by year, the bad habits had crept in. Of course he could hit a drive through orthodox mid-off but if he did it would get wedged behind a downpipe at the side of the house. A square cut from the textbook would threaten his father's cold frames, and the M.C.C. approved hook shot would decapitate the herbaceous borders. So instead of a ball being treated on its merits he learned to play according to circumstances. Adjustments were made, liberties taken, and indulgences allowed to take root.

By the time he became a capped county player Richard was, like most batsmen on the circuit, infected with bad habits, theories and nervous tics. Instead of one step forward or one step back he would shuffle sideways before committing himself to the back or front foot. He was fond of changing the position of his hands on the bat handle and experimenting with different guards at the crease. If he was out of form, his anxiety would cause him to overbalance to the off, placing his foot in line with the ball rather than his bat.

At such times, he suspected the psychological aspects of the game had gained the whip hand over the physical, his battles fought more against himself than the opposition. But as he prepared to face another Upton delivery his turmoil was so complete that the mental and the physical had become wholly disconnected. He could think of nothing but his wife, her lover, his children, his home, and the utter discontinuance of his future.

This anguished absent-mindedness meant that with no one at the helm, his batting reverted to the fundamentals. Back to the bat-shape drills of the playground and the coaching mantras of his youth. The result was a purity of method which, had he been conscious of it, would have brought him as much pleasure as it did to Julian Lycett, purring in the Press Box.

AN INNINGS TO MATCH THE BEST
By Julian Lycett

Richard Hastie has been a county cricketer rather too long to be regarded as an exciting discovery. A revelation may be a better description after his innings at Edgbaston yesterday. Those lucky enough to witness it can rarely have seen such finely accomplished batting. That his effort came when his side was subsiding badly only added lustre to his achievement.

Richard had been dimly aware of Jim Rook calling the start of the final hour. Thereafter a minimum of twenty overs would be available for the batting side to achieve their target or survive defeat.

Topsy Turner had come and gone, making the score 214 for seven. The middle order collapse after Brennan's dismissal had been precipitous and 'Doc' Holliday arrived at the crease intent on putting up the shutters and playing for a draw. Richard remained off limits even to 'Doc', neither joining him for a chat between overs nor calling when runs were to be taken. 'Doc' had sufficient nous not to take offence. In any case, though he was clearly in distress, his partner was batting out of his skin and in no need of advice or encouragement.

'His eye saw the ball early out of the hand, allowing him to judge immediately the line and length. As a result his footwork was decisive and the execution of his strokes a matter of conviction.

Nothing demonstrated this better than the three consecutive strokes he played off his toiling brother, Philip Hastie, to bring up his century. The first was a sumptuous front-footed drive bisecting cover point and mid-off that left both fielders statuesque in admiration.

The second was a stroke played with a straight bat off the backfoot to a ball pitching barely short of a length. Getting high up on his toes, Hastie caressed the ball off his hip through mid-wicket for four. The fielder placed there, Chatterway, must have been fooled by the languid timing into believing he had the shot covered but before he could bend, the ball was past him and on its way to the boundary.

When Gledhill brought his field in closer to prevent Hastie from taking the single that would take him to his century, the batsman simply scooped the ball over the in-field with the air of an uncle patronising his nephews in a game of beach cricket.'

'Well batted, Dick. Great knock,' said 'Doc'. In response he thought he detected a slight inclination of the head but no more. Even if Richard was aware of the spectators' applause there came no acknowledgement. He had engineered the single as a conditioned reflex to appropriate the strike for the next over rather than to provide another statistic for Mr Wisden's almanack.

9

Tessa could sit and wait for Richard to return home or head towards the sound of the guns. She thought neither could make matters worse, so unwilling to endure the suspense she chose to be pro-active. The dull thrumming sound of tyres on macadam provided a suitable accompaniment to her mood. Cocooned inside the capsule of the car, she found it a palliative of sorts. The late afternoon traffic was bunching at pinch points along the city ring road and people's impatience to get to the weekend was palpable. A driver in front had wound down his window and was drumming his fingers on the roof of his car as, bumper to bumper, they crept to their gardens in the suburbs.

Tessa's desire to set off for her destination seemed to imply an urgent mission to correct a terrible misunderstanding but truthfully she could think of nothing to mitigate or explain her behaviour. It had not been for love on either side but nor was she willing to confess to a purely sexual motive. What was done was done, and what she had done she could scarcely believe herself.

It had begun at Jephcott's house on the evening she and Richard were invited to dinner. She had spilt a dash of wine on her dress and Jephcott had joined her in the kitchen as she tried to sponge away the stain. Lightly inebriated, he had kissed her neck from behind. When startled, she had spun round, he planted another on her lips. He was the host and also her husband's team boss and her response was more muted than propriety properly demanded. Over the following days he phoned her repeatedly to apologise for his indiscretion. She told him it was forgotten and that she had not told Richard of the incident.

It would be their secret.

Jephcott's subsequent invitation to Tessa to have lunch with him was wrapped up in his hopes for Richard's career and his future as captain. Naturally it had to be confidential since nothing had been confirmed by the Committee, but it would be helpful to give her an insight into the life of a captain's wife.

It was a plausible enough pretext for a clandestine meeting during which he had been attentive, charming and increasingly aware of her susceptibility. He said he understood the stresses and strains of being the wife of a professional sportsman. Self-involvement came as part and parcel of the job, especially a player as single-mindedly ambitious as Richard. Tessa had hung on Jephcott's words, bathed in his empathy and lost herself completely. They skipped the coffee and within an hour of leaving the restaurant she was naked but for her wedding and engagement ring.

Afterwards she was shocked by her insouciance. There was no dark despair. No feeling of guilt. Only the sense of being a curious bystander in her own life.

From the ring road she took the dual carriageway and drove west. Having set out so resolutely she was struck by nerves and in less hurry to reach her destination. Would she be able to tell the truth? Did she even know the truth of why she had let it happen? She had already said farewell to her integrity, would she have to surrender her dignity as well? Would she beg for understanding or put up a smokescreen of self-justification?

By Spaghetti Junction she hoped she would have the answers but as the miles ticked by the only straw she was able to clutch was the one bearing Laura Kyle's name.

10

Gledhill was no slouch when it came to teasing out a finish. Although there seemed nothing either he or his bowlers could do to disturb the fluency of Richard Hastie's batting, he was sure 'Doc' Holliday at Number Nine had come in with instructions to shut up shop. Accordingly he left gaps in the field to tempt Jephcott's men to continue their pursuit of the target. And as they chased, he knew errors would creep in and the remaining wickets would fall.

'What d'you think?' said 'Doc'. Up until then he had observed Richard's right to silence but now circumstances demanded a common strategy. The two men had shared a stand of forty taking the score to 254 for seven with ten overs remaining. The required run rate of four and a half per over was undemanding but if either 'Doc' or Richard got out, only Badel and KC were left to bat. KC was a renowned no-hoper with the bat and judging by Badel's first innings effort, he was using the Senior Pro as a role model. Not for the first time 'Doc' had cause to rue that most perverse of cricket's characteristics, namely that at crucial moments when batting skill was most called for, the players at the crease were those least able to provide it.

'Are we going for them?' 'Doc' persisted. Richard appeared not to hear. He was visualising his wife and Brennan screwing on the stairs, unable to contain their passion until they reached the bedroom. He imagined himself discovering them and dragging Brennan away, his rival's superior strength nullified by the hobbling effect of his 'Y' fronts tangled round his ankles.

'Dick, are we going for them?' Richard turned away with what appeared to be a shrug of the shoulders. Despite his partner's apparent indifference, 'Doc' knew that win, lose or draw, his immediate task was to push singles and give Richard as much of the bowling as possible. But within an over he had shuffled across his stumps and been given out LBW.

Though Richard Hastie was playing like a man possessed, the loss of Holliday threatened to derail the visitor's assault on the target. He quickly lost another partner when Badel was caught behind off Upton to reduce his side to 264 for 9 with five overs of the final twenty remaining. At this point Hastie was unbeaten on 124, but with only Colclough to keep him company, the thirty-five runs needed for the win seemed beyond their reach.

Throughout his stay at the crease, Hastie had demonstrated a technique that married an impregnable defence with an elegant simplicity of method, all the while refusing to let the misfortunes of his partners disturb his composure. As such, he showed himself to be a man able to rise above an ordinary game and decide its destiny. The England selectors might well take note as they convene to select the party for the winter tour.

The way KC held his bat told observers all they needed to know about his run-scoring potential. Whereas an accredited batsman walked to the crease using the bat as if it were a walking stick or a rolled umbrella, KC made his way to the middle holding the bat low on the handle like a cudgel. He believed batsmen were employed to bat and bowlers were there to bowl and he adopted a rustic style that invited no confusion.

As a time-served member of the fast bowlers' union, KC expected opposing members to pitch the ball well up to him. In return he would take a few comical swipes at the ball and surrender his wicket in the process. But brevity was all. Any tail-ender tempted to outstay his welcome was quickly reclassified as a batsman and on the receiving end of the sort of rib-ticklers that encouraged him to think again.

Nevertheless, with the game on a knife-edge, normal rules of engagement were suspended. Unaccustomed as he was to putting his bat to serious use, KC would prop forward like a saw horse and block for as long as his luck might hold.

Wherever Gledhill deployed his fielders, Hastie contrived to find the gaps. Such was his nerveless command of the situation, it seemed the bowlers were colluding with him to provide the closest of finishes for a small but increasingly excited band of spectators. Frustrated by Hastie's ability to farm the strike, the home bowlers had few opportunities to test Colclough's rudimentary defence. When they did they found the Number Eleven at his most obdurate, taking blows to the body with disdain as Hills tried to unsettle him.

Twenty five runs off the last five overs became twelve runs required from two. Under pressure, Hills now bowled a magnificent over to concede just three runs, leaving the visitors nine runs to get from the final over to be bowled by Philip Hastie to his brother, Richard.

Hills' containing over had raised the mercury appreciably. Three days of often-soporific endeavour had come down to the last six balls and still the match could end in any one of three ways. The game was already ten minutes past its advertised finish but no-one was leaving. Newspaper sellers absconded from their kiosks to watch. Tipplers evacuated the bars. Even Wilf Bristow sauntered to the boundary edge to witness the conclusion.

As he had done for the previous hour, Gledhill took time to place his field. Though Speedy had been unusually expensive he could normally be relied upon to deliver the ball well up into the block hole where a batsman's first instinct was to dig it out and survive rather than try to score.

Richard stood unbeaten on 148. He had scored 76 out of the 104 runs added since tea. At that stage a show of nerves would have been understandable, yet his demeanour remained that of a person wholly detached from events. KC had pottered to the middle of the pitch in the hope of inducing a response and drawn only a blank stare. He was not even sure if Richard was aware of the state of play but decided to give him the benefit of the doubt rather than break the spell that had taken them to the brink of victory.

Speedy joined his captain in fussing with the field placings. Since being told of Tessa's infidelity, Richard's domination of the bowling had been absolute, a paradox which Speedy belatedly realised was consistent with his brother's innate bloody-mindedness. He knew from past battles that if Richard took a blow to the body he was twice as difficult to get out. Clearly emotional trauma had had a similar effect in sharpening his focus and stiffening his resolve.

A delicate balance had to be struck between defence and attack but when at last Gledhill had arranged the field, Philip Hastie began the final over. Fuelled with nervous energy, fielders dried sweaty palms on their flannels, each knowing a spilt catch or a mis-field would probably decide the outcome.

Speedy's first ball was a mite short of a length and angled in from the off. Unwilling even at this stage to spurn the textbook, Richard glanced the ball wristily into a gap on the leg-side for two runs. The following ball, he unfurled a flowing straight drive. Given a modicum of justice, the stroke would have given his side a clear advantage. Instead, with nobody to stop the drive going for four, the ball hit the stumps at the bowler's end and stopped dead. With the visitors needing to score seven runs from four balls, Hastie played a similar stroke to the next delivery and on this occasion gained due reward.

KC had to shift smartly to dodge Richard's straight drive. Even though the ball was destined to reach the boundary from the moment it left the bat, KC felt obliged to run to the far crease in case it was cut off. He turned as the ball hit the fence in front of the pavilion and ambled back down the pitch to find himself talking to Richard's back.

'Great shot. Bloody great.' Richard stayed rooted to the spot, his eyes fixed on a stand to the side of the pavilion. Looking over his shoulder to share his view, KC saw Tessa standing alone at the top of a concrete staircase. Though only a faint sun permeated the clouds, one of her hands shielded her eyes. She had a cream cardigan draped around her shoulders, a handbag clutched under her arm. Richard recognised the shirt-dress she was wearing as one they had bought together on holiday. He recalled her coming out of the shop's changing room – her smiling face, the way the dress hung closely over her hips, the scooped neckline framing her holiday tan. 'Come on,' said KC quietly. 'You can sort things out with her later.'

'What?' Richard murmured distractedly.

'Later. You won't need to bother with Jephcott. I've dealt with him.' The steely profile Richard had maintained melted as if he had re-entered the earth's atmosphere.

'What d'you mean?'

'I've put the bastard in hospital.'

'What?'

'Come on. Three runs in three balls – a piece of piss the way you're playing.'

'Jephcott'? Richard thought. What the hell was KC on about?

Gledhill re-jigged his field placings to surrender a single but cut off a four or two. His fastidious adjustments gave Richard time to decipher KC's words. Jephcott 'dealt with'? Jephcott 'in hospital'? Jephcott and Tessa? A new maelstrom threatened to drag him under.

Like an animal sensing a rival has lost the stomach for a fight, Speedy paused at the end of his run up and detected a change in his brother's manner. It was doubtful if anyone not of the same blood and internal circuitry could have sensed it so quickly. Gone was Richard's composure and intimations of weakness had returned – the nervous tweaks to the peak of his cap and the flaps of his pads. What Speedy would give to topple him now – to snatch victory at the eleventh hour to win the points, the money, and the kudos. That would be a story to tell Sheila and the boys when Uncle Richard came to visit.

Three runs were required in three balls and with Hastie still in assured command, the odds had swung in favour of the batting side. But then contrary to all that had gone before he appeared suddenly overcome by doubt. Having dispatched his brother's previous ball so scornfully for four, he groped at the next and missed it by the width of a barn door.

'Well bowled, Speedy.' Gledhill's cheerleader shout was directly in Richard's ear but he heard it only as a muffled sound in the distance. In the same way he had speculated on Rod Brennan's overnight absences, he now began to piece together Jephcott's movements. Sickeningly, he recalled the occasions during the season when the captain had made 'private arrangements'. He felt pulses of painful pressure behind his eyeballs and his bat took on the weight of a railway sleeper.

Speedy placed his first and second fingers either side of the ball's seam and ran in. His delivery angled into Richard then straightened. Minutes earlier, his brother would have played the ball late, adjusting his stroke to take account of the deviation. Now he pushed myopically forward and got an outside edge that would have carried to second slip if a man had been stationed there.

As the ball ran down to third man, KC realised they would have to take the run, a single that would leave him facing the final delivery with two runs needed to win. 'Shit, shit, shit,' he grizzled to himself. He had spent his days bowling his boots off, his nights nannying delinquents, now he had been left at the business end of a do-or-die last ball finale – a man who barely knew which end of the bat to hold. 'Stupid bastard game,' he cursed.

The crowd was generating an atmosphere out of all proportion to its size. Barked exhortations and excited yelps had accompanied each of the last five deliveries but as Speedy waited to bowl the final ball even the hum of traffic from the Pershore Road seemed to quieten.

Speedy's thoughts were only of victory and with it the personal epithet of the man who held his nerve while others quivered. In the reasonable expectation of KC lunging at the ball and missing, he resolved to aim for the wickets and finish the match with stumps spread-eagled. His captain, meanwhile, was tinkering with his field settings again. With KC on strike he had to factor in a host of new angles, none of them predictable.

'Stupid bastard game,' repeated KC, looking round the field for gaps. Normally there was no need for such a futile gesture but circumstances demanded a feigned display of competence. He possessed only two strokes. One the block that had served him well so far, the other a cross-batted heave which, on the rare occasions he connected, went in the direction of cow-corner.

The pragmatic professional inside KC desperately urged him to block the final ball and settle for a draw. Despite his partner's heroic innings, he believed that over three days it was as much as his team deserved. In any case, though his signature hoick to leg offered an outside chance of scoring two runs for a win, it was rather more likely to mis-fire and hand outright victory to the opposition.

It was sad to see so seasoned a professional in such a bind and no disgrace that when the moment came his mind went blank. True to his intent, Speedy ran in close to the stumps and bowled the ball wicket to wicket. KC picked up his bat and swung it. By some miracle the ball struck the middle of the blade – in the dead spot just below the splice. A well-timed stroke springs sweetly off the bat like a pebble out of a catapult. Despite investing as much strength as he could summon, it felt to KC as if he had hit a medicine ball with a stick of celery. The ball reluctantly took off over Speedy's head. All eyes followed the ball's looping trajectory.

'Run!' shouted KC to Richard.

From an angle square of the wicket it was obvious Upton at deep mid-on could comfortably cover the ground to take the catch. But Speedy was also in the hunt, turning from his follow-through and dashing back as the ball arced over his head.

It was usual when a catch went up between two fielders for the captain to shout the name of his favoured catcher. Normally he would choose the man closest to the drop-zone but with Upton charging in from the boundary, and Speedy racing directly away from Gledhill's point of view, the captain could not assess their respective distance from the dropping ball. Hearing no call, both men kept their eyes skywards and assumed ownership of the catch. Sensitive souls might have chosen to avert their eyes as they converged and collided, their outstretched arms crumpling like fenders in a motorway pile-up. As the two fielders landed in a tangle on the grass the unclaimed ball bounced free, enabling KC and Richard to complete the second and winning run.

It was an improbable end to an exhilarating day of cricket, the game swinging first one way and then another. Above all Derbyshire's victory was a richly deserved reward for Richard Hastie's magnificent effort. His innings of 157 not out was unhurried at first, accelerated thrillingly in its middle stages, before a final murderous assault left the opposition beaten in his wake.

'Eh, fantastic knock.' KC punched Richard gently in the chest with his gloved fist. 'Even if you did leave the hard bit to me.'

Gledhill's thwarted team and the band of disappointed

home supporters gave the batsmen a generous hand as they walked from the field. KC saw that his partner's gaze remained focused on the stand in which Tessa was sitting. 'A bit of advice – start by giving her a hug, then take it from there.' A hug seemed an unlikely preparation for the dark hours of recrimination that lay ahead, but Richard did not demur. Reading his thoughts perhaps, KC grabbed him round the shoulder and pulled him into an awkward embrace as if to infuse his partner with some chin-up resolve from his own inexhaustible stock.

Richard had not lifted his bat to acknowledge the applause. 'Give 'em a wave,' urged KC. Head bowed, his features shaded below the peak of his cap, Richard perfunctorily raised his bat as he strode into the pavilion. Inside, team-mates greeted the heroes with more glad-handing.

'Great stuff, Dick.'

'Well played, Dick.'

'Superb, mate, superb.'

'You beaut, KC, what a finisher.' Amid the hearty back-slapping and the cheerful scragging of his neck, Richard remained unmoved. Not until Ibbo gave him a pint of beer from the team tray did he take off his batting gloves and slump exhausted into his changing place.

11

'Nice piece to write for your readers, Grimmers,' said Lycett. Grimley was already trying to figure out how he could cut his copy to the stipulated length. Doubtless his editor would remind him yet again that at the tail-end of the season, cricket had to doff its cap to soccer no matter how remarkable the story.

'A crisp five hundred.'

'Only five hundred words to cover a famous victory? Surely not?'

'We have to make room for the footy,' said Grimley shamefacedly.

'Ah yes, the footy.'

'And the speedway.'

'Really?'

'Not to mention the angling column, the ping pong, and the darts and dominoes leagues.' Lycett looked genuinely shocked. Provincial journalism was indeed another country. 'What about your piece?' asked Grimley.

'A doddle. Your man Hastie's written it for me.'

'I mean the one you came to write.'

'Not sure I'm with you, old thing.'

'Badel.' Lycett crimped his fleshy lips and one of his eyebrows ticked upwards.

'That one will have to wait.'

'No sacrificial lamb? HQ will be disappointed.'

'Why's that?' Lycett replied disingenuously. 'Who am I to say he throws? I'm just a hack, old boy. I don't decide these things.' Grimley allowed himself a thin smile. As his father used to tell him, principles change according to circumstances.

12

Having parked in a relatively unoccupied section of the car park, Tessa watched players haul their gear from the pavilion and stow it in the boots of their cars. One by one they drove out of the ground until only KC's and Jephcott's remained. The wait had become almost unbearable. Her mind continued to race through grim scenarios, each one leaving her lost or abandoned. She thought about bathtimes, holidays and birthdays. Simple family moments made mundane by repetition that seemed more precious now than she could ever have believed possible. She had risked so much for so little. How could she convince Richard that her duplicity was not that of a woman who believed she had nothing of value to lose?

KC and Richard had been the last to shower. They sat in silence, towels round their waists amid the detritus of newspapers, empty glasses, and wet towels. 'Bad do,' said KC finally. 'I wish there was something I could say. Aye, bad do.' There was another long pause before Richard rose and started to dress. The door was open and he could hear the dressing room attendant whistling cheerfully in his room across the corridor. 'Lucky there's no game tomorrow. You'll have all on, I expect.'

There was something touching about KC's clumsy attempt at pastoral care. He was not used to choosing his words so carefully and knocking heads together was not an approach he could use in this instance, much as he wanted to.

'Course, you're not so lily-white yourself, are you?' Richard shot KC a wounded look. 'None of us are,' he added, ignoring the fact that he had remained resolutely faithful to his wife throughout his playing career. 'What's happened is diabolical, but you shouldn't do owt in a rush. You've the kids to think about. It's a blow, lad, but Tessa's a grand lass and everyone makes mistakes.' The homily, heartfelt and commendably brief, brought a thickening to Richard's throat.

Tessa saw KC and Richard walk into the car park. She felt gloomy enough to think Richard might load his gear into KC's car and leave without speaking.

'Good luck,' said KC. 'And well played. You're on the boat for sure.' As he watched Richard trudge away across the tarmac, he regretted striking such a note of celebration. He should have put a sock in it as his wife was always telling him.

Richard's coffin-sized case weighed a ton and the tumult of the day had left him with nothing in his legs. Taking what seemed like an age to stow his kit, Richard eventually climbed into the car holding a soft toy that had been left in the boot – an eyeless giraffe. They sat silently staring at the giraffe, neither knowing where to start.

'Where are the girls?'

'At June's.'

'Do they need collecting?'

'She says they can stay over if I'm delayed. You batted well.' He stared out of his side window, unwilling to respond. She looked at the wound and bruising above his eye and felt the pain of not being free to touch him. Jephcott's car remained in the car park and Tessa, unaware that he was having his jaw surgically repaired, was afraid he might appear. The feeling was not merely one of embarrassment but of dread, as if she had been in thrall to someone who might suddenly emerge and enslave her again.

'What do you want to do?' he said after a lengthy silence.

'I don't know.'

'Do you want me to go?'

'No.'

'Can you think of a reason for me to stay?'

'I can think of three. The girls need you. So do I.'

'Sure,' said Richard reproachfully.

'I love you.'

'Then why?' He looked at her for the first time.

'I don't know.' Her reply sounded like an evasion but it was the truth.

'It feels as if you've taken some sort of revenge – for what I don't know.'

'It wasn't revenge. I wasn't trying to hurt you. It was how I'd come to feel about myself. You left me a grass widow for too long.'

'So you screw another cricketer?'

'He said what I wanted to hear.'

'And I don't?'

'Not often enough.'

A knuckle tapped on the side window. The gates to the ground were to be locked in ten minutes the white-coated attendant informed them.

They made unhindered progress against the flow of late rush-hour traffic leaving the city. It would be more congested once they traversed the centre and joined the eastbound exodus. The weather had reverted to close and mardy. Though the sun stayed hidden behind thin cloud, it generated enough heat to make the air clammy inside the car. The radio, burbling at low volume, took the edge off the silence observed by Richard and Tessa after leaving the ground. The quirky bus-driver position at the wheel of the Austin 1100 gave Richard the appearance of someone in charge. In reality he was struggling to steer a course. How had he let this happen? How had the quotidian lapping of their lives detached them so far from their moorings?

'How long?' he asked. His mouth was so dry he could barely speak. Tessa remained silent. 'How many times did you screw him?'

'Don't – '

'How many times!' She bit her lip. They drove through the last set of lights before climbing the incline towards the lanes of traffic racing around Paradise Circus. 'Why, Tess?'

'I just wanted to be noticed again.' Her words, she knew, were unequal to the task. He shook his head in disbelief, his rage ready to explode. His hands tightened on the wheel, the Austin almost at the roundabout.

'That's bollocks! You're 'noticed' wherever and whenever you walk into a room.'

'By you?'

'Of course by me,' he snapped. 'Noticed, admired, and desired.'

'Like Laura Kyle?' Richard flinched involuntarily.

'What?'

'Laura Kyle.'

'What's she got to do with it?'

'I thought you could tell me.' He was stunned. One moment his finger had been on the trigger, the next he was looking down the barrel. From fight to flight in an instant. Fumbling distractedly for the gear stick, he muffed his change-down and the car drifted unchecked into the whirl of rushing traffic.

'Richard!'

There was nothing the on-coming Commer van could do to avoid a collision. Freighted with ladders, it ploughed into the side of the Austin, threatening to bend it in half. There was a loud bang, an explosion of dust, and a drawn out convulsion of twisted metal and glass as the conjoined vehicles dug into the tarmac and juddered to a halt. The shock to its hydro elastic suspension had made the Austin's bonnet rear up like a speedboat at full pelt. The front offside tyre, torn off by the impact, rolled drunkenly across the carriageway causing more chaos as vehicles zig-zagged to avoid it.

Richard's body had moved into its own collision with the interior of the car. His legs were wedged between the steering wheel and the caved-in door panel. His upper torso had twisted and been forced against Tessa, their faces locked together, wind-shield glass scattered over them like chips of ice. 'You alright?' he moaned.

'Are you?' His face was so impressed upon her's he could barely nod. He could feel movement in his fingers and toes, but his leg was trapped against the handbrake and clearly broken. At first Tessa feared the wet sensation on her face and neck was caused by blood trickling from a head wound, but then she tasted tears and heard him sobbing into her cheek. He felt her squeeze his arm. 'It's okay,' she whispered. 'We'll be okay.'

After a short, eerie silence, voices could be heard and Richard became aware of faces peering into the cabin. Miraculously, the radio had continued to transmit the evening news. The final item was an announcement of England's touring party to the West Indies. Seventeen names in all, the last one his.

Chapter Sixteen

THE CAPTAIN'S REPORT

At the start of the season many commentators were as convinced as I was that we had a team capable of mounting a realistic challenge for championship honours. In the event, sixth place represented a commendable improvement on recent seasons even if it did disappoint some of our supporters. Unpredictable weather robbed us of two certain victories and a mid-season crop of injuries also prevented us reaching the top three spot our combined talents warranted.

Our bowling attack was never less than competitive. Ray Turner continued to add craft to his undoubted natural abilities. Though he has become a regular bowler on the national scene, he remains vulnerable to injury. This is a story familiar to young pace bowlers. When he was fit he gave our attack an altogether different dimension. Though the generally damp pitches blunted his speed a little, on a dry bouncy surface he could be as hostile as any bowler in the country.

At the other end, Ray was fortunate to have in support our senior professional, Ken Colclough. I have expressed my appreciation of KC's contribution to the team in all my previous Year Book Reports. The records clearly summarise his outstanding deeds but behind the impersonal statistics is a man who is a role model for any professional cricketer. On rare occasions I have seen KC bowl without success at great players on shirt-front pitches. Apart perhaps from a quiet curse in the direction of the groundsman's lodgings, he carried on in his own staunch manner, accepting his successes in the same spirit as he withstood his disappointments.

The principal batsmen of KC's era have, almost without exception, voted him the bowler they most feared. Yet top honours continued to elude him. The reasons for such an injustice I will leave for others to consider but as his captain for the past six years, I could not have wished for a more willing team man. On behalf of myself and the playing staff, I wish Ken the pleasant and happy retirement his unstinting efforts have earned.

The batting averages were dominated by two players. During the season Richard Hastie came to the fore as a batsman of substance and class, a development not unconnected with the arrival from Tasmania of Rod Brennan. In the past Richard has proved himself to be a consistent batsmen with a sound technique. Of Rod we knew little in advance, but players and spectators soon came to expect fireworks whenever he walked to the wicket.

These two batsmen's contrasting styles seemed to combine perfectly and resulted in a number of match-winning stands. Richard's outstanding season culminated in a memorable unbeaten century to carry us to victory at Edgbaston. The innings had sealed his selection for England's winter tour only for a car accident to condemn him to months of rehabilitation. Our delight at his almost complete recovery is tinged with regret that he will no longer be playing for the county. Following Richard's request, the committee reluctantly agreed to his special registration by Sussex. We all extend to him and his family our best wishes for their move to the South Coast.

The loss of such an important batsman would have proved even more damaging had the committee not been able to persuade Rod Brennan to renew his contract. Happily he, together with his new wife, will return for another season when hopefully he will strike yet more fear into the hearts of opposition bowlers.

There is never enough space in this brief captain's report to pay due credit to those who contribute so much to the team effort, often without regard to their personal statistics. By his own high standards Barry Picken had a disappointing season. However, Neil Ibbotson grew in stature, particularly during the drier first half of the season. Keith Holliday proved again a model of consistency behind the stumps and was an influential figure in maintaining dressing room morale.

As the season drew to a close, a bowler of whom much had been expected became mired in controversy. Alvar Badel, having emerged from the local league, caused a stir on his debut. His action however aroused comment and in a climate when throwing had become such a hot topic, he was put immediately under the spotlight. After receiving advice from Lord's, the player was withdrawn from the side and after attempts to iron out his action had failed, the committee regretfully decided not to offer the player a contract. We wish Alvar well in his new career in the Council Parks Department.

Sadly for me this is also a parting of the ways. Sport of most types is an ephemeral activity and it is a wise player who knows the moment to leave the stage to younger men. It has been my pleasure and privilege to lead the county for six years but the time has come to devote myself full-time to my family's business interests.

If I had my time again I would not wish to change my county or the teams I have had the good fortune to captain. To a man they have given unswerving loyalty to myself and to the club, and I thank them wholeheartedly. My thanks also go to the committee and members of the club for their unwavering support. Lastly but importantly, I must express my gratitude to my wife, Pamela. The lot of a captain's wife is not an easy one. The misfortunes that dog a cricketer's life tend to follow him home and I have relied heavily on Pamela's forbearance.

Members will understand from this report that the team for the coming season will be a much-changed one. In fact it provides a wonderful opportunity for the new incoming skipper to shape a side to reflect his own ideas. Accordingly, I believe the appointment of Philip Hastie as captain will mark an exciting new chapter in the life of the club. Philip is a proven high-class performer and though his former county was understandably reluctant to let him go, they were unwilling to stand in the way of his ambition to assume a position of ultimate responsibility. He will be the county's first professional captain and I wish him the very best of luck.

With his customary modesty, Robin Jephcott has omitted to mention himself in the above report. As in previous seasons his contribution with the bat was not inconsiderable, as can be assessed from the averages. However it is his leadership for which the county is most in his debt. Though composed almost entirely of homegrown players, the team has never been less than competitive under his leadership. But discovering, as others have before him, that the job is an arduous one, Robin felt that fatigue had begun to affect his judgement and form. This belief, together with a wish to devote more time to his family and business interests, resulted in his decision to retire at the end of the season. We thank him for his invaluable contribution over the years and wish him well in the future – YEAR BOOK EDITOR

Acknowledgements

I have been fortunate in having the help of a number of people whose encouragement was invaluable in completing this, my debut novel.

My thanks go to staff at Methuen for their support. I am also grateful to those who submitted themselves to my early drafts: Anthony Edwards, Robbie Kingston, Tony Marks and David Baggett; former playing colleagues David Smith, Fred Rumsey and Geoff Miller.

Others: Stephen and Sue Chalke, Jim Graham-Brown and Nick Smith were generous with their time and perceptive in their detailed responses.

My thanks are also due to Anthony Garner and Ian Sharp for their enthusiasm at moments when my reserves of confidence might have run dry. Most of all I thank Carol for her unwavering support and assiduous close reading.

Finally, a collective thank you to those with whom I shared the field of play. None should recognise themselves as portrayed in my cast of characters, but if I have done my job properly, they might find some slight affinity with any one of them.